About the Author

Dermod Judge has been a designer, typographer, copywriter, dramatist, actor, broadcaster, international award-winning filmmaker, film and stage director, script writer and editor, international lecturer on storytelling and filmmaking. Now, having some time on his hands, he has turned to writing novels, of which the second is *Two Jam Jars For The Manor*. His first novel *Clash* came out in 2017 from the same publisher.

TWO JAM JARS FOR THE MANOR

Dermod Judge

The Book Guild Ltd

First published in Great Britain in 2017 by
The Book Guild Ltd
9 Priory Business Park
Wistow Road, Kibworth
Leicestershire, LE8 0RX
Freephone: 0800 999 2982
www.bookguild.co.uk
Email: info@bookguild.co.uk
Twitter: @bookguild

Typeset in Minion Pro

Printed and bound in Great Britain by 4edge Limited

ISBN 978 1912083 053

British Library Cataloguing in Publication Data.
A catalogue record for this book is available from the British Library.

Printed on FSC accredited paper

This book is dedicated to all the film practitioners who fed the day-dreaming part of my young nature and provided an escape from what was a pretty unstimulating lifestyle. It is also dedicated to those who, like me, sat and sighed in a cinema seat.

1

Relentless poverty throughout working-class and boredom throughout lower middle-class Dublin dampened the spirits and dulled the intentions of many pinch-faced, inadequately clothed and spiritually parsimonious denizens of the gloomy suburbs of a dull city, right up to the 1950s. While primary-level education was compulsory and free, there were insufficient employment opportunities to engender widespread respect or appetite for secondary education. Consequently, far too many young Dubliners left school as soon as they could, in order to add to the family's income, in however small a degree, so perpetuating the cycle of disinterest which was closely allied to a despondent despair. Leaving school, permissible at the age of twelve, meant leaving behind any possibility of changing the cards that were dealt by an uncompromising society in an unwinnable game of 'beggar my neighbour as myself'. A stultifying stasis descended on all but the most intrepid and life became a dreary journey from one self-destroying predicament to another. Well might James Joyce, the bête noire of the all-pervasive priests, describe Ireland as *the sow that eats her farrow*.

In Dublin, for grown-ups, a newspaper-wrapped packet of hot chips, a few pints and a good kick up the arse for eejits comprised the universal panacea for the world's ills. Here, for those who would, with increasing frequency, be called teenagers, a pair of your own long trousers, an occasional fag and a very infrequent *coort* with a grudging young girl kept itchy body and errant soul together. But there was many a light in the darkness and many a brave soul that pushed against the chains and the boundaries of cynicism and ennui that kept the working class in their place.

But in Western Europe, the youth of the 1950s were preparing themselves and the major cities for the 1960s, which showed the working class that the world was indeed its oyster and the chains and boundaries were there for the breaking. The restlessness that these souls felt was the longing for escape, that deep, primeval urge that set us walking on two legs to stride through the savannahs, using opposable thumbs to make effective tools, and made us see stars not as mysterious, detached gods and weird creatures, but as beacons to guide us to distant horizons and new lands, while the rest stayed in a world of darkness, sleep and insecurity.

Before these restless youths took the lonely road into exile and/or drink, there were two distractions from the boredom: sin and cinema. Sin was what would later be called the default route. It was free, ready to hand and could pass away many a desultory week until the weekend, and the 'occasions of sin' hove to again at the weekend. The only price to be paid – if the girl didn't fall pregnant of course – was the mandatory confession and subsequent penance.

But for those who wanted to escape from the dusty sweat, guilt, even (Gawd helpus) semen-smelling confessional into a cheap but a glorious world of glamour and excitement, beautiful women and handsome men, derring-do and heart-stopping adventure, there was the local cinema. Here the dreams of a somnambulistic nation were acted out on demand, and while the strenuously cynical customers applauded the actions on screen, they decried and denied any sign of emotional involvement in the lives of the screen characters, but deep down, most of them were secretly moved by the emotional stresses they were put vicariously through by cunning screenwriters.

Typical of the fodder that was strewn before the eyeballs of the cinemagoer was the Saturday-morning follin'-upper (following-upper or serial), during which the audience shouted for such stars as Hopalong Cassidy (the chap) and his sidekick (the pal), groaned at the girl (the mot) and rooted for Captain Marvel – even in baggy pre-Lycra tights that made his legs look like badly-lagged drainpipes and vests that barely contained his sagging belly. These short films and others like them were screened in half-hour episodes before the main feature. The entrance cost thruppence. The smoke-fug was strangely comforting, if a little throat-catching. The local cinema was the womb of stillborn desires and the vault of shrivelled ambitions. When the more expensive city-centre movie palaces had finished with the reels they were sent on to the local flea houses: the MGM musicals, the powerful dramas, the goofy comedies, the restrained romances, the gangster shoot-'em-ups and the stately Westerns. All on scratchy celluloid reels with fuzzy sound, so even these harbingers of dreams were second-hand. Each feature was started with a cast list and the names of the technicians involved, of whom only the director had any chance of registering with the average audience. The other arcane credits flipped or scrolled by, uncomprehended. These were the days of the continuous performances to which patrons could enter at any time of day they chose. Danny Kaye sang a song about them which contained the lines:

This is a picture that begins in the middle
For those who came in in the middle.

Customers who arrived at a dramatic point had to go through all the attendant settling-down processes before trying to fathom out the plot. Of course, this played havoc with the screenwriter's and the director's intention to tell a story which had a carefully plotted beginning, middle and end.

The Manor Cinema in Stoneybatter in Dublin North was a tatty old place, slumped amidst dreary shops and lace-curtained, two-storey houses, but, in the eyes of the swarming Saturday children, it was a palace in which they could escape from the tawdry reality of Dublin into the glittering dream world of American mainstream fantasies. They hollered for the chap in the follin'-uppers until they were hoarse; shouted, "Shazam!" on cue to help get Captain Marvel out of a weekly scrape. During the features, they hid their heads behind the seats in front at the delicious unravelling of various mummies and screamed with the best of them at Bela Lugosi's pale face. They worried about the credibility of Randolph Scott and Jeff Chandler and succumbed totally to the presence of Edward G. Robinson. Cowboys and comics, gangsters and grovelling villains were the grist to their Saturday mill. Laughter, tears, thrill and rage were generated by the exploits of people who were, sometimes, more real to them than their neighbours. Who did they know in real life who bared his soul more openly than Jimmy Stewart? Who could they trust more implicitly than Spencer Tracy? Who could they rely on to 'get them out of here' more than John Wayne? Who could face up to the sort of trials they faced with more native wit than Leo Gorcey? What girl did they know in Blackhorse Lane who had the grace of Margaret O'Brien?

On some days, newspaper boys would run through the dense clouds of tobacco smoke which billowed from the balcony where the adults and older children sat loftily above the yelling and struggling kids below.

"*Herald* 'r *Mail*?"

4

"Come up here with your fecking papers," would come a deep voice from the balcony.

The aged commissionaire would stride down the aisle with a pump-action spray, covering the children on each side with a mist of disinfectant. Some lad would invariably stand up in his seat and inhale the spray into his open mouth, to the laughter of his friends. Suddenly the lights would go out, to a great deal of shushing. Onto the screen would come the images that they had invested their thruppence to see.

After one such screening, young Johnny Moore made his way homeward, his head full of stories and dreams and dramatic intentions. His mind was still buzzing around those heavenly beings on the screen whose lives wove themselves around dramatic events which threatened their sanity, their sense of humour and even their physical existence. But however horrendous the dangers they had to face, they all emerged in the final scenes intact and victorious. He knew that the events shown weren't real. That they were devised, that they were experienced by actors, some of whom, having died magnificently in one film, appeared again and again in subsequent films, just as good, just as innocent and just as ready to plunge into danger. But always, as he entered the cinema, he handed over his sense of belief with his thruppence and was prepared all over again. Sometimes he wondered who made these pictures, who thought them up. He was dimly aware of a place called Hollywood, full of beautiful women, handsome men and clever, very clever picture-makers.

As so often happened after a Saturday morning at the Manor, he needed room to think about the world he had inhabited for the past hour and a half, and the shortest way home was along Blackhorse Avenue, towards and into Blackhorse Lane. The further he would walk, the closer would seem the horizon and the lower would seem the clouds. And he knew that, as he came to the lane and passed the low, dark-roofed cottages and damp, echoing yards, bedraggled trees and car-free roads, he would be infected by the physical, mental and spiritual inertia that hung there. But now he had to dwell on the picture he had just seen and conjure up some of the wonderful things the people in it had said and done.

The Phoenix Park was the place for that. Winter or summer, there was room there to dream, to talk aloud when alone, to imagine anyone he liked appearing from behind a tree and stepping into his life with new sensations, strange quests and marvellous adventures. As had thousands of Dublin boys before him, he considered the park his private space. Only he knew its secrets, its hidden treasures. Only he could creep up so close to the placid fallow deer that browsed and wandered there in complete safety. Only Johnny Moore knew the way to get into the Zoological Gardens without paying. Only he knew the terrors that lurked in the low, dark tunnel through which flowed the feeder stream to the lake in the Furry Glen. Only he could cross the deep ditch the surrounded the American Embassy and dodge the CIA men that surely lurked there. He had even wormed part of his way into grounds of the Papal Nuncio but his courage had failed him at the thought of excommunication if caught by the priests that crawled all over it. Johnny had climbed nearly halfway up the massive walls of the Magazine Fort, on the side away from the road, thanks to a great tree that grew close to its stones and some ivy that clung to them. By his next birthday, he would reach the top. He did not know that two hundred years before, when the Magazine Fort had been built, Jonathan Swift, the Protestant dean of St. Patrick's, had declaimed:

Now here's proof of Irish sense
Here Irish wit is seen
When nothing's left that's worth defence
We build a magazine.

Sometimes Johnny would position himself on the railing around the Garda depot while the policemen were marching in the huge square. Daringly, he would shout out instructions to halt, wheel right, about-turn or wheel left, and wonder if the marching men could tell his voice from that of the bellowing instructor. Strangely, the men guarding the gate never gave out to him.

Once he had turned smartly in through the gates of the McKee Barracks on the avenue side, past the sentries who were barely taller than him in their baggy uniforms, and marched across the grounds towards the park side without getting caught or even noticed. He found the gate into the park and walked home, somewhat upset at the sheer carelessness of the sentries. Supposing he had been a German spy, making a map of the barracks? What then?

But most of all, he could be an Indian in the park, slipping from tree to tree, creeping up on the Huron dogs like Uncas or his father, Chigasomethingorother, or even Hawkeye, but that was Randolph Scott who he never really believed. Besides, he preferred being an Indian because Indians never gave in under torture and never got lost, even in a blizzard. Uncas froze at a movement among the low-slung branches but it was only a deer, so he released the string of his bow and lowered it to the ground. Hey. He was nearly at the gate to the lane and he hadn't worked out what he was going to say. Was he getting old?

2

It was Saturday again, and Sean was the first to weaken.

"Jay, Johnny, I'm bursting."

Sean was the youngest of the Moore children, the pet of the family and the perpetual worry of his mother. His brothers and sisters, thin for the most part but wiry and tough, were considerate of Sean and always aware of his physical vulnerability. They were careful, also, to include him in all their activities, with that tolerance which comes easily to large Dublin families. The fact that Sean was at the bottom of the clothes chain meant that he was always wearing fourth-hand hand-me-downs, and the fact that he was much smaller than his elder brothers meant that he was always slipping around in the clothes, giving the impression that if you grabbed him by the scruff of the neck, he would slip out one of the cuffs of the trousers.

Nonetheless, Johnny, the eldest boy in the Moore family, fixed him with a gimlet eye as he whined, nasally, "Eat the lovely jam, my Artful Dodger, or I'll get Bill Sikes to come and eat your heart out."

This was too much for Sean. A tear ran from his eye down into the thick smear of jam around his mouth. Sean's face was often smeared, usually with a particularly viridescent mucous, but jam was an unusual glazing and generally indicative of plenty – an infrequent phenomenon in the Moore cottage. Siobhan, his eldest sister and surrogate mother to the rest of the brood, expressed concern, so the rest of the family left Sean to her. She wiped his face with a damp piece of material that served as a tea towel when dishes needed to be dried, a fly swatter when the weather was hot and a casual facecloth when faces needed to be made reasonably presentable.

"Now look what you've done, Johnny Moore. Don't mind him, pet. Down the little red lane," she said as she coaxed Sean's habitual smile back.

The Moore children were all raggedly dressed but what they wore was clean. The kitchen in which they stood was also clean but very much the worse for years of wear. The furniture and fittings were sparse and most items had been procured at auctions, through casual trades or from deceased estates within the extended Moore family. The decorative value of the lot was, to say the least, minimal. The grey walls, with shreds of long-departed wallpaper in the corners, were pocked with damp. The floor was covered in thin linoleum which had once boasted a floral pattern. The fireplace was little more than a hole in the wall with a flue that poked through the slate roof. Ceiling there was none. Altogether the kitchen was a cheerless space, opening directly onto the back yard which sported sparse grass running to seed, nettles in the corners, a tattered privet hedge along its edge and a multi-knotted clothes line that sagged wearily from the roof above the kitchen, across the length of the yard, athwart the back lane to the top of the high wall on the other side. This drying apparatus was supported in the middle by a warped length of two-by-four deal with notches along its flank to snag the line at different heights. Along each side of the cinder track that ran between the back door and the gap which at one time had contained a gate, there had been a brave attempt to grow marigolds. The little hollows surrounding each languishing plant indicated a degree of careful, if ineffectual tending.

Inside the kitchen, Johnny was moving along the row of his siblings, spooning jam into their mouths from an almost-empty jar.

"I want to go to the lav," Attracta complained.

"When the lovely jam is gone, my dear," crooned Johnny, spooning away.

"But it's the jam that's making me want to go."

"Why can't you throw the fecking stuff away?" said Albert.

"Don't say 'feck' in this house," came the chorus.

A thin voice yelled from the lane, "Oowa, oowa, all the gang!"

"She coming."

The spoon went into overdrive. The mouths of Siobhan, Albert and Attracta did stalwart work and the jam jar was replaced, empty, on the shelf. Johnny turned and surveyed his assorted brothers and sisters, rubbing his hands and speaking with a lisp. His hunched shadow stretched across the floor and up the wall.

"Well, my dears, you have done well for old Fagin. Soon another story shall be heard in the lane."

The doorway darkened as Rita Moore came in. She stopped and looked at her children, standing around, suspiciously idle as Paul came sidling in behind her. She looked as mothers of six children, with inadequate income, usually look: tired, worn and resigned to a life that was hard for the most part and dreary for the rest of it. The prettiness of her teens had been of the type that seldom survives the twenties and never survives the drudgery and perpetual pregnancies that were all too often the lot of such as her. Her formerly pert features now looked pinched. Worry had creased her brow and the sides of her mouth. Weariness had slouched her shoulders and weakened her posture. Sometimes, however, when one of her children, usually Johnny, made her laugh and forget her worries, she could look nearly beautiful.

"What are you terrors up to?"

"Nothing," came the chorus.

Rita shrugged out of her dowdy coat and handed it to Attracta. She placed the shopping bag she was carrying on the table, untied her headscarf and sank gratefully onto the chair that Johnny pulled up for her.

"Thanks, love. Siobhan, get my slippers, there's a dear."

All eyes fastened on Johnny as he leaned on the table and fixed his mother with a steady gaze. "Mother, who carries all the cares of the world?"

"What? The cares of this family are enough for me, Johnny Moore. Attracta, pass me my pinny."

"To the world, it is only an empty jam jar, but to me, it's the Holy Grail, Aladdin's lamp, the treasure of Sierra Madre."

Johnny glanced at the rest. They all nodded, impressed. Rita tied the apron on.

"There's no empty jam jar."

Siobhan eagerly took the jam jar and held it out. All eyes fastened on it.

"There is, Mammy."

"Sacred Heart! Who ate all that?"

"It was gone yesterday," said Paul.

"It bloody well wasn't."

Rita took hold of the jar and made as if to throw it out through the door. The children's intake of breath was simultaneous. Fighting a smile, Rita offered the jar to Johnny.

"All right. Take it. Now out and play, all of you."

With a cheer, they all crashed through the door. Sean, slow as always, made to follow them. Rita spoke to him gently.

"Sean?"

He approached her. There was a smear of jam on his cheek.

Rita wiped it off and offered her fingers for him to lick. He shook his head and made a face.

"Are you all right, pet?"

"Yeah. I'm grand."

"No running around now."

She pushed him towards the door and from the bag took a few – a very few – purchases and lined them up carefully on the table. One for the all-too-fleeting teen years when beauty was the secret desire. Two for the handsome beau you prayed for and fought against the minute he appeared and tried to drop his hand. Three for the labour pains that nobody said would be as bad as they were, and which followed all too quickly on the short, shabby and uncomfortable fumbling. Four for the children that resulted in serried ranks until your innards or some other unknowable force stopped the functioning of your womb. Five, and she had lined up little milestones on a life that had settled into a dull throb, like an incipient toothache.

Had Rita been asked, she would not have described her life as very hard. She knew no better. She had been the youngest of four girls reared in a cottage a little better than this. She had left school at the lowest legal age, as all her sisters had done, and taken up maid's work in a convent in the parish. She had to keep house for twenty domineering nuns who treated her with the bare minimum of respect. There she existed from eight in the morning until nine at night, when she was reluctantly allowed retire to her tiny, ill-shaped room under an iron roof that provided no insulation from the stifling summers or the ice-cold winters. She was allowed Sundays off and spent them at home where there was room for her, since three of her sisters had married and moved out into the same sort of cottage in the same sort of ugly street in the same sort of unlovely suburb.

On Sundays, she associated with other girls in the neighbourhood and would join them at the Sunday-night *ceili* in the local church hall, under the watchful eye of the parish priest. There, in spite of the clerical vigilance, she had met and 'done a line' with Tom, who was a nifty dancer and a good singer, accomplishments that marked him out as being above the average in attractiveness. One thing had inevitably led to another and, since he had what appeared to be a steady job in a mental hospital, they were married and she was pregnant at the usual working-class speed. She left the nuns, Tom left what would be a succession of jobs and they moved into this cottage. And there her life shrank to that of a provider and nourisher of a brood of children who seemed to have as restricted a choice in lifestyle as she and Tom had had.

Johnny's head appeared around the doorjamb.

"Listen, Ma. About the—"

"Hurry along now. You'll be late and they'll all be waiting."

He made fine bow and disappeared. Rita gazed for a few moments at the spot where he had stood. Then she glanced at the mildewed picture of the Sacred Heart on the wall.

"Isn't there anything you can do about the price of jam?" she murmured.

3

The old cast-iron pump stood guard at the entrance of the back lane. Piles of rubbish, discarded prams, bedsprings and mattresses were strewn about. Down one side stretched the remains of several ramshackle fences and stunted bushes. These bordered the back yards of the row of dilapidated cottages. It was from this back lane that the inhabitants entered and left the cottages, rather than the official front doors which looked out onto the paved Blackhorse Lane.

On the opposite side of the back lane was a high, dressed stone wall, crenellated at the top and a great thing to climb. It was the wall that bordered the Phoenix Park, the lung and recreational space of Dublin city. Above the wall loomed several broad-leaved trees, twisted and gnarled, their foliage gone for months now. The park contained deer to stalk, chestnut trees to strip of their conkers in the season and the Furry Glen to take your girl. Next to the rambling wildness of the western parts, the tidy People's Garden was a boring place to be. So was the Hollow, where prim Dubliners sat listening to the police and army bands during the day and secretive couples lay about whispering during the night. The great turf stacks, erected during the war, had dwindled to untidy heaps and the huge mound that covered the carcasses of thousands of cattle slaughtered because of foot-and-mouth was slowly subsiding. The park was a playground made in Heaven and the Moore family, like every Dublin family, considered it theirs.

Several hundred dark starlings exploded, chattering insanely, from one of the trees as the Moore children rushed out of the cottage and up to the pump. Albert and Paul struggled to gain possession of the long, curved handle, shiny from thousands of hands. As it descended under their combined weight, Siobhan rinsed the jam jar in the sparkling, cold water that gushed from the spout.

"Why is it always Johnny?" asked Paul.

"When we sent you once, we couldn't make out what it was: cops and robbers or cowboys," replied a scathing Albert.

Johnny emerged from the cottage and approached the pump.

"Johnny, where's the other jam jar?"

Johnny immediately adopted a tough-guy pose, hitched up his collar and pushed the children aside to get to Siobhan.

"It's in the mean end of town. Down some dark streets. Outta my way, punks. There's man's work to be done."

He grabbed the jam jar, tugged the imaginary brim of a fedora at Siobhan and pushed through the children again to stride out of the lane. They were delighted.

Siobhan gave Paul a look. "See?"

Just before he turned the corner into the road, Johnny stooped and picked up a rusty old tin. He turned back to the children and gave them an exaggerated wink.

Out on the larger road, Johnny approached the windowsill of one of the small houses. On it were several pots and jam jars containing bedraggled flowers and plants. Sidling up to the window, he pressed himself against the wall and reached slowly out to take one of the jars. He took the flowers out, placed them in the tin and set the tin on the windowsill. One flower flopped over and Johnny tried to make it stand upright, just as the grim face of the houseowner peered through the glass. Johnny smiled at the face, gave the flower a final little flick and moved off, the jam jars hidden behind his back.

The road got wider as he approached the suburb's centre and the houses became a little more substantial. There was an increasing number of motor cars parked at the sides of the roads and Johnny made a mental note to study the names of the different cars and the signs they had on their bonnets. He must keep up with the times. There was an Opel, and he wondered where that was made; and there was a Ford – America, of course. Johnny moved out onto the road to avoid two hopelessly drunken men fighting each other silently and ineffectively. He started to skip and shadow-box down the centre of the road, a fist thrust inside each jar.

"A left hook. Duff! A right cross. Duff! John L. Sullivan is down! Eight! Nine! Ten! Gentleman Jim is the new champ. The Corbetts have done it again!"

Suddenly, out of a side street appeared three rough-looking boys slightly older than Johnny. He had seen them before on their way to the park. They lived in Cabra, a sprawling housing estate which now accommodated those who had been moved from the inner-city slums. Ripped from the community which had nurtured them in its own rough way, the children of such estates that ringed the city seemed almost feral to the people of the neighbourhood. No orchard was safe from them; nor was any stray boy with jam jars. They saw him and started to howl gleefully.

The tallest said, "Come here. I'll bleeding kill you."

"He's got two jam jars. Get him."

Johnny took to his heels.

"Mother of Mercy, is this the end of Rico?" he gasped.

Fast as he was, the boys gained on him, no breath spared for shouting. In front of Johnny, Father Mulligan, a dark-clad priest, came out of a house and started to walk towards town. Johnny caught up and fell into step with him. The Cabra boys fell back, muttering, and started to follow like jackals. The priest looked down at Johnny.

"Johnny, isn't it?

"Yes, Father."

"Off to the Manor, I see. Good, it'll keep you out of mischief for a few hours. Run along, you'll be late."

Johnny cast a glance at the following boys. "Erm… bless me, Father, for I have sinned."

"But I only hear confessions in church. Unless, of course, it's very serious."

"Oh, it is."

"And very urgent."

Johnny clutched his chest. "I felt awful this morning."

"We better hurry up, so. How did you sin, my son?"

"I stole nearly a whole half a jar of jam."

"And did you eat it all?"

"No, we all ate it."

"All? How many of you are there, now?"

"Six, last time I was home."

"Well, you better say six Hail Marys for your penance, seeing as how you appear to be the one who had the main benefit from six… sins. Fair enough?"

The Cabra boys had by now given up following and drifted away.

"When the chips are down, Padre," said a relieved Johnny. "You can't say fairer than that."

"Say an act of contrition now and run along or you'll be late."

Johnny ran off, crossing himself.

"Oh my God," he said as he crashed into the middle-aged Mrs Murphy, who had stepped around a corner and into his path. "I am heartily sorry," he exclaimed as she recovered her balance, "for having offended thee," he shouted back as he sped on towards his destination.

4

Father Mulligan walked on to the church he had been serving in for what seemed like all his life. It was confession time and he felt the familiar headache gather inside his skull. His flock was obsessed with sin and he suspected that some of it was the church's fault, although he could admit that to nobody. He dreaded the weekly immersion in the dark confessional, when the foetidness of the sinners crept through the grille, with the aura of anxiety hard upon its heels. Strange; they were always on edge, even though most of their sins were tawdry, shabby exploits and thoughts. With the best will in the world, he tried to take them seriously, but after two hours he always became bad-tempered. The regulars knew that and came early to avoid a penance made sharper by irritability.

His headache vanished when he moved into the church, having donned his vestments. Paddy Fortycoats was first in the pew and his rare confessions were cheerful affairs. Back from a month or two spent tramping the roads of Ireland, he was always full of nonsense and smelling of hay and turf-smoke and freedom. If he wasn't the original of that nickname, he was fit to carry it. His bulk was augmented by layer upon layer of ragged coats, cloaks and jackets, all with capacious pockets and secret crevices containing the Lord alone knew what loot, treasures and assorted mementos collected here and there in his far-flung travels. It was a wonder that he could fit into the confessional. The priest had often argued with the bishop as to whether Paddy's countrywide peregrinations didn't disqualify him from the title because the original Paddy was supposed to restrict himself to the streets of Dublin, but if he had commandeered the illustrious name illegally, who was to challenge him? He was still great value in a town that prized its characters and supported them generously. What was a city, after all, without its eccentrics who managed to live long, unproductive and apparently aimless lives with equanimity and a certain grace? They did no obvious harm, except to the sensibilities of those who were fixed irrevocably in place by penury and inertia, shackled to a motley collection of indifferent possessions and haphazard habits. Father Mulligan nodded at Paddy and went into the confessional. Paddy was not far behind him as he slipped into the side booth. The priest slid the intervening panel open.

"God be with, my son."

That set Paddy off.

"And his Holy Mother and Joseph – his worldly and saintly guardian – and St. Patrick and Bridget and the entire plethora of sainted and blessed intercessors. May they all be with you."

"Thanks," said Father Mulligan.

"Not all at the one time, mind you," continued Paddy. "But when you need them, may they be queuing up at the parapet of Heaven to leap over to succour you, like every year was a leap year, one after the divine other."

"Thanks again," replied the priest, amused at the manoeuvring for the spiritual high ground. "Are you ready to make a good confession?"

"I'm certainly ready to make a confession. You'll tell me whether it's good or not. The penance you give will tell."

"Do you think the size of the penance raises the value of the sin? What is this, a game of sacramental poker?"

"Poker? Ah, I remember that game. Tell me, does a stout hawthorn stick still beat four aces?" Father Mulligan could hear Paddy settling down for a good old chat. "It's so long since I've been to confession that I've forgotten the rules."

"How long is it since your last confession?" he asked.

"Let's see now... there was a King of Ireland then."

"Brian Boru, I suppose?"

"No, he was in the grandad's time. I'm talking about one of them English gurriers that was always getting their pictures on the pennies. Edward or George or some such toffy-nosed name. I got thirty days in Kiltimagh for shouting out all that bleeding king's shortcomings. Didn't repeat myself once."

"You deserved thirty days," said the priest, feeling like the straight man in a comedy routine, which he knew he was. "Public obscenity is an offence, you know."

"Ah, it wasn't for the cursing they put me away. It was for revealing state secrets."

"How long is it since you were shriven?"

"Shriven, is it? That's a grand word, haven't heard that in a good while. That's one of the things that's changed for the worst, Father – the words. The words have got shorter and they mean less. We should never have given up the ould tongue, the Gaelic."

"We'd little choice in the matter."

"That's true. Shoved their language down our throats, the English did. But sure, we get our own back on them by improving it out of all recognition."

"I'm inclined to agree. But we're here for confession and—"

"The Irish words were more mellifluous. *Bolscaraght!* Bejaysus – ye need to be in the whole of your health to say that. The Irish could spell, hey? And the names we used to have! Caoindealbháin, Ó Mathghamhna, Ó Muircheartach, Ó Tíghearnaigh. When I hear those names, I want to invade

England. And then there was Mac an tSagairt (son of a priest). No offence, Father. It was before your time."

"None taken. Now, your confession!"

"Easy now, Father. I'm getting round to it. Sort of creeping up on my sins, in case they'd slip out of my mind in fear of forgiveness. Do sins have a life of their own, I wonder?"

Father Mulligan was enjoying himself, but the scraping of feet on the floor and the subdued coughing indicated that a few parishioners were becoming impatient. They were such a demanding lot, he thought, as if another second without purging their souls would plunge them into eternal damnation. Well, they would have to hang a little between Heaven and Hell for a few more minutes. He parted the curtains on the confession box and glared out. As expected, Mrs Murphy was first in the queue but they all shut up like a box of Jacob's cream crackers when they saw his face. Should he really have such power over this lot, he asked himself? Yes, he should, he concluded. Paddy was good value.

"Well, sins have a way of multiplying themselves," he said. "That's a form of life, I suppose."

"That's a powerful, intellectual thing you've just said, Father. It's a pleasure to meet such cleverness. But as I was saying, I try to keep up the standard of the language in my travels, for fear it'd degenerate altogether."

"You do, do you?"

"I do, I do. For example, I might say to some woman who opens the door to me, 'Good morning, my good woman, would you like to bestow on me the infinitesimal bit of a rasher, for the deification of God?'"

"And does it work?"

"'Deed it does. Another time I might let rip with, 'God save all here, and is there a superfluity of sustenance in this house that could alleviate a touch of the malnutrition?'"

"That's a good one. But your confession…?"

21

"Oh, it's coming, it's coming. The trouble is, Father, I'm not sure what's a sin and what isn't any more, it's so long since I thought about it."

"The real sins haven't changed since... since God gave Moses the Ten Commandments."

"Now that's a good place to start. I remember them. Let's see now if I can jog the ould conscience with them as a sort of mnemonic. First, *I am the Lord thy God... any... whatsit... strange gods before me.* No, pure as the driven snow on that one. Second, *thou shalt not take the name of the Lord in vain* – ah, bejaysus, that's a divil. Not that I mean any disrespect when I—"

"How would you feel, do you think, if day and night, somebody thoughtlessly called out your name in almost every sentence, and you could hear it, clear as a bell, every single time?"

"That'd be a terrible pain up the—"

"And supposing, just once, that person actually wanted to attract your attention because he was in need of help? What then?"

"I'd ignore the garrulous ould reprobate."

"Exactly." For a moment Father Mulligan actually thought he was winning but Paddy soon disillusioned him."

"All right. That's one against me. Where was I? Three, the Sabbath, keep it holy. Now, I don't indulge in what I would call 'work' on a Sunday but perforce, Father, perforce."

"What do you mean?"

"Sure, it's no use begging when all the ould fellas are at home – they won't let their ould wans give me anything. So I find a barn or a haystack or a hedge, and I while away the Sabbath in benign and beneficial thought."

"That's not keeping it holy. Don't you ever think of church on a Sunday?"

"I do, when it's raining."

"Not good enough. That's another one against you."

Another cough came from outside. Mrs Murphy was undoubtedly feeling the weight of her sins. Father Mulligan opened the curtain again and let out his late-Saturday-morning glare. Silence immediately descended. It was broken by Paddy.

"That's two out of three so far. You wouldn't like to lay a little bet on the outcome?"

"I would not! Carry on."

"Only asking. What's next?"

"Four, *honour thy father and thy mother.*"

"Why wouldn't I? Next?"

"*Thou shalt not kill?*"

"Wouldn't hurt a horsefly."

"*Thou shalt not commit adultery.*"

"Ah, sure, who'd want the likes of me? Next?"

"*Thou shalt not steal.*"

The silence was pregnant.

"*Thou shalt not steal.*"

"I was doing well there, Father, wasn't I?"

"*Thou shalt not steal.*"

Paddy cleared his throat noisily.

"Do I detect a guilty conscience?" asked the priest.

"I wouldn't call it 'stealing' exactly."

"What would a Garda call it?"

"Oh, he'd call it stealing all right."

"And he would know, wouldn't he? I mean, that's his job, isn't it? Distinguishing stealing from an actual loan. What sort of things?"

"Oh, nothing that would upset the financial viability of anybody's estate."

"What sort of things?"

"I mean, nothing they'd want to leave in their wills. Fruit. A fair bit of fruit. And vegetables. The odd hen."

"Yes?"

"The occasional bottle of milk."

"Yes?"

"A bike, once. But somebody stole that from *me*, so that doesn't count."

"Yes it does. What else?"

"I stole an ashtray from Moran's pub in Bundoran. A great, heavy thing with *Sweet Afton* written on it."

"And what, I wonder, would a gentleman of the road want with an ashtray?"

"Nothing. I found that out the hard way. I lugged it all around the west, till I threw it at a dog once that was molesting me."

"However, you stole it. What else?"

"I... er... I stole a thing from a priest's house once."

"I see."

"It was one of those glass balls with a little church inside, and when you shook it, the snow flew around and slowly settled on the church roof and the road. It was great gas looking at it around a fire at night. Then I gave it to Shifty Connor, an ould tramp from Cobh. I found him lying half naked on the ground by a dead fire, coughing his lungs up. September, it was, and getting very cold. Shifty shouldn't have been out in that weather. So I gave it to him to look at, lit the fire again and left him there. He looked so peaceful."

"So poor Shifty spent his last hours gazing at a wee church he could never enter."

"Divil a bit. He stuck it into a sock and used it as a cosh at the next Puck Fair. Broke many a head with it that year, he did."

"All right, all right! How about bearing false witness against your neighbour? How are you on that?"

"Gameball, Father."

"Are you sure?"

"Would I lie? Unless..."

"Unless...?"

"Unless you'd call getting Tadgh O'Donnell into trouble for something he didn't do 'bearing false witness'?"

"Yes. I'd call that bearing false witness."

"Even though he's always got a crooked mouth on him and deserved it?"

"Even though."

"Well, we were cutting the red seaweed on Arran a few years back. Terrible work, it is. You're in a greasy forest that's lying on its side, up to your oxter in the slippery, slithery stuff, following the tide out, bent over until you think your back'll never be straight again. Tadgh and me had been given knives to cut the stuff and I felt the blade heave in the hilt when I hit a stone with it. Now Tadgh had put his knife down on the half-tide rock while he was dragging the weed out of the way of the waves. Quick as a flash, I swapped the knives and went back to my cutting.

"When the tide came in and we handed back the knives, the old josser tested each one. 'Who was using this knife?' he bellows.

"I look at it and I say, 'I can't tell a lie – that's Tadgh's knife.' I got my two florins for the day's work and Tadgh got nothing."

"So that's another one against you. You're not doing so well, are you? Now, what about coveting your neighbour's wife?"

"And what would the likes of me need with a wife? I'm told they have a way of imposing themselves on you and upsetting the equilibrium."

"And coveting thy neighbour's goods?"

"From what I see, them fellas that have goods have their hearts broke with them. If it's a house they have, there's rent to be paid or a... whatdoyoucallit?"

"A mortgage."

"A moooortgage! Imagine letting them banking yobbos get their claws into you with a moooortgage. And them motor cars! I hear you have to be filling them up with petrol every minute. Sometimes I think I wouldn't mind a donkey, but look at the price of grazing! No, I can't say as I've seen many goods worth the coveting. Is that the lot?"

"Yes, that's the ten of them."

"How did I do?"

"Six out of ten. I've seen worse. Will you change your ways?"

"I'll do my best, Father."

"That's fair enough. Now say an act of contrition. Do you know how to?"

"I think so."

He muttered through the prayer and Father Mulligan gave him absolution with a free heart. Paddy started to rearrange his various layers of clothing, out of which wafted a not-unattractive aroma of grass, dust, damp and ancient ways.

"That's a load off my mind, Father," said Paddy as he fumbled. "I'll be on my way, so. Unless there's a smidgen of a sausage suppurating on the stove next door?"

"Any sausages in there are Hafner's sausages and, as such, are reserved for those in holy orders. However, if you ask the housekeeper nicely, she might be able to lay her hands on a tincture of turnover with a soupçon of jam on it."

"Sure, that'd go down very well, Father. May you continue to bask in the benevolence of the Almighty."

"May your road be downhill to the next dosshouse."

"And may your novenas nestle in the eardrums of the saints."

"May there be seraphim at your shoulder and cherubim at your cheeks."

Paddy stood up and paused for the coup de grâce. "May the holy hordes of Heaven hover over your every endeavour."

He stepped smartly outside before the priest could counter-attack and said to Mrs Murphy, "You're in luck. The ould priest is in grand form."

5

At the junction of Manor Street and Prussia Street the resulting road to the south was wider but did not confer any additional stature on the buildings on either side. They comprised a motley collection of single- and double-storey homes, the occasional one-storey shop and the very occasional substantial 19th-century edifice or three-storey dull brick dwelling. There were kids everywhere in the space between the converging roads. A swarming knot of them was milling around an old, scruffy man with a precarious barrow laden with jam jars. He was examining each jar handed to him, refusing chipped ones and handing over thruppenny bits from a greasy bus conductor's bag for each two jars that passed his careful scrutiny. He kept up a bad-tempered tirade all the while.

"Jam jars for money. Good coin of the rellim. Mind, ye little feckers. Yiz'll knock over me barrow. Lemme look. Are they chipped? All right, that's sixpence. Jam jars. Jam jars for coin of the rellim. A penny ha'penny a jar. Satisfaction guaranteed."

By dint of shoving and gouging, Johnny managed to force his way through and swap his jars for a thruppenny bit. Clutching it to his bosom, he turned to approach…

The Manor Cinema.

He ascended the steps, humming the 20th Century Fox fanfare, and stopped to examine the two posters mounted on the wall. He drew a bead at the one advertising *High Noon* and was ungluing his eyes like Stan Laurel at the Laurel and Hardy *Block-Heads* poster when he was grabbed by his collar and hurled down the steps towards the queue. It was the commissionaire, dressed in a greasy blue coat sprinkled with bedraggled gold piping and dandruff.

"If you're going to the pictures, get in the queue," he bawled.

The queue was a screaming mass of children from which, every so often, a child would be expectorated in tears. Johnny crashed into this tumult and collided with a brawny young thug called Flaherty by everybody because nobody knew his first name. He had the precarious confidence that his bulk gave him. He had the cunning that came from having to cope with a dangerous, alcoholic father. His slow progress through school meant that he was mostly in the company of younger children whom he could bully with impunity. He could write in a surprisingly adult hand, even though he couldn't spell, so the other children got him to write notes from their mothers, asking for time off school or excusing them for not having written homework. His slow thinking process made him resentful of bright children, such as he knew Johnny to be, and this resentment triggered quick violence.

"Watch where you're going, Moore, or I'll beat the shite out of you," he growled as he sucked on a cigarette butt.

"Another fine mess you've gotten us into, Stanley," murmured Johnny as he joined what appeared to be the end of the queue.

"Who's smoking there? Children can't smoke in my cinema."

"We're not in your cinema yet, ye stupid eejit," said Flaherty out of the side of his mouth as he threw the butt away.

"Who said that?" bellowed the commissionaire, lunging towards the queue.

Flaherty and two of his pals took advantage of the confusion to dodge to the front, Flaherty cuffing one youngster who was about to complain. At that moment, the doors of the cinema were opened and the children ran screaming up the steps.

Within ten minutes the cinema was full. A dense cloud of cigarette smoke billowed from the balcony where the adults and older teens sat. The ground floor was crammed with yelling and struggling kids.

Eventually the lights went out, to a great deal of shutups. Onto the screen came the image of Stan Laurel in army uniform, rifle on his shoulder. Cheers greeted his first appearance and laughter followed at the sight of him striding up and down in a deep trench worn in the ground outside an army hut.

Johnny squirmed into his seat, grinning delightedly.

Several hours later, the Moore children were seated on one of the mattresses in the back lane, totally absorbed in what Johnny was saying as he stood in front of them.

"The people are hiding in their houses," said Johnny. "Looking out at the only man who can bring law and order to their town. Gary Cooper knows what he has to do. He walks down that street, where four men are waiting to kill him. His wife is in the train. She's going to leave him. But he's the sheriff and he's got to kill Miller."

Johnny suddenly sang:
"*Or lie a coward, a craven coward in my grave.*
Do not forsake me, oh my darling,
On this, our wedding day."

He turned to see his father, Tom Moore, coming into the back lane and smiled briefly at him. Tom had casual, Celtic good looks: a pale, symmetrical face; jet-black curly hair and a dapper way of moving. There was, however, a sulkiness that appeared readily and which stemmed from vague dissatisfaction with a life that had thrown him from feckless teens into demanding paternity with bewildering speed.

The other children, wrapped in the story, were unaware of Tom, who drew an imaginary gun and fired a shot at Johnny. Johnny smiled again and carried on, matching his actions to the words.

"Cooper hears glass breaking and ducks behind a house. 'Miller!' he calls. One man comes out wearing a woman's bonnet. Cooper ducks. Cooper fires. *Kuush!*"

Tom clutched his breast at the shot and staggered up the path and into the cottage. Rita was standing at the window, listening to Johnny. She moved away as Tom came staggering in.

"Shot by my own son. I'm done for," he said.

"We're all done for if you didn't get the job."

"I got the job."

"Thanks be to the Sacred Heart for that."

"Thanks be to Jacko," Tom replied, and Rita frowned. "The last job in Dublin. On the fecking buses."

He grabbed Rita and did a few tango steps.

"Don't say 'feck' in this house."

"*Kuush!*" shouted Johnny from the lane, and the children started to cheer.

Tom buried his face in Rita's neck. "Feck, feck, feck, feck," he said, and a smile lit up her face. Through the window the sound came of Johnny leading the children in song:

"*Do not forsake me, oh my darlin'*
On this, our wedding day-aaay
Do not forsake me, oh my darlin'
Wait. Wait along."

6

In the small, prefabricated schoolroom adjoining the main stone buildings of the Phoenix Park National School, a sweating Flaherty was on his feet, reading laboriously from a book clutched tightly in one hand. With a dirty, bitten fingernail, he was tracing each word. Every so often he would pause and look up into the corner of the ceiling to see if the meaning of the difficult word lurked there.

"...But Oisín's saddle... g-g-girth broke as he... heaved the stone and he fell to the ground."

All the children, except Johnny, who was sitting directly behind Flaherty, were following, or anticipating the reading in their own books. He was listening to Flaherty with an absorbed look on his face. He loved the Fianna, the powerful but vulnerable Finn, Diarmuid of the fatal beauty spot that smote Grainne, and Oisín, the gentle giant who left magical Ireland for an even more magical Tír na nÓg and three hundred years of bliss. This was the best bit of the story: when Oisín returned to Ireland.

"Suddenly, he was no longer a... power-ful young Fenian... warrior, but a man strick-en with... ex-ex-treme old age, white-bearded and with-ered."

Whack! A cane descended on Johnny's back, wielded by the irascible headmaster who was teaching the class.

"Dreaming again, Moore? Why can't you ever pay attention? Come."

The headmaster walked to the front of the class, swishing the cane. Johnny followed him and, as he passed a relieved Flaherty, the latter stuck his foot out. Johnny kicked Flaherty's ankle hard. Flaherty let out a yelp. The headmaster turned.

"You too, Flaherty. You seem to be keen on joining the fun."

The two rueful boys walked to the front where the head administered two cuts on each of Johnny's hands, interspersing each cut with acid comments.

"You never pay attention, do you?" *Whack.* "When are you going to do this school a favour" *whack* "and get a job?" *Whack.* "I've had enough of you." *Whack.* "Flaherty? You're next."

Flaherty stepped forward to receive the same treatment, glaring at Johnny. After the smarting two had regained their places, the headmaster appointed another boy to carry on reading and specifically instructed Johnny to keep his eye on his book, while he fondled the cane.

The headmaster liked the cane. It made what he considered his job – subduing boys – easier. It had a direct, uncomplicated effect on boyish behaviour which no degree of shouting could accomplish quite so satisfactorily. It fitted snugly into the hand, made a pleasing sound as it swished through the air and an even more pleasant sound as it connected with cringing flesh. Besides, the little gobshites deserved plentiful applications of its whippy, stinging length. For forty years he had been trying to get even one of them to listen, really listen, to no avail. It was as if the younger generations had been bred into some sort of dumbness. Thank God he had no children of his own. Just imagine if he had and they too were dumb, incapable of taking in even the rudiments of knowledge, let alone wisdom? No, thank you very much, no sawn-off, short-arsed, snot-nosed sniveller would ever disappoint him in his own immaculately waxed semi. At least he could leave them all behind in the school at the end of each day.

That afternoon, Johnny and his friends Tomas and Michael were walking towards the local field where they often played their games, which were made exciting by the possibility of being chased by one of the bulky, wellington-booted cattle and sheep tenders. They were all carrying hurley sticks and as they passed an old, weathered Anglican church, each rattled his stick along the railings. Michael stopped and looked up at the noticeboard.

"Wonder what it's like in there?"

"It's a sin to go into a Protestant church, isn't it, Johnny?" piped Michael.

"They say it is," said Johnny. "They say you'll go to Hell," he added with relish.

"Do Protestants go to Hell?" Tomas wanted to know.

"Yeah, 'cause they don't have confession."

"They can't go to Hell. There's no room. Hell's full of feckers like you."

Johnny tapped the ball along the ground, and Michael and Tomas followed, trying unsuccessfully to get the ball away from him as he started to chant:

"*Proddy, Proddy on the wall*
Doesn't know how to hit a ball."

They moved on until they came to a fence and clambered over it into the field. Quickly, they placed their jerseys and jackets to represent a goal and Michael took his place as goalie. The other two tried to get the ball past him, with little success. All of a sudden Johnny cocked his head as a song was heard in the roadway.

"*Sons of toil and danger*
Will you fear the stranger
And bow down to Burgundy?"

33

Johnny stopped playing and joined in:

"Forward, forward, march against the foe
Onward, onward, the lily banners blow."

It was Tom Moore, who climbed easily over the fence. The boys greeted him.

"What sort of song is that?" asked Tomas.

"That's the song the ould cow died of. Give us a belt of that ball."

Tom took Johnny's proffered stick and caught the ball that Michael tossed to him. With a surprisingly lithe movement, he tossed the ball and hit it straight up in the air. Without moving from the spot, he raised his hand, caught the ball again and tossed it back to a delighted Michael.

"He won the distance puck at Croke Park," said Johnny, not without some pride.

"The longest puck in Leinster," Tom assented, handing back the hurley.

"You could have played in the all-Ireland," said Michael.

"True," said Tom, "I could have."

"But you gave it up." Johnny was disapproving.

"I had more important things to do with my life. Well, see you later. I've some business to attend to."

He strode across the field towards some men who were standing in a circle, alternately looking down and then looking up. Groans and laughter were heard distantly.

"Business, my arse," said Michael, and ducked as Johnny took a swing at him with his hurley.

The men were playing pitch-and-toss, a form of gambling that the police had deemed illegal and the priests had declared immoral. Tom had joined them and was looking desperate as he held out his index and second fingers. One of the men placed two ha'pennies on them and stood back. Muttering, Tom tossed the coins and swore as they landed. The other men gathered up the coins that they had placed around the grass and Tom looked around at a burly, hard-faced man who was standing just outside the circle.

"Skin the Goat, let's have a pound," said Tom.

"It'll cost you two."

"Two?!"

"That's the deal."

Sighing, Tom held out his hand. With a smooth, unhesitating movement, Skin the Goat placed a pound note in it. Tom took the money and with a preening glance at the other players, threw the pound on the grass and held out his two fingers. Two coins were placed on them and Tom tossed. He groaned as the coins landed and looked down to where another pound note was being offered.

Sometime later, Tom and Skin the Goat were leaving the field.

"I'll give you your two pounds on payday," said Tom. "That suit you?"

Skin the Goat nodded. His seeming casualness was due to the certain knowledge that no man in his right mind would renege on a debt to him. Tales abounded as to the many men who had been badly hurt or had left town because they hadn't understood 'the deal' according to Skin the Goat. He never lent large amounts of money but he lent to large numbers of men, and he charged 100% interest because on a small amount, repayment of such usury was possible if inconvenient. He knew better than most the problems of paying – and collecting – if a man borrowed out of his league.

"I'll have better luck at the cattle market next Wednesday," continued Tom. "Those drovers are always game. If you let me have another two then, I'll pay you back out of my winnings."

"I hear you're on the buses now. Good money, that."

"Not bad."

"Regular, though."

"As clockwork."

"You'll need more than a two-pound stake to beat them culchies. I'll meet you at the park gate, just after they've had their lunch-hour jars. They get a bit brave then. And don't *you* drink before the game. This is business."

Skin walked on, leaving Tom a bit bemused as to how he had suddenly gone into partnership, as it were, with such a dangerous man. He'd always wanted a quiet life, or so he said. In fact his life was so quiet it was killing him. It was years since he had woken up looking forward to the day that lay ahead. He couldn't stand the cottage, with the kids yelling and Rita avoiding his eyes most days and nowhere to put himself. But where could he go? He used to go out to the seaside a lot, but carting the kids all the way out to Sutton got worse each year. It used to be OK with just him and Rita, but Jaysus, that was ages ago. What was happening to his life? It was going so fast, like the school holidays used to.

You could lose yourself in a job, but jobs were sporadic and never lasted long. The culchies had the civil service sewn up, and besides, you needed Irish and good marks and exams and all that shite to get in there. A few jars with Jacko was the only diversion he had available and that cost money, and Jacko was, well, a bit limited, always talking about the things that happened to him on the buses. The buses, for Chrissake! And here Tom was now, starting on the buses, the worst fecking job in Dublin.

He'd dreamed of being a singer once, a real one, not like Ollie Flanagan who sang with that lousy four-piece at the tennis club every Saturday. Jaysus, he was dire, hadn't changed his repertoire in years. No, Tom'd sing in big halls, at the Royal Cinema in the supporting programme. Maybe even on tours, too. Or the radio. Real songs with real meaning in them. Thomas Moore always brought the house down. His *Believe Me, if All Those Endearing Young Charms* was good, or *Beautiful Dreamer* by Foster. But the marching songs and the ballads from the light operas were best of all; you could get real energy into them. And where did he hear those songs? On the BBC Light Programme, mostly. He hated to admit it but the English seemed to have more respect for a good song, even though the Irish were always bragging about their singing.

But Christ, the stuff they tried to teach you at school! *Philib a'Cheoil* was a hoor. Them drawn-out notes took the breath out of you. He was put in for the *feis ceoil* once and had to sing it. Down to the Father Matthew Hall he had trundled with his little card that was supposed to be signed and brought back. He'd never been there, except in the night for the yearly pantomime. Those principal boys – girls with great legs – always put him in a state, except when they sang with their arms around the leading mot. Jaysus! Dire.

Anyway, he had gone into a building next to the Father Matthew Hall and into a room where an ould fella sat behind a high desk, marking in a big book. Tom put his card on the desk and sang the fecking *Philib a'Cheoil*. The ould fella said nothing, so Tom took the card and left. There were no marks on the card so he never took it back to school and nobody ever asked him how he'd done.

In fact, the office was that of an accountant in a firm of importers and exporters of jute sacking, which had nothing to do with the *feis*. The accountant dined out on the story for ages. He always said that Dublin would be a better place altogether if a small gurrier came into your office once a day and gave you a song.

Years later, Tom found out the true name of the song was *Ceol Na Pioba* – pipe music, not the name of a fella. It just fecking shows you!

He joined the choir at the Pro Cathedral for a while but the way they drew out the notes got on his nerves: *Faith of our faa-aaa-aaa-thers* (pause) *hooooooooly faith…* That was wojus, and the young fella who kept scatting jazz breaks like Louis

Armstrong or Tommy Dorsey in a low voice only made things worse.

Tom tried singing to a mot once, but he never did it again. He was giving her a bar home after a hop and he sang *Ah, Sweet Mystery of Life* into her ear. When she got off she refused to give him a *coort*, merely called him a dirty-looking eejit and flounced off. Come to think of it, he used to sing to Rita and she enjoyed it – well, she said she did, before they got married, of course. It all stopped after he walked down the aisle in a borrowed suit, with all the lads gawping. Here he was now, with six kids. Still a singer looking for his song.

7

Moving slowly under the stunted, bare trees of a small hawthorn plantation, an unkempt, middle-aged man approached the stone buildings of the school, pushing an old bicycle. He paused at the edge of the plantation and watched the children playing in and around the schoolyard. The school bell clanged and the children started to pile into the various buildings. The area suddenly seemed very quiet.

The man reached into his pocket and produced a baby Powers. With slightly trembling hands, his unscrewed the top and tipped the contents into his mouth. The trembling stopped and, wiping his mouth, he threw the bottle in amongst the trees and started to move out of their shadow towards the school. He dreaded going in. He knew this position wouldn't last, and that this was his last chance.

It wasn't so much the drinking, he was quite good at hiding that. It was the disillusionment that made him quick to anger, with boys and colleagues. The boys were, for the most part, doing just enough to get into the next class. He couldn't remember when he had last met a child with a spark of originality in his thinking. Of course, it had to do with the level of schools in which he had taught in recent years. Back in… oh, so many years ago, when he had been teaching in schools in the better areas, there had been some bright kids. Kids worth teaching. Kids actually hungry for knowledge. Kids who knew that knowledge carried power with it, power to do whatever you wanted to do. Kids like… well… best not think of *him*. Ten years of age, bright as a button, active as a ferret, mercury in short trousers, a perpetual joy and a terrible loss. No more children after that.

His anger with his colleagues was because, to them, teaching was a way of earning a living without too much mental or physical effort. They didn't encourage brightness, it upset the even tenor of their days in the classroom. Brightness called for effort from them, for knowing more answers, for deeper thinking and more careful probing. For his colleagues, it was easier to prod all the class along at the same tempo and try not to let too many fail at the end of the year. And his anger with himself… well… best not think about *that* either.

Declan Gallagher opened the school gate and went in.

"The year, Moore, the year?" bellowed Mr Wilson.

Mr Wilson, an erratic, excitable teacher, had the ability to make an entire class nervous just by entering a classroom. When he directed his ire at a particular pupil, that pupil's heart rose instantly into his throat, making thinking and talking difficult. Wilson liked the flush that such nervousness brought to most young boys' cheeks so much that he couldn't resist pinching those cheeks. In self-defence, he pinched so hard that any thought of the guilty pleasure that the fleshy compression could possibly bring to anyone was banished from the mind of the boy who experienced it and the boys who witnessed it.

"I just know it was when the Protestants were fighting the Catholics and—"

"Did I ask you that?" hissed Wilson. "It was 1690. Get that into your head. Sixteen ninety. Class?"

"Sixteen ninety," howled the class, glad it wasn't them that was being pinched.

Johnny's look of frustration was so intense that Wilson was tempted to squeeze him around his thin, smooth neck.

"But yes," said Wilson grudgingly "the Protestants *were* trying to destroy our Catholic and holy way of life. And nothing's changed in modern Ireland, I can tell you. And when in that year did the Battle of Aughrim take place? Eh, Moore?"

He reached out encouragingly and rubbed Johnny's lower back, just where the spine curved out on its way to the buttocks.

"January?" answered Johnny hopefully.

Wilson smacked Johnny's bottom, but not too hard.

"July, you eejit. And I don't suppose you know the month of that year that saw the magnificent Siege of Limerick?"

Johnny's face lit up. Wilson reached for his arm, but Johnny stepped away.

"But I know that Patrick Sarsfield signed the surrender, and when the French came in plenty of time to relieve them he said, 'Too late. Our honour is pledged.'"

Wilson advanced on Johnny, forcing him towards the front desk, against which he had to lean backwards.

"When I want to know what Sarsfield said," he hissed, bending closely over Johnny's arched body, "I'll ask you what Sarsfield said."

He placed both hands on the desk on either side of Johnny, surveying the class over Johnny's shoulder. The lower parts of their bodies touched.

"Now, who can tell me how many Irishmen chose to serve with the Catholic French king?"

Just then the door opened and the headmaster came in, with Gallagher close behind him, wiping his mouth. Wilson turned quickly away from Johnny. The boys rose to their feet. The headmaster glared at Johnny.

"In trouble again, is he, Mr Wilson? Hardly worth the effort of educating him, is it? Class, this is Mr Gallagher, your new teacher."

To his surprise, Johnny saw Gallagher looking at him with what seemed like sympathy. But that emotion was so rare in the school environment that he wasn't sure.

Later that day, Gallagher was walking around the edge of the classroom, more interested in what was outside the window than what was in the room. Flaherty was on his feet, sweating again. Behind him, Johnny was drawing stickmen in the lower margin of a thick schoolbook.

Finally Gallagher sighed and turned to face the class. It was clear that he didn't enjoy doing so.

"Come on... erm... Flaherty, who was known throughout Ireland as the Great Liberator?

Johnny leaned forward and whispered something to Flaherty.

"Houdini, sir," Flaherty said with relief.

As the class exploded, Johnny lowered his head over his book. Gallagher's hand came into his line of vision and took the book.

"You're Moore, aren't you?" asked Gallagher as he examined the stickman on the pages.

"Yes, sir."

"Well, you'd better fetch the mechanism of chastisement. Do you know what I'm talking about, Mr Moore?"

"The cane, sir."

"The cane. Good. Off you go. Mr Flaherty, your grasp of Irish history is astounding."

Johnny didn't hear any more; he was out the door and staggering down to the teachers' room where the single cane in the school was usually kept.

"The swine make us fetch the shovels to dig our own graves, but they will not break our spirits."

In the room, the headmaster and Wilson were perusing some exercise books when Johnny entered. Without a word, the headmaster took the cane off its shelf and handed it to him. Johnny took it and left the room. The headmaster looked at his watch.

"Sixpence, I believe you owe me."

"Flaherty won't be far behind," said Wilson, reaching into his pocket.

Back in the corridor, Johnny marched up to the classroom door, the cane on his shoulder like a rifle. He lunged at the door as if with a bayonet.

"Halt. Only those with the password shall pass."

Just then, the door opened and his classmates erupted out, slamming him against the far wall. Gallagher emerged and beckoned him inside. As he walked to his desk, Gallagher was flipping through Johnny's book.

"Stony ground, Moore. I don't expect a reprobate like you to understand the scriptural allusion. We, my colleagues and I, scatter the seeds of knowledge in all directions and some of them, unfortunately, fall on stony ground. I dare say this book it is not the greatest literary work extant, but the story has some merit."

"Yeah, I know."

"You have actually perused it, Mr Moore?

"Yeah. The day I got the book."

"And was it so badly written that you had an overwhelming urge to deface it?"

"No. I was drawing the story. I do it for my youngest brother on all the books. Well, the ones that have stories. Look."

Johnny came around the desk and, taking the book, he flipped through the pages from back to front and the stickman animated as he spoke.

"See. The young man is kicked out of his home with a few bob by his father. He has a great time until he runs out of money and then goes back to his parents to beg for forgiveness."

"And does he get it?"

"Oh, yeah. Fathers always forgive their sons. It's the prodigal son story."

"Interesting," said Gallagher. "Why do you think that story has lasted for so long?"

"Well, it's an easy story to tell."

"What else?"

"Erm…"

"What can we learn from it?"

"Well, when the son was spending all the money, he did bad things."

"Yes, he did."

"But he was sorry for it. Real sorry. And his father was glad that he was sorry, and that he came back."

"Was he not angry with him?"

"Yeah… but he was gladder that he came back and was sorry."

"Yes. Because he was lost, but also because he was found."

"Oh, yeah. I forgot that."

They looked at each other silently for a moment.

"Has the entire Moore clan read the Holy Testament?"

"No, only me. No one else is interested."

"What else, I venture to ask, do you read?"

"Not a lot. As well as the Bible, we have an old, battered encyclopaedia that Daddy brought home once. And I read the schoolbooks."

"Do you have any hobbies?"

"I draw a bit. And I go to the pictures."

"Often?

"Every Saturday."

"An expensive pastime, I dare say."

"No. We collect jam jars and there's a man who gives a penny ha'penny for a jam jar and it takes two to get into the Manor."

"The Moore mansion has many siblings, I suppose?"

44

"Siblings? Oh, yeah. Six of us."

"Are there enough jam jars in Dublin?"

"I'm the only one who goes. But I have to tell the rest of them the story when I come home."

"You've been hiding under a bushel all this time, haven't you, Moore?"

"Erm… wait… a light. Right?

"Right."

For one moment there, Gallagher thought later, he had felt the draw of a hungry mind. He had been warned that Johnny Moore was a handful, of course, always getting into trouble. But that's where the ideas were, in that mystical sideline between the strict rules enforced on the playing area and the all-too-ready condemnation of the crowd. Mustn't get too excited, though – Moore was as ragged-arsed as the rest and would probably drop school as soon as it was legal, wasting all efforts. Still, well worth watching.

What had drawn him to the story of the prodigal son, he wondered? Trouble with the father? Wanting acceptance from the father? Forgiveness from Gallagher? Forgiveness! That's a good one! His wife had never forgiven him for losing their son, that's why they parted. As if the thing was that he had never forgiven his son, for leaving him.

Gallagher paused, bent down to fiddle with his shoelace and glanced up and down the street. Nobody he knew in sight.

He straightened and wheeled his bicycle quickly into Cummiskey's front yard.

8

The bus was almost full. The smell of damp, unwashed wool was stifling. The passengers next to the windows were rubbing the condensation off the glass and peering through as if the outside world was more interesting than that inside the bus. Every so often, several passengers would cross themselves as the bus passed a church on the side of the road, in acknowledgement of the Holy Eucharist that was stowed in the tabernacle on the altar. The 'well-travelled' among them crossed themselves as the bus passed a church which lurked out of sight down some side street, and this knowledge of the liturgical geography of Dublin imbued them with a certain sanctimonious smugness.

Tom, with his conductor's badge and cap, his money bag and his low-slung ticket machine, was moving down the aisle, balanced on the balls of his feet, swaying easily with the movements of the bus. It was nearly the end of his first week on the buses and it wasn't so bad. Jacko had shown him what was what and had shared a few tricks with him to make up for the lousy wages, even though he had to sort out the clerk at the depot because the tickets and the money had to balance and he couldn't do that himself; he was never good at sums. The clerk and Skin the Goat, they all wanted a bit of him, even though he took all the risk. Jaysus! Even stealing cost money. It wasn't fair. Anyway, he'd be paid tomorrow and would have enough for a few pints, so he was singing as he took the coins and dispensed tickets and change, to the subdued amusement of some of the passengers and the embarrassment of the rest.

"Give me some men
Who are stout-hearted men
There you are, Mam.
Who will fight for the right they adore.
Thruppence, is it? Right. All the way? Rightho.
Give me ten men
Who are stout-hearted men
And I'll give you ten thousand more.
Change? Don't worry about change. The CIE has plenty of change.
Shoulder to shoulder
Hold on. I'll give you your ticket in a minute. The ould machine has stuck.
And bolder and bolder…"

All this was accompanied by some very slick punching and issuing of fresh and used tickets, manipulating of coins and fast hand movements. Tom ended his song standing next to the ticket bin, collecting fares from and issuing tickets to departing passengers. Just as he pretended to issue a ticket and throw it into the bin, he caught the eye of a grim-faced man sitting in a rear seat.

"Where to, ould son?"

"To the depot."

The grim-faced man took a Córas Iompair Éireann inspector's card out of his pocket and showed it to Tom, who sighed and shrugged resignedly. The inspector then stood up and rang the bell four times. The driver slowed the bus to a crawl and looked back. The inspector walked to the front of the bus, waved his card at him and indicated a stop. The bus pulled in to the side of the road. The inspector then addressed the passengers as he moved to the back of the bus.

"Sorry, ladies and gentlemen. You'll all have to transfer to the bus behind. It's an emergency. Sorry for the inconvenience."

He leaned out and flagged an approaching bus to a halt. The grumbling passengers disembarked and the inspector addressed Tom as the empty bus pulled away.

"We're a habitual people, us Dubliners. Haven't changed our hairstyles since we left school. Always buy the same colour suits and overcoats. Drink the same beer. Smoke the same cigarettes. Go to the same Mass every Sunday. *And* we catch the same bus every day. Do you think we don't know how much this bus makes in fares? The third day you did your Mandrake the Magician tricks with the tickets we were on to you. You're finished on the buses. That's for sure."

"It's a poxy job anyway."

"You should stick to singing. Are you not ashamed of yourself, robbing the poor passengers like that?"

"I'm not robbing them. They get taken to where they're going and they would've had to pay the fare anyway."

"Then you're robbing the CIE."

"The CIE? Them gougers?!"

The Moore children were waiting in the back lane. Albert was at the entrance, looking out. Suddenly, there was a strangled, vaguely dove-like call. The children looked at each other in puzzlement. Siobhan got it first.

"It's a call. Wait."

Albert hurried back to them and they stood looking at the entrance to the back lane. Through the hedge behind them came a long stick. Sean sensed something and turned to look. He saw Johnny's face peering at him through the hedge. It had two sooty stripes across it and he was holding the stick, which had various additions stuck onto it, making it look vaguely like a rifle. A matchbox was fixed underneath and the long handle of a comb jutted backwards from it. The trigger was a hair clip and a knitting needle hung under the 'barrel'. A metal coat hanger had been bent around the back, to give the effect of a stock. This was covered with brown sticky tape. He moved the rifle around until it was next to Paul's ear.

The poke in Paul's ear and the fiendish yell from Johnny came at the same time. Paul got the fright of his life and the children scattered.

Johnny pushed through the hedge and raised both arms in the air.

"Peace, palefaces. I, Hawkeye, will take you to safety."

Later, in the kitchen, Johnny had drawn war-stripes on Albert's face with soot from the stove and tied a tattered hen feather around his head.

"You, Uncas, last of the Mohicans, are destined to die with Cora in your arms."

Albert tentatively put his arm around Attracta and Johnny grabbed Siobhan, who had difficulty stifling her giggles.

"I will take this woman, Alice, to safety to her father in the fort, in spite of the Hurons that lie in our path. Then I will ask for her hand in marriage. Follow me, loyal Delawares."

Within a few minutes the Moore boys were ostentatiously stalking a file of schoolgirls being escorted along the side of the road by a nun. The last girl heard something and looked back at them. Johnny, in the lead, drew his hand across his neck and spat on the ground. The girl hurried to catch up with the rest. The stalking went on until it came to an inconclusive end when the girls turned into and through a gate and the nun stood as they passed and glared at the Moore boys, who crossed the road with studied nonchalance, heading towards the park.

"You couldn't bloody well hang on to it."

Rita was taking her anger out on a sheet she was wringing dry. Tom was trying to brave it out.

"I can do better than the buses."

"If you could, I wouldn't have to take washing in."

She slapped the sheet down into a bucket of rinsed linen on the floor. Johnny's head came around the door. He was still in warpaint, and in his hands he clasped his rifle. He sensed the atmosphere and ducked out again. Rita followed him with the bucket and, taking a sheet, shook it out and started to hang it on the line. Johnny was nowhere in sight. Tom came behind her.

"Give us a hand with these," said Rita briskly.

"That's a woman's job," Tom said as he slouched on out the gate and down the lane.

Rita sighed and carried on hanging the linen. Into her line of vision came a stripe-faced Albert, leading Attracta along the top of the wall.

"Sacred Heart!"

The two stopped, and Johnny's voice wafted on the breeze.

"There is only one way to escape, Uncas, last of the Mohicans."

Attracta crossed herself as Albert grabbed her hand and jumped.

9

One of Johnny's favourite spaces was that which stretched through the branches of the row of laurel bushes bordering the big house owned by the intimidating Major Brennan. The broad, glossy leaves sheltered and hid from view the tough branches along which it was possible to clamber from one end of the row to the other. From this safe, invisible haven Johnny aimed his rifle – and imprecations – at passers-by. Sometimes he made what he considered to be owl hoots through cupped hands. This time he was involved in guarding the big house from the war party of Huron dogs that he was expecting to explode over the Phoenix Park wall in a torrent of red rage. Well, Hawkeye and Uncas were waiting for them.

His attention was aroused by the *clip-clop* of approaching hooves. Down the road towards the big house came a smart pony and trap. Major Brennan was driving and flicking the long whip around the pony's ears with a deftness that Johnny decided had to be practised at the first opportunity. He took aim at the major and released a shot at his head. Then he took aim at the young girl seated beside the major. His rifle – and his jaw – dropped. He had never seen a girl so neat, so worthy of rescuing from the clutches of the Hurons. Her pigtails, the yellow ribbons that held them and the touch of fur around the neck of her coat were immediately and indelibly etched into his mind.

The pony slowed at the impressive gateway to the big house as the major let a man on a bicycle pass. Then the major steered the pony in through the gates, which stood wide open. This gave Johnny enough time to scramble through the laurels and up to the gate on the inside of the hedge. He took his place as the pony and trap passed inside, his rifle at rest and his hand raised in salute, relieved that the lovely girl was safe inside the army fort and out of the clutches of the savages in the Phoenix Park. The major raised his whip in reply, and he and the girl exchanged amused glances.

Johnny moved to the gate, calling out, "I'll close the gate after you."

As he grabbed the gate, the major turned in alarm.

"No! Don't touch that gate!"

It was too late. The gate was not fixed to the hinges because the brickwork of the pillar was being repaired. It toppled in slow motion and pinned Johnny to the ground. His last thought was gladness at having died for the lovely girl.

When he came to, Johnny half-opened his eyes. Through the slits came the glow of sunshine on golden and silver things. He opened his eyes fully and ignored the pain in his head as he took it all in. The room was opulent. More than any place he had ever been in. Everything seemed to glow: the picture frames, the mantelpiece with its ornaments, the glass-fronted cabinet with gleaming treasures inside, the tall lamps and the highly polished, dark wood furniture. He was lying on a deep, comfortable sofa, upholstered in a light golden cloth. On a small table next to it stood a cut-glass tumbler. He took it up, marvelling at the weight, and sipped the cool water inside. Then he surveyed the room again through the glass, enjoying the distortions and refractions.

"Of all the gin joints in all the towns in all the world, they had to choose this one," he murmured contentedly.

His gaze fell on a portrait of the lovely young girl hanging in an alcove. He decided it was very like her but not as nice as the real thing. He sat up to get a better look and winced at the pain. Putting his hand to his head, he found a large bandage around it. So that Huron dog had wounded him as he ran from their camp through the woods. Lucky the waterfall was too dangerous for all but Hawkeye to jump down. Unca had been waiting for him downriver and, using plants known only to the Delawares, had fixed his wound and—

The door opened and the major entered, followed by the local doctor, Dr Jones. The lovely young girl followed them. The doctor smiled at Johnny.

"How are you feeling, Johnny?"

"I'm grand."

"I'm surprised you've survived as long as you have. How old is it you are now?"

"Twelve. Nearly thirteen."

The major indicated the rifle at Johnny's feet. "You lead a very adventurous life, I see."

"Sure, that's only play, Major Brennan."

"I'm sorry about the gate, Mr Moore."

"That's all right." Johnny tried to shrug carelessly, but it hurt his head. "Doctor, will I be able to wear a hat again?"

"Oh, there's no serious damage to the ould head. A few stitches that I'll take out next week. No heading the ball till then," said the doctor.

"Angela," said the major, "won't you escort Mr Moore to the kitchen and see if there's something there to build up his strength again?"

"Yes, Papa." She moved to the door and opened it, smiling at Johnny. He smiled back and then climbed carefully off the golden sofa, turned and bowed gravely to the men before walking out.

The major moved to the liquor cabinet. "Drink?"

"Thanks. He's a gas man, that Johnny. Bright, too. Stands out a bit from the snotty-nosed orphans in the lane."

"When that heavy gate fell on him, I…"

"Oh, you needn't have worried. It would take more than half a ton of iron to put him out of action for long. I've treated him many times for bumps and scrapes but never anything broken. Except for the skin, of course. The lane breeds a hardy lot."

"I've seen him around. In places where he shouldn't be, sometimes."

"Your apples?"

"My apples."

"Ah, we've all pinched a few forbidden apples in our time. A residue of the original sin, I suppose."

The major handed the doctor a generous glass of whiskey and proffered the water jug.

"Thanks. Just a touch. Thanks again."

"Good health."

"*Slainte*. It'll be good to have your daughter back again. It's a big house for one man."

"Yes, it is."

"She's so like her brother, God rest his soul. How long will she be staying?"

"A year. Then off to a finishing school in Devon."

"You'll be very proud of her when she's… finished."

"I intend to be."

"Well, enjoy her while she's here."

"Oh, I will."

In the kitchen, Johnny was stuffing himself with a plateful of pie and a glass of milk.

"This is great."

"It's ham and veal pie."

"Two meats?"

"I'll give you some to take home, if you like. You have brothers and sisters?"

"Yeah. Five. You?"

"I'm… an only child, now. I had a brother. A twin brother. His name was Darcy."

"What happened?"

"He died two years ago."

"That's terrible. Children shouldn't die."

She watched him as he finished the pie in silence.

"Are you really, really poor?"

"Yeah." He raised the glass of milk. "Here's looking at you, kid."

"Where did you learn to talk like that?"

"I go to the pictures at lot. Have you ever been?"

"To a cinema? No. It's not fair, you being poor."

"Sure, the lane is full of poor people. Some are really, really poor and that's awful. I won't always be poor, though. One day, I'll have a house like this, with pictures on the wall."

"And whose… picture will you have on your wall?"

"Someone easy to look at and good to come home to."

She smiled as he finished his milk.

"Well, I better mosey along," he said.

The car, driven by a chauffeur, pulled into the entrance of the back lane. The driver decided he wasn't going any farther. Angela gazed out the window, quite appalled.

"Is this where you live?"

"Yeah. Can I… have one of your ribbons?"

"Yes. You can take it off."

He did so with trembling hands. The children of the lane started gathering around the car, peering in, giggling and whispering. The chauffeur got out, opened the boot and took out a basket full of fruit, vegetables and prepared foods, and, at the bottom, the remains of the pie wrapped in a white cloth.

Johnny stuffed the ribbon in his pocket and got out. He took the basket from the chauffeur, thanked him and turned back to Angela.

"I'll bring back the basket as soon as I can."

"There's no hurry," she replied. "Go and mosey."

Johnny pushed through the children and ran to his cottage. Rita was ironing and Tom was sitting at the table reading a newspaper when he came in. They both looked at the basket as Johnny placed it on the table. Tom was the first to speak.

"Where the hell did you get that?"

"Major Brennan gave it to me, because his gate—"

"Did you go begging?"

Johnny's jaw dropped in astonishment. "I didn't beg! He gave it to me because—"

"Because he thinks I can't feed my own children! Jaysus! As if I hadn't enough on my mind!"

"What happened to your head?" asked Rita.

"Bloody Protestants! Jaysus!" said Tom.

"His gate fell on me."

"Think they're better than us!"

"Does it hurt, pet?" asked Rita.

"This? This doesn't hurt. *This* doesn't hurt at all."

Johnny ran out of the room. He wanted to suffer in solitude, smell Angela's ribbon, rescue her from the Hurons and return her to her very grateful father.

10

The children were glassy-eyed and Gallagher looked exhausted.

"Tomorrow, God help us all, we shall be delving into grammar. I know that you all—"

The bell rang and the children ran for the door. Gallagher caught Johnny's eye.

"Moore. A word."

Johnny took up his things and approached. Gallagher handed him an exercise book.

"When I asked for an essay on *Electricity in the Home*, I didn't expect the first episode in *The Adventures of Captain Shocking*. Eight out of ten for making me laugh. Tell me, are you going to carry on at school next year?"

"Yes."

"Then you'll have to improve your marks in all subjects. Especially maths."

"I wish I could only do the subjects I like."

"That's just not possible in a national school, and I don't think it should be. Whatever you want to do, you need a groundwork in all subjects to excel in one or two. What education is all about, or should be, is to turn out a well-rounded person who can make a contribution to society in all walks of life. Being good at maths is not much use if you don't have a working interest in, say, literature. No sane person spends his entire day doing the same thing over and over again. A person should be familiar with all sorts of human endeavour. Do you know what you want to be?"

"I want to work in pictures."

"Pictures?"

"Stupid, hey?"

"No. Not stupid. Difficult, though."

"There's millions of pictures being made, and there must be millions of jobs to make them. I'd be ready to do anything."

"I'm sure you would." Gallagher gathered his thoughts. It was a long time since he'd had such a conversation with a pupil. "Let's say, though, that you did get into pictures, as, I don't know, a cameraman. You'd learn your trade, get familiar with your tools, make many pictures and earn a good living. Then what?"

"That'd be plenty."

"Would it? You wouldn't want to spend your entire day working. What about literature? About music? About theatre?"

"Theatre?"

"Yes. Where storytelling first started. Long, long before they made the first picture, great stories, great plays that changed the world, were being told on stages, in front of people who wanted to find out about other people's lives and problems. That's why your picture-makers call the script for a picture a screen*play*. And they study the playwrights who have been writing them for thousands of years. And suppose you did become a cameraman. I don't know much about cameras but I promise you that understanding such a clever machine would require a sound understanding of mathematics."

"Yeah. So, I better do better at maths."

"Yes. You better. That story you drew on your textbook. Do you know why the figures move when you flick through them?"

"Yeah, well, they just do."

"No. They don't *just* do. Each picture moves forward just enough to make the eye see it as if it did move that distance. Now, supposing you had to build a camera that would make thousands of pictures seem to move in front of thousands of watching eyes. You would need to work out just how far to move each picture forward, and just how fast. And you'd need maths to do that. So, the next time you see Hopalong Cassidy draw his gun faster that the baddie, it's all to do with the number of very short images moving so fast it seems like a blur. It's maths at work."

"You seem to know a lot about pictures. Do you know how I could get in?"

"I know little enough about pictures, but what I do know comes from a good general knowledge, and a good general knowledge only comes from what you learn at school and carry on into your working life. As to getting into pictures, I dare say there *are* ways, though perhaps not in Ireland. But, as with any job, Moore—"

"Yeah. My marks. I know."

"*All* your marks."

"Yeah. I suppose it's all a dream, isn't it, Mr Gallagher?"

"Don't be afraid of dreams, Moore. Sometimes they are the only things that get us out of the mire."

"Mire?"

"Muck, bog, swamp, slough, marsh, mud. *Two men look out through the same bars. One sees the mud and one the stars.*"

The school bell summoned them back to class and Johnny went with Gallagher's last words ringing in his ears.

When the lunch break finally came, it found him sitting next to a fire that had been lit by a team of corporation workers. They were cutting down and sawing up some of the diseased broad-leaved trees that grew next to the wall in the Phoenix Park. He admired the ease with which they climbed up and lopped off branches and the confidence with which they felled the trees. He was fascinated by the way, with notch, saw cut and axe blows, they could bring down a towering trunk exactly where they wanted it to fall. Once down, they could reduce the huge mass of timber to manageable logs in a morning and ready them to be carted away. The men invariably lit roaring fires with the smaller branches, and it was at these that several of the schoolchildren toasted the cheese or jam sandwiches with which they were supplied by the school service.

Johnny loved the calm taciturnity of the men as they destroyed the massive trees and the casual ease with which they pulled the long, two-handed saw backwards and forwards through the wood with a faint singing noise. He admired the glittering axes that left such clean, bright gashes in the wood at each stroke. His one disappointment with these heroes was their raucous laughter when he referred to them as lumberjacks. However, he forgave them because of the splendour of their work.

He was returning to school from one of these breaks, working out in his mind how he could create an axe head like theirs and sipping from the half-pint bottle of milk which was also supplied to schoolchildren. Suddenly he was confronted by Flaherty and two of his cronies. Flaherty snatched the milk bottle.

"Hey, Moore," he said. "I see you're sucking up to Gallagher, the dirty drunkard."

"Well, you'd know about all that, wouldn't you, with your da and all?"

"Yeah. He's just like my da. And I'll show you what *he* does to me when he comes home stocious, you little shite."

He finished the milk and threw the bottle away. Then he and the other two started punching Johnny.

Johnny lay there, passive, until they had finished and run, laughing, towards the school. Then he sat up and touched his bruised lip.

"When you call me a shite, smile."

He smiled, and winced as his lip hurt.

Window dressing has become a universal industry, staffed by sophisticated and artistically attuned men and women instructed by statistically guided marketers who have a deep understanding of the attractive power of a shop window. In the effort to attract, entice and activate passers-by, every known seductive colour, shape and texture is brought into play. In Johnny's day, such windows were beyond his imagining because irrelevant, beyond his means because ridiculously expensive and beyond his understanding because such spaces were in another world, promising consumer benefits beyond his terms of reference. But in the smaller shops in the meaner streets of his immediate world, his attention and sometimes avarice could be and was aroused by higgledy-piggledy displays of bright and shiny things, the use of which he understood, albeit vaguely in some instances. Such was the grimy window of Bourke's Photographic Shop, which guaranteed satisfaction in photographic coverage of weddings, first communions and special occasions, with portraits a speciality and a major part of the window dressing.

However, other attractions crept in from time to time, which gave the window additional interest. A corner of the window had recently been devoted to small displays of postage stamps. Johnny pressed his nose against the glass and cupped his hands on either side of his head to eliminate reflections and look at the stamps with their fine colours and details. The wonderfully coloured San Marino stamp had been exciting him for days but the price, thruppence, was an awful lot of money. Johnny had delivered a bag of washing to the priest's house next to the church that morning and now he had an unaccustomed thruppenny bit in his pocket which Father Mulligan had unexpectedly given him, and so the San Marino beauty would be the start of a collection of truly beautiful stamps which he would leave to the National Museum on his death, to be marvelled at for generations.

He stepped back from the window to ponder and his eye was caught by a shiny black-and-silver item in the far corner of the window. It hadn't been there last time he'd looked. He went back to the window and peered in at it, shading his eyes again. He read the engraved name on the side: a Bolex. A movie camera! A Bolex H-8. His heartbeat speeded up. What could the H-8 stand for?

The thing had a lovely, chunky look to it, with three lenses at the front, what looked like an eyepiece along the top and a shiny handle folded into the side. *Must be for winding*, he thought. And the round container? For the film, of course. His hands itched to hold it.

He felt eyes upon him and, looking up, saw old man Bourke looking at him over the display panel at the back of the shop window. He would have loved to look longer at the Bolex, but was embarrassed. He walked away, imagining the eyepiece glued to his eye and the weight of it in his hands. He held his cupped hand in front of one eye and viewed the street through it. A cyclist passed, freewheeling, and he followed the moving figure through the circle formed by his thumb and forefinger. He became excited about the blurred movement of the houses behind the seemingly static bike and rider. Oh, what it must be like to capture movement on film and then see it on a big screen!

Behind him, Bourke emerged from the shop with a cloth in his hand. He wiped the window where Johnny's face had been pressed against it.

Johnny walked on, thinking of the various items at home he could use to make a movie camera. There was the cylinder from a gas mask he'd been saving. That had a nice, heavy feel in the hand. And the tube from a roll of lavatory paper he had pounced on that time in the jacks of the cinema in town. Neither the jacks at home nor the one at the Manor Cinema boasted such things! If the tube were fastened to the gas-mask cylinder, it would serve as the eyepiece, especially if he made a cone of cardboard and stuck that on the back end to shade his eye as he peered through. Then there was the handle of the broken meat mincer he'd found outside Mullarky's shop – he could stick that into a bracket on the back of the cylinder as the winding handle. It would be better on the side but there was no way he could bore a hole in the cylinder; the back would have to do. It would be nice to have a container for the film on top. A polish tin, maybe? There might be one in the yard of the priest's house. Father Mulligan's shoes were always shiny. The rest he could make up from that roll of fish-glue brown sticky tape that he'd stolen from the school office. Even though licking it to activate the terrible-tasting glue was torture and most times he cut his tongue, it was his great forming material. Then some of the priest's boot polish to blacken everything, except maybe for a panel of silver paper at the back for effect. The lens turret in front? That would be a problem. Hold on – lemonade-bottle tops would do. He headed home, stamps forgotten at the thought of having his own movie camera.

11

An interminable Dublin drizzle had set in. From a tattered poster on a rain-darkened brick wall, the 'hero' sailor from the Player's cigarette pack looked down onto a gloomy, wet street. A torn piece of the poster next to his head flapped in the gusty wind, adding a jaunty look to his otherwise expressionless mien. Directly below the poster a thin man in a sodden mackintosh was unevenly voiding the contents of his stomach over his shoes and the gutter. He straightened up, spat and moved towards the pub. The dull gold 19th-century decorated typeface of the name, painted on a dark green fascia, glistened in the lamplight as the man reached the pavement, paused and reached carefully for the kerb with his foot. He found it, transferred his weight and lurched bravely towards the door. Unfortunately for him, it was closed against the weather. He cannoned backwards, regained his balance with difficulty and moved more carefully for the door again. Reaching it, he turned the handle and almost fell through as the door opened. A dull shaft of light and the sound of a voice raised in song emerged, to be shut off as the door closed behind the man.

The pub was thick with cigarette smoke and noisy conversation. Through the fug, two soberly-dressed young men were moving amongst the throng, handing out leaflets for the Pioneer Total Abstinence Association. They were tolerated in most working-class pubs in Dublin, probably because of the lack of impact on the pub-going public. Some of the drinkers just looked away when addressed; some nodded in a friendly manner and took a leaflet, which they jammed into their pockets. Others grinned and turned their lapels around to display the distinctive Pioneer pin, a symbol of the pledge they had taken to give up drinking alcohol permanently. This was worn outwardly during the day and tucked out of sight when they went to the pub.

Jacko was at the bar, half an eye on the harassed barman who was juggling a dozen pints in various stages of pouring. The other half of his eye was on two old Dublin men crouched at the dingy bar and dawdling over the remains of their pints. They were at that stage of inebriation which loosens both the tongue and the inhibitions.

"Do you know what they're doing to our cows?" asked one of the other.

"Whaaa?"

"They're feeding them cement."

"Whaa?"

"Not enough to poison them. Enough to make the meat heavier."

There was a long pause while the other finished his pint. Jacko's pints arrived. He threw some money onto the bar.

"Oh. So they can charge more for the meat?"

"Right."

"Bastards."

"You can say that again."

"Bastards."

Jacko scooped up the change and his two pints and headed towards the section of the pub from which Tom's voice was issuing.

"*And so I go to fight the savage foe*

Although I know I'll be sometimes missed
By the girls I kissed."

Jacko arrived at the corner where Tom was holding forth, placed the pints on the table and slipped into a seat next to Tom. Tom sang on.

"Goodbye, goodbye
I wish you all a last goodbye
Goodbye, goodbye
I wish you all a last goooodbyeee."

As the people around Tom clapped lightly and murmured appreciatively, a furtive, damp man edged in and sidled up him.

"Goodbye, yourself. Skin the Goat is looking for you."

Tom and Jacko exchanged horrified glances and scurried for the door. The two old men left the bar, slipped into their vacated seats and attacked the brand-new pints.

Outside, Tom and Jacko dodged across the street and into the park. They walked along under the widely-spaced street lights, shoulders hunched against the rain and the icy north-east wind. Tom, perturbed, spoke.

"That Skin the Goat is a right gouger."

"He's not the worst."

"A hundred per cent, he charges!"

"If you're gambling," agreed Jacko. "But if you're skint, he's negotiable and much more amenable."

"Is that why he's called Skin the Goat: 'cause he'll skin you?"

"No. He got his name from somebody who skinned a goat for eating straw out of his horse's collar. He was on the Invincibles."

"Them fellas who killed…?"

"Yeah. The Phoenix Park murders. They killed some fucking English officials."

"How do you know about all this?"

"Jaysus, I don't know. The ould fella, I suppose. He was always going on about the Fenians and the like."

"So was my ould fella, but I paid no attention."

"Well, you should have. It's who we are."

"Who who is?"

"The Irish. We—"

"Ah, don't you start. The Shan Van Vocht and all that shite. Jaysus!"

They walked on, getting damper by the minute.

"Jaysus! But whatever you do," said Jacko, getting back onto safer ground, "you pay him back when he says you pay him back. That's—"

"The deal. Yeah, I know."

"What's he into you for?"

"Ten pounds."

"Jaysus. Pay him. Do yourself a favour."

"Ah, what can he do?"

"What you don't know, you won't grieve over."

Later that night, Rita was in bed, her overcoat supplementing the blankets. Tom was seated on the end of the bed, looking out at the bare trees, etched by the moonlight.

"What's wrong?" asked Rita.

"Nothing. Everything."

"There's a packet of fags in the drawer."

"Where did you get them?"

"Light one and give us a drag."

Tom lit a cigarette, took a long pull and passed it to Rita. She inhaled and blew the smoke at him.

"I haven't heard you sing in a while."

"What's to sing about?"

"I always love to hear Thomas Moore."

"Him? Yeah, he lived in London and sang about us."

"Well, that's the first time I've heard you say a bad word about him."

"Well…"

"Give us a couple of bars of *The Meeting of the Waters*. Softly, so you don't wake the kids."

"Agggh!"

"Go on. It was the first song you ever sang to me."

"Avoca. I've never been there. Don't even know where it is."

"You don't have to go there if you can sing the—"

"I'm off on the B&I tomorrow. I've been wanting to tell you."

"Oh!"

"No point in hanging around this kip."

"There's always work over in England, I suppose."

"Yeah, the bastards. They do it to exploit us."

"But why so sudden?"

"What's the point in hanging around?"

"I hear the Tin Box Company is hiring."

"Yeah, women! And paying them less than they'd have to pay men."

"Well, there's many a woman around here desperate with no man earning. They're glad of it."

"But they don't see… the men need work and…" The unfairness of it all flummoxed Tom, and he gave up. "I'll be back for Sean's first communion."

"It's too soon."

"I'll send money for his suit."

"Sure you will. No. You finish it."

Tom finished the cigarette and slipped the butt end out through the top of the window. Then he started to sing, very softly:

"There is not in the wide world a valley so sweet
As that vale in whose bosom the bright waters meet…"

Rita lay back on her pillow and looked at the man who had taken her out of a large family of mostly girls and, with the best will in his adolescent life, made her his wife. Dear God, he really believed the song and all that it offered.

"Sweet vale of Avoca, how calm could I rest
In thy bosom of shade, with the friends I love best"

Right now, he was almost a ghost of darkness against the

gloom of the room, but the side of his body facing the window and the inconstant moon were etched out in a sliver of white face, light shirt and slim, expressive white hands which moved melodramatically with the yearning lyrics of the song. He looked young again, as he had when he first proposed marriage to her. Now she was glad they had never been to Avoca. To lose that idealistic image was to lose all dreaming. Tom sang with all the heart he was prepared to share with an indifferent world.

Johnny was in the kitchen, fiddling with his maths homework but listening to Tom as he finished.

"*Where the storms that we feel in this cold world should cease And our hearts, like thy waters, be mingled in peace.*"

He was still sitting there when Tom came in carrying a small case, the dark brown leather of which was thick, and it was scuffed on the corners. The stitching, lighter in colour, was frayed in places but the case was solid and rigid and the fasteners were brass. A brass key was in the lock and a harp was embossed on the lid. Johnny has seen the case under the bed many times but something about its officiousness has deterred him from opening it. A respect for its stolid respectability had overcome his usually irresistible curiosity. Besides, he couldn't find the key.

"Here," Tom said. "I thought you might like this. I kept it because your grandfather asked me to. But I never looked at it."

Johnny turned the key and opened the case, enjoying the hard *click* as the levers flew back. It was lined inside with dark green baize and was full of documents, notebooks, loose sheets of paper and several mysterious items that begged to be examined. It was a fine case, and had a fine, decent, musty smell.

"It's his old IRA stuff. He was high up in the organisation. The old lot. Not the young bowsies that are causing all the trouble now."

"Commandant John Moore," said Johnny. "He used to tell us stories."

"That's all they were. Just stories."

"No, they weren't."

"He was a miserable ould bollix, anyway. Erm… I'm off to England for a while."

"England? Why?"

"To find work. You'll have to look after your ma. You're old enough now to get some sort of job."

"What about school?"

"You've had as much school as I had."

Johnny started to speak and then changed his mind. Tom's eyes flashed.

"What? *What?*"

"Nothing. I could get a part-time job."

"What fecking use would that be? Don't be an eejit."

"Will you be long gone?"

"No. And keep that stuff out of sight."

He left the room. Johnny sighed and looked into the case. He took out a bullet and looked at it for a while. Then he clasped his arm above the elbow and screwed up his face.

"Captain, I've got a little bird here. Wounded in the left wing."

In the early hours of the morning, Tom emerged from the cottage carrying a brown-paper package. He paused at the gate and lit a cigarette while he looked back at the cottage. Then he strode down the back lane, singing softly.

"Where the desert sand is nice and handy
I'll be full of grit.
You won't see my heels for the dust."

One of the curtains was pulled back and Johnny's pale face looked out at his departing father. He dropped back onto the bed, clutching the IRA case and, to keep his mind off his father, he thought about his grandfather.

He had spent a lot of time with him after his release from

the Curragh and before he left the country. He had been incarcerated along with hundreds of others who had refused to accept the legitimacy of the Irish Free State. Commandant John Moore hadn't told Johnny much about his personal experiences in the Easter Rising, the war of independence or the subsequent civil war. He harked back to and told stories about the Wild Geese, the remnants of the old Catholic aristocracy who, in an unparalleled haemorrhage of nobility, chose exile rather than the honourable surrender offered to them by the warrior Prince William of Orange after their defeat at the Siege of Limerick in 1691. With Celtic fatalism, they searched nature for an image desolate enough to match their departure and found it in the grey geese that deserted the shores of Ireland every year after a bitter winter. Carrying their battered arms and their burning resentment of Protestantism, the Wild Geese, as they became known, sold their lethal skills to the kings and marshals of Europe and Asia. Irish surnames, thinly disguised by exotic first names and prefixes, dotted the annals of the world: Count Francis Lacey, Austrian Minister for War; O'Cleary, father-in-law and advisor to Bernadotte, King of Sweden and Denmark; de MacMahon, President of France; Peter Lacey, field marshal to the czar; Dom Ricardo Wall, Prime Minister of Spain; and Mountcashel, founder of Louis XIV's beloved Irish Brigade.

Johnny had thrilled to the tales of these heroes and the lesser personages among the Wild Geese, the younger sons who treated the courts and battlefields of Europe as their playgrounds. His grandfather had told of them all. There was Richard Hennessy from County Cork, who tarried long enough at Cognac to nurse his wounds and found a brandy business. There was Chevalier Wogan, who escorted a Polish woman across war-torn Europe to meet her Stuart bridegroom and then sank into oblivion, his sense of honour and drama satisfied. There was also Tomas Armstrong of Granard, aide to George Forbes, the founder of the Austrian Navy, who had captured the colours of the Coldstream Guards at the Battle of Fontenoy. Another member of the family, Tomas Francis Armstrong, had fought against the Zulus in South Africa and caught the reins of the riderless horse that had galloped away from the corpse of the Prince Imperial Napoléon Eugène Louis Jean Joseph – how the name rolled off the tongue – and around whose body they found twelve dead Zulus after the last great battle at Isandlwana. His grandfather had made him pronounce that name properly.

A firing squad from Thomas Francis' regiment had executed his brother in the early 20th century for running guns to the Irish rebels, with the twists of fate that were common in Irish recruits to Britain's armies. Finally, there was Major John MacBride, who had led the Irish Brigade in the Boer War with a Colonel Bo Blake of West Point, fresh from fighting Apaches in Arizona. MacBride had been shot by the British after the rising in 1916, refusing the blindfold with the words, "I have looked down the barrels of their guns before." All these, Johnny had heard about from his grandfather, who considered himself one of the latter-day Wild Geese when he went abroad. Unhappily, he only got as far as Scunthorpe, where he died of bronchitis.

His thoughts flitting between the Wild Geese and his emigrating father – a not-unusual occurrence in his part of Dublin – Johnny fell asleep.

12

"What's keeping him?" said Johnny with an impatience he rarely displayed.

"You must pay special attention," said Siobhan.

"It must be the best picture ever made," piped Sean. "Is it the best picture ever made, Johnny?"

"No wonder it's extra to get in," said Attracta.

"You must remember every word of it," said Siobhan earnestly.

Johnny paced up and down the lane, three jam jars clutched in his arms. "I should have gone myself," he said.

"Oooowa! Ooowa! All the gang." Albert appeared, calling the signal; the precious fourth jam jar held aloft. Johnny grabbed it and was off like a bullet. Siobhan looked after him dreamily.

He was about halfway to the Manor when suddenly three Cabra boys blocked his path. An ambush, hey? Well, this was his territory; he'd show them a thing or two. Nobody, but nobody knew the dark streets of this town like Philip Marlowe. Jamming his fedora down firmly, Johnny ran up a side lane. Another Cabra boy dropped from the wall ahead of him. Hell! Somebody musta squealed. He turned to face the oncoming children, his heart in his mouth. The largest boy spoke.

"Four jam jars."

"Worth a few fags, them," said another.

Johnny drew himself up. "OK, you punks. See if I care."

And he smashed the four jam jars at the feet of the astounded boys.

The queues were gone. The Manor doors were closed and the old man was packing his jars securely into his barrow.

"Mister?" came Johnny's voice from behind him.

"What do you want?" asked the old man, without looking up.

"I need sixpence. I'm here every Saturday. I'll bring four jars next week. I'm your best customer."

"I never seen you before," said the old man when he finally looked up. He'd certainly never seen Johnny like this before: lips bruised, eyes swelling, blood on his cheek and chin. "Feck off, ou'a that."

He pushed his barrow away and Johnny crossed to the Manor and mounted the steps. He approached the poster for *Gone with The Wind* and started to examine it closely. It was an illustration of Clark Gable carrying Vivien Leigh in his arms while behind them a city burned.

Distraught, he turned away, the long Saturday morning stretching ahead of him, endless and empty. From inside the cinema, he could hear the faint sounds of merriment. Abbott and Costello were in the supporting programme.

He descended the steps, muttering, "Who's on first?", the start of his favourite routine between Bud and Lou. "Watts on second and I don't know's on third." He paused at the bottom and looked up the alleyway beside the cinema. He'd never noticed it before, being too keen to get into the cinema on arrival, and to get home afterwards.

"Jay? It's Quasimodo." Two older boys were perched precariously on a ledge high up on the side wall. One was peering into the cinema through a crack in a boarded-up window, while the other waited his turn at the crack. Johnny ignored them and passed on and around the back of the building. There was nothing of interest there, but when he gained the other side, he was excited to see a metal staircase leading up to what he guessed was the projection booth. He crept up it to the metal door at the top and pressed his ear against it. Sure enough, he could hear a whirring noise which could only be the projector and, fainter than that, the familiar high-pitched voice of Lou. He sat there, thinking of the beams of light passing through the fast-moving film, spanning the distance across the vast space of the cinema and weaving those magic images on the screen, at which the audience inside was laughing. Inside! While he was outside, jarless and storyless. Siobhan would kill him.

He sighed and set off on the long way home through the park, planning his military funeral as he trudged along. At the Garda depot, he toyed briefly with the idea of running away and joining the Garda and living a life of being told what to do and not having to make the painful decisions he was expected to make, all on his own. As he passed the back of Áras an Uachtaráin, he kept an eye out for the damson tree that grew conveniently next to the railings. Yes, there it was, but the fruit was still hard and green and bitter. Then he thought of Siobhan and her bitter disappointment at not being told the story she most of all wanted to hear. Squaring his shoulders and thinking hard, he set off home, his mind whirring.

"There's this fella with a great head of black hair, and a big hat, like a Stetson but much posher, and a great little ronnie on his upper lip. He's Clark Gable and he's in love with a scarlet woman who's always fainting 'cause she's from the South, Southern bells they called them, and they're very delicate… So he has to keep carrying her around all the time."

The Moore children were staring at him in disquiet. Siobhan had a scathing look on her face.

"The thing is that the place where they live is set on fire by the soldiers and he has to carry her away to safety. He has millions of fights with the soldiers because they want to… ravish… the scarlet woman—"

"What's ravish, Johnny?" asked Albert.

"It's… erm… you're too young to know. But it's not nice anyway. But the man wins every time because he's… well, he's Clark Gable. And then him and the scarlet woman are standing on a cliff with the city burning behind them and all the horses and cattle are screaming with agony. Suddenly a great storm comes up and the wind sucks her out of his arms and she's blown over the cliff. She's gone. Gone with the wind."

Later, as she was bathing Johnny's swollen face, Siobhan dabbed a little harder than was necessary and Johnny winced.

"Who did it?"

"Some Cabra boys. They were after the jam jars but I threw them at their feet. I'm sorry, Siobhan. You wanted to hear it so much."

She dabbed very gently.

"Blown off a cliff by the wind. Jay. I never heard the like."

13

School was over for the day. Gallagher stood at the gate holding his bicycle. and called out as Johnny ran through. Johnny approached him.

"Moore. There's a place I wish to take you to. Today, if you're not otherwise engaged? Excellent."

Gallagher mounted his bicycle and Johnny sat astride the metal rack on the back and clutched Gallagher's hips.

Half an hour later, with some heavy breathing from the rider and some agonising cramps in the thighs of the passenger, they were in the local library; the first time for Johnny. He was mesmerised by the reflection of the bright lights in the shiny, dark brown lino on the floor. Gallagher went up to the desk, behind which sat a sharp-faced woman in black-rimmed spectacles. Her glance went from Gallagher to Johnny, and it was immediate war.

"I wish to enrol my young colleague in this house of explication," said Gallagher.

"Does he live in the area?"

"His abode is in the immediate vicinity.

"Who'll be responsible for books borrowed?"

"Books borrowed shall be his responsibility and he shall be mine. I am his teacher."

"He doesn't look very responsible to me."

"You above all, madam, should know the old adage about books and covers."

"What happens if he loses a book?"

"Should that eventuality come to pass and the world not come to an end, the required monies for replacement shall be forthcoming from me."

"He doesn't look as if he could afford to pay any fines for overdue books."

"He wouldn't dare let a book from this well-regulated establishment become overdue."

"We cannot allow our books to become shabby and grubby."

"Shabbiness and grubbiness are anathema to my young friend, especially pertaining to books."

"He doesn't look as if he can read."

"You are looking at a young prodigy who has read the scriptures."

The librarian struggled with her doubt.

"Fill in this form and I'll get the tickets ready." She had one more go at it. "He *won't* be wanting three, will he?"

"The allotted quantity, madam, the allotted quantity."

She handed Gallagher a form and turned to stamp – very loudly – the book of a borrower.

Shortly afterwards, they were seated at a table on which Gallagher had laid three books.

"It is in the nature of things that the custodians of sacred places should be formidable creatures, with enormous stamping powers. I have chosen three books for your virgin foray into literary society."

He placed *The Count of Monte Cristo* in front of Johnny.

"It's thick, isn't it?" was Johnny's first comment.

"It needs space for all the great deeds it has to relate. When you are counted amongst the greatest storytellers in the world, as Alexandre Dumas was, you need elbow room. Besides, I wouldn't have one single word removed. The story concerns a man wrongly accused and, on the eve of his wedding, imprisoned for life in the most horrific jail imaginable. After ten years in this hell, he climbs into a sack destined as a coffin for a dead fellow prisoner. He's thrown over a cliff into the sea, claws his way out of the sack. He discovers buried treasure and comes back a rich man. He spends twenty years seeking revenge on the people who harmed him, and when he has driven one of his accusers mad and killed the man's wife and son, he is about to kill himself what he realises he has been playing God – the greatest sin of all. So he renounces the world and seeks an unrevengeful life with a beautiful woman who had loved him all along. There's seven hundred pages of action so nail-biting you'll whizz through it as if it were a bus ticket. Do you think you will like that?"

"Yeah!"

Gallagher proceeded to get all three books loudly stamped by the librarian and they walked back into the darkening street. They mounted the bicycle and, pausing frequently for breath, Gallagher carried on.

"The other book is about the finest swordsman in Paris, a giant of a man, who is feared by every soldier in the King's army. But he has the biggest nose ever seen on a human face, at which nobody is allowed to look directly. He falls in love with a beautiful lady, as all heroes are required to do. Her name is Roxanne and he woos her with wonderful speeches about love and Heaven and the deaths he will die if he doesn't have her love. But he hides his face from her because of his enormous nose. It is a play."

"A play?!"

"Some of the world's finest stories have been written for the stage. I told you before: every moving picture on which you expend your jam jars was written as a play."

"By special people?"

"By very special people called scriptwriters, who can make

people all over the world laugh, or cry, or feel frightened or angry or happy, no matter what language they use."

"But how can people follow a picture in another language?"

"Because they tell their stories in pictures. What people do in a picture is much more important than what they say."

They reached a rather steep incline and Gallagher stopped the bicycle. They both got off and went ahead on foot.

"It's all about the story," said Gallagher when he had recovered his breath. "Ever since we first learned to talk and gather around a fire at night, we told stories to each other. It was the only way we could make sense of the great big, strange world we had been born into. We told stories about each other, then about the bravest among us, then about the birds and the animals and the strange gods who must have made it all. Each story had something to tell us about life, about survival, about how to be content and how to live a good and safe life."

"Just like in the pictures."

Gallagher waited for Johnny to absorb the thought and make sense of it. To his satisfaction, it didn't take more than the length of a narrow street for it to happen.

"Just like the pictures," Johnny continued when he had things straight in his mind. "There's always the chap and the pal and the... mot... and the baddie, and the chap has to beat the baddie because..." Johnny struggled for a moment, and Gallagher let him.

"Because...?" Gallagher finally asked.

"Because there's something he has to do and he will *not* let a baddie or a..."

"Mot?" suggested Gallagher helpfully.

"Yeah! A... mot stop him. No matter what," Johnny finished lamely, and walked on, thinking furiously.

"Congratulations, my boy."

"For what?"

"For putting the essence... you understand?"

"Yeah!" said Johnny impatiently.

Gallagher stifled a smile. "The essence of a story is just that. A quest that the… chap has to go on, no matter what how hard it is and no matter who's trying to stop him."

"Jay. I wish I was a storyteller."

"But you are. You tell your family the stories of the pictures."

"Yeah, but I don't make up those stories."

"Why don't you?"

Johnny walked on silently, stunned by the notion.

"Why don't you get a notebook and start writing a story?"

"About what?"

"About John Moore and how he overcomes all obstacles and all the people who are trying to stop him."

Johnny remained silent for a long time until they passed Mullarky's shop in the lane. Rita was walking towards it. She surveyed the two of them as Gallagher doffed his hat.

"Hello, Mammy. We've been to the library."

"That's nice. Mr Gallagher, isn't it?"

"It is indeed, Mrs Moore. I'm delighted to meet you and I apologise for keeping Johnny out so late."

"That's quite all right, Mr Gallagher, I'm pleased that you take such an interest in my boy."

"I do indeed. He's the most intelligent boy in the school and he is destined to go far."

Rita was stunned for a moment, but she recovered quickly. "I'm glad you think so. Johnny, dinner's on the stove. I'll be home soon."

"OK, Mammy."

Rita entered the shop and Gallagher, glad to be off the bicycle for a moment, started to walk on. Johnny was still enthralled by the library books.

"These books are dinging, Mr Gallagher. And that one?" Johnny waved the third volume.

"Does your mother do all her shopping with that… fellow?"

"Yeah. He's the only shop that's near."

"Pity." Gallagher collected himself and they walked on. "The other book is also… dinging. It is a book about how moving pictures are made: the director's role, the cameraman's and all the relevant technicians. It describes most of the cameras they use and the stages of production. It even includes a small section on scriptwriting. Aha! That seems to have aroused an even higher degree of interest."

"I never knew they had book on how to make pictures."

"In the Temple of Enchantment, guarded by the Dragon of the Rubber Stamp, there are books on everything."

They stopped at the entrance to the lane and Johnny stood there, clasping the books and looking steadily at Gallagher until the latter began to feel a trifle uncomfortable.

"Well, Johnny, I hope you will enjoy the books. Remember you have to return them in two weeks."

"I'll have read them long before. And can I take out some more books then?"

"As many as you like. Three at a time and only for two weeks each."

"It was there the whole time?"

"The library? Yes. The whole time."

"And I never knew. How is that?"

"I don't know. But you do know now."

"Are there more libraries?"

"Plenty more. Some with a much wider selection of books. Some with books on specialised subjects. And all of them can be accessed mostly for free, like this one."

Johnny started to walk up the lane, but stopped and looked back. "I thank you, Mr Gallagher." He turned and walked away, and Gallagher was, strangely, the more grateful one.

14

The shelves in Mullarky's shop rose to the ceiling and they were laden with boxes, tins, sacks and cartons. Along the front of the counter there was an array of wide-topped, sloping sweet jars. Inside each, under a congealed glaze of sugar and smudges of groping, dirty fingers, bulging with temptation, were a sticky mass of liquorice allsorts with their wicked geometrics; sweet jelly-baby succubae; dull, tooth-decaying toffee lumps; gobstoppers to make your spit bloody and glaring; and baleful bullseyes. All bought in bulk and doled out in ha'penny handfuls. At the back of the serving area, a marble slab contained cheese, joints of cold meats, a large tin of tea and a tub of pickled onions. From hooks above these offerings, sausages and black and white puddings dangled. From racks in the centre of the shop hung an assortment of garments. Shoeboxes were everywhere. With the exception of the sweets, the choice of product was limited. Choice was restricted to town shops. The regional shop offered basic products and relatively high prices.

The shop owner, Mullarky, was a presentable man in his forties, well into that venerable Dublin institution, bachelorhood. Years of good, selfish living showed in his plump face, which always had a faint sheen of perspiration. Such was his reputation for thrift and shrewdness that it was rumoured that he still had his first communion money. Indeed, his frugal lifestyle left very little room for anything other than the careful garnering and nurturing of capital.

Right now, he was behind the counter taking several matches out of each of the matchboxes in front of him, and he was in a terrible mood after his annual confession. Last month Father Mulligan had gone on about camels and needles (the nerve of him!), and this morning he'd started as soon as Mullarky knelt down.

"*And Jesus went into the temple and overthrew the tables of the money changers...*"

Oh, one of his quare moods, all right.

"*And the seats of them that sold doves...*"

"Racing pigeons, Father, I'm a pigeon fancier myself," he'd replied. Well, he wouldn't let a priest walk all over him.

"Will you listen?!" The priest went on. "*My house shall be called a house of prayer, but you have made it a den of thieves.* Do you understand that?"

"Can't say that I do, Father."

"Money changers in the house of God?"

"In here? There's hardly room for a bit of decent commerce."

He could hear from the heavy breathing that that had shook him.

"Have you something to confess?' Father Mulligan asked after a pause.

"I have, Father."

"Yes? Yes?"

"I overcharged on an order last Tuesday for... for the orphanage." There. Say what you will; he always felt better when it was off his chest. "By seven and six." Then there was a silence from himself. "I suppose it was nearer ten bob." Still no sound. "Maybe it was twelve and six." Jaysus! They were a hard lot. "It was a pound, it was a pound!"

"Well, put it in the poor box."

"The whole pound?!"

"No! Not the whole pound. Two pounds."

"Ah, come on, Father."

"Three pounds!"

"Ah, you can't expect me to—"

"You stole from orphans. Four pounds."

"I'll not pay it."

"Then I'll deny you absolution. Five pounds."

"Then I'll go elsewhere. To the deaf priest in Phibsborough, maybe."

"Aha! It doesn't work like that. I've got you there. Oh no. If I deny you absolution, then it's denied you totally. Six pounds."

"I'll see the bishop."

"The bishop'll refer you straight back to me. Seven pounds."

"I'll go to the Pope!"

"Won't do you any good – and it'll cost you a great deal more than… eight pounds. Just imagine – no absolution, ever again."

Eight bloody pounds! What could he do? The bleedin' priests had you by the balls. Look what they did to Parnell! And then refusing the sacraments to the poor devils in the Curragh! It's worse than the selling of indulgences, so it is. Is it any wonder that Martin Luther threw thirty-two theses in their teeth? They learned nothing from the Reformation.

A bell clanged as the door of the shop opened. Mullarky snapped out of his anger and hurriedly hid what he was doing as Rita entered.

"Hello, Mr Mullarky," she said as she went towards the bread counter. He eyed her up and down and dabbed at his forehead with a dirty handkerchief.

"How are ya, Mrs Moore? Any word from Mr Moore at all?"

"No. Sure, he's probably too busy to sit down and write."

"Probably. What can I do for you?"

"Have you any stale bread left?"

"It's all today's. And that's full price, I'm afraid."

"You'd better let me have a turnover, then."

She counted out money as he wrapped the bread in a sheet of newspaper. She moved along and looked at the jam on the far end of the counter.

"That jam is terrible dear."

"It doesn't have to be."

She looked sharply at him, but he was all innocence.

"Tell you what," he said. "I could always put you in the book. Not for much. Until your man comes home, like."

"Once you start…"

"Now, a sensible woman like you wouldn't let a thing like that get out of control."

Making sure she was not looking in his direction, he reached below the counter and took out a notebook.

"I keep many of the families round here going till the money comes in the post. I charge a little bit of interest but it's so small they don't even notice."

"I'd die if anybody knew."

"Who would know? I'd never tell anyone. It'd be our little secret."

He paused as Rita looked at the jam flavours.

"Jam's good for filling up the young ones' stomachs, so it is."

Rita took a jar and rushed out in embarrassment. Smiling, he took out a pencil and wrote Rita's name and cottage number in the book. Thumbing through the pages, he was pleased to see that he had most of the households beholden to him. Camels and needles, indeed! He closed the book and slid it back into its place. Time for a cup of tea and a sip of that French brandy he'd been saving.

As Johnny came out through the school gate, carrying the library books, Flaherty made a grab for them. His cronies were in attendance.

"Don't you touch them. I'll…"

"What? What'll you do, you gobshite?" Flaherty's face was half an inch from Johnny's when a well-wielded schoolbag connected with his ear and he staggered. Siobhan stood there, breathing heavily.

"Gobshite yourself. You go near my brother again, Flaherty, and I'll take a bread knife to your goolies."

Flaherty half-sauntered, half-slithered away, totally intimidated. Johnny looked at Siobhan with very much increased respect as they walked homewards.

"*Gone with the Wind* is on in town," said Siobhan. "I just have to see it. The thing is, it costs a shilling there."

"To what do I owe this… honour?" asked Dr Jones, as he looked at the three elder Moore boys swarming all over his car, washing it.

"Dr Jones," said Johnny, "we need a shilling."

"Well, here's thruppence towards it."

They singled out the 'buildings' in Stoneybatter, where pride in one's home extended to the pavement outside. It was swept as often as the front room and the doorstep was scrubbed at least once a week. Johnny and Paul both managed to pry a scrubbing brush out of the wrinkled hands of a kneeling housewife and wield it vigorously enough to earn a ha'penny. So they covered the street. Slave labour, Johnny said it was, and he suspected it was against the law.

On another occasion, Johnny mowed a lawn, Paul raked the cut grass into heaps and Albert carried these heaps to bottom of the garden, while the owner of it all relaxed on a chair, smoking and directing the work. The lawn was almost finished when a shrill woman's voice was heard from the house.

"Is that lawn finished yet?"

The owner leapt to his feet and threw his cigarette away.

"Here," he said, offering a penny. "Away with you."

Paul and Albert ran out the back gate but Johnny dawdled, pushing the lawnmower slowly towards the shed. The voice shrilled again.

"I said, is it finished?"

It worked. The anxious owner thrust another penny into Johnny's hand, so Johnny ran through the gate.

Later, Johnny was in Mullarky's shop to see if there were any jobs. He stood there feeling embarrassed for some reason when Mullarky said he would get a penny if he would just give a message to his mother. Mullarky didn't release the coin when Johnny grabbed it.

He leaned over the counter as he said, "All you have to do is give your mammy my regards and tell her the communion suits are in."

Johnny took the coin and left. Outside he stopped and looked at the penny long and hard and, in a flush of incoherent rage, he flung it over the hedge as far as he could. Feeling better, he wiped his hand on his trousers and went to join his brothers.

The final job for the last few pence was collecting horse manure with a shovel borrowed for the purpose from the local market gardener. Johnny was stationed, with a bucket, at the market gardener's gate, at a relatively busy road junction. A passing dray horse raised its tail and obliged. The carter, sitting amidships, spread his toes apart to let the steaming balls fall to the ground and the boys swooped, scooped and dumped the load into Johnny's bucket. He carried it into the market garden, collected a penny and went outside again; then stopped at the gate in horror.

The major and Angela, in the neat pony and trap, were paused at the side of the road. The major was talking to a passer-by and Albert and Paul were crouched down behind the trap, looking at the pony's rear end in hope. As Johnny stood there, in shock, the pony dropped a load and the boys ran to the front and attracted the major's attention.

Oh no! thought Johnny.

"Oh, Major?" shouted Albert.

"Oh please, can we have the sh… the manure?" screamed Paul.

The major obligingly flicked the whip around the pony's ears and the trap moved forward. The passer-by moved with it and the major continued the conversation while Albert and Paul made short work of the contents of the pony's bowels.

Freeze-frame as Johnny saw his brothers approach him with a reeking shovel. Tilt to Angela as her gaze followed them to where Johnny stood with the bucket. Close-up on her face as she smiled in recognition. Extreme close-up on the manure as it dropped into the bucket. Cut to a wide shot of the Angela and the major as they smiled at him. Zoom in as they conferred and the major nodded and called out.

"Mr Moore – recovered, I see. Call around this afternoon. All right?"

"Papa could do with some help," said Angela.

Part of Johnny's soul died and the other, bigger part soared as he nodded dumbly at the departing pony and trap.

Paul nourished the dying part when he mimicked, *"Papa could do with some help."*

Johnny started to throw the contents of the bucket at them. They ran away, laughing.

15

With Siobhan packed off to the downtown cinema, the shilling and bus fare nestling safely in her purse, Johnny was among the highest branches of an apple tree in the major's orchard. He picked the big, glossy, heavy apples with a turn of his wrist and tossed them down to the major, who caught each one in his broad-brimmed hat and laid it carefully in a basket.

The effect of bruising on apples prior to being stored for the winter had been explained to Johnny, who, until that moment, had considered apples as being purely for immediate eating. From his vantage point, he could see the wall which he had scaled many a time to raid what he considered the best orchard in the neighbourhood. He paused in his labours, remembering the delicious stomach-loosening feeling prior to an orchard raid, but the major cut into his thoughts.

"Just the big, ripe ones, and try not to break the branches."

"No," muttered Johnny, "I'll break my neck instead."

"All picked?" asked the major.

Johnny scanned the branches around him. A few smaller, unripe apples remained, but he relaxed and enjoyed the view. The houses amongst which he had grown up looked too small to contain people, never mind the huge feelings he had had over the years. He could see right into the Phoenix Park through the bare branches of the broad-leaved trees that girded it. The canopy stretched away into the distance.

"All picked?" asked the major again.

"Yeah," called Johnny. "I'm coming down."

Back on the ground, he looked at the overflowing basket of apples and, in spite of himself, thought of how few apples ever made it into his house.

"I've another job for you, if you have the energy."

"Yeah," replied Johnny.

The major turned towards the house. He led Johnny inside and up three flights of stairs, turning briefly into a side room to fetch a torch.

"I'm too old to climb into the attic and Farrington thinks it's beneath his dignity," said the major as he stopped on a dark landing and reached for a thick rope. He pulled on it and a ladder descended from the ceiling, revealing a trapdoor into the attic. "It's safe up there, but cramped and quite dusty. Are you up to it?"

"What are you looking for?"

"A picture which I haven't seen for… for several years. It's towards the front, that direction. It's a portrait of… a young boy. You'll know it when you see it but you'll have to clear some things away to get at it."

He handed the torch to Johnny, who ascended the steps and disappeared into the attic. The major followed him up the ladder and stopped with his head poking through the trapdoor. Johnny pointed the beam at the treasures that were piled around and about.

"Jay. There's so much… stuff," he said in awe.

"The discards of five generations of Brennans."

The beam played over a large, framed diagram with a crest on the top.

"What's that?" asked Johnny.

"That's the family tree of ten generations of Brennans. It's as far back as we can trace my family, although the name Brennan goes back to the 4th century in Northern Ireland. The name O'Branain was found among the Eoghan sept, descendants of Eoghan Rogh O'Neill, we think."

"I never thought families could…" Johnny groped for words.

"The history of Ireland, indeed the history of any country, is composed of the actions of the great families." It had been so long since anybody had expressed any interest in the arcane subject that the major's tongue was loosened. "If you look halfway down on the right – yes, there – you'll find the name William Brennan. He was 'Brennan on the Moor', the famous highwayman."

"The song?"

"The song." The major hummed the tune faintly and briefly. "According to the song, his trigger finger was shot away, and that's why he was captured. We had a wrestling Dr Brennan too, and a Brennan who was considered the most learned poet in Australia."

Johnny sat perfectly still.

"After that," continued the major, "the two branches of the family parted. One branch, not mine, helped found the Irish civil service. My branch is, unfortunately, coming to an end."

"An end?" Johnny was snapped out of his reverie.

"The name descends through the male line and…"

The major paused. It was clear that he had given Johnny much food for thought, and he quite enjoyed the palpable hunger of the boy's mind, reaching out across the dusty attic space for knowledge. Eventually the beam of the torch crept back to the family tree.

"So our names are connected in some way: Brennan and Moore," said Johnny.

The major suddenly became aware of their rather ludicrous positions: he on a ladder, Johnny crouched in the attic. He cleared his throat.

"All right, behind that, behind the chest, there should be a portrait. Can you see it?"

The beam played over the items and landed on a portrait of a young boy, uncannily like the portrait of Angela in the lounge. It even had the same frame. Johnny knew immediately it was Darcy. He placed the torch down carefully and lifted the picture over to the trapdoor. The major climbed down the ladder and then reached up to take the picture from Johnny's outstretched grasp. He held it and looked at it in silence while Johnny climbed down the ladder.

Johnny, in sympathetic silence, tugged on the rope which sent the ladder skywards. The major stood looking at the picture.

Eager to break the painful pause, Johnny asked, "Do you know if the Moore name goes back far?"

"What? Oh, yes, all over the country. The name Moore is derived, I would hazard a guess, either from '*Mor*', meaning 'big', or 'moor' because they lived beside a moor or were associated with a Moor – a Negro."

"A name can tell you all that?"

The major started down the stairs. Johnny followed.

"I seem to remember that many Moores were forced to live in Munster because they resisted the English so much in Dublin," said the major.

"The Moores? *My* Moores?"

"Well, you should look up your family name in the library."

"Would it be there?"

"Undoubtedly. That's what libraries are for."

"The only one of my family I've ever heard about is my grandad, Commandant John Moore, Irish Republican Army."

"Oh well, we've had some trouble from that quarter. The IRA wanted to burn this house. I dare say your grandad had a hand in that."

"What happened?"

"Well, *my* grandfather had some powerful friends, so the

house was spared. There's another Moore you know about: Sir John Moore. He was a fine soldier. You'd be interested in him, seeing as how you are yourself a rifleman."

"Ah, that's only play. But what did—"

"Sir John Moore was one of the founders of the Rifle Corps two hundred years ago. Up until then the infantry had only muskets—"

"I know what they are."

"Do you? Good. Well, when the first rifle came along, it was more accurate, up to two or three hundred yards – that's as long as this estate is from my front gate to the orchard wall. Moore trained a body of men in its use. He dressed them in dark green – they've been called the Greenjackets ever since – and they learned to think for themselves in a war, to move forward alone, to use the cover and unevenness of the country to hide from the enemy and to shoot to kill and waste no ammunition. Moore changed warfare forever. I have one of the early rifles in my study, if you'd like to see it."

"That'd be dinging, Major." Johnny was wondering if he had anything green to wear at home. "Was he was related to Grandad at all?"

"If you go back far enough I'm sure he was." They reached the study and the major led the way in. "There you are. One of the early Baker rifles." He placed the portrait on the floor next to the window and reached for a highly polished brass-and-wooden rifle hanging on the wall. "What do you think?"

He handed the rifle to Johnny and watched to see how he would handle it. Johnny took up the weapon, instinctively grasping it firmly; the barrel in one hand and the stock in the other. It was surprisingly heavy but he adjusted his grip and stance to accommodate it. Having looked at it closely for some moments, he stroked the brass-and-wood stock and moved his hand up to the hammer. His thumb slid into place on the curved brass and he looked at the major for permission. The major

94

nodded and Johnny, with some difficulty, cocked the hammer and, pointing it at the floor, pulled trigger. It slammed into place with a satisfying metallic thump. He savoured the moment and handed the rifle back.

"It's great."

The major took the rifle and returned it to its wall bracket. He left the study and Johnny followed. They exited the front door and walked back towards the orchard. When they reached it, the major handed him some coins.

"Your wages."

"Thanks, Major," said Johnny.

The major selected four of the best apples in the basket and handed them to him. "And a bonus."

"Thanks, Major," said Johnny again as he ran off.

The major called after him. "It will save you and your brothers climbing over the the wall this evening."

Without turning back, Johnny grimaced to himself and ran on. He could still feel the weight of the rifle in his hand. Turning over the problem of adapting his own rifle to reflect the glory of the solid, smooth and heavy weapon he had just fallen in love with, he was back in the lane in what seemed like no time. Most of his siblings were sitting on the mattress, looking decidedly forlorn.

"Funny, you not being the first to see it," said Paul.

Siobhan came around the corner. She walked towards them and paused as they came into register. She looked at them with a beatific smile.

"Well?" said Attracta.

"What was it like?" asked Albert.

"Siobhan, aren't you going to tell us?" pleaded Paul.

"Fiddle-de-dee, how you do run on!" replied Siobhan.

"We're dying to hear!" exclaimed Attracta.

"Frankly, my dear," replied Siobhan, "I don't give a damn."

She walked past them into the cottage. They were all angry, except Johnny. He understood, even though he felt redundant.

16

Inside the kitchen, Sean was standing on a chair in his new communion suit and Rita was adjusting the trouser hem. Siobhan passed dreamily through. The others followed, flopping onto various perches. Johnny came in last, dejected. Rita looked at him.

"You'll see it yourself soon."

"It doesn't matter, Mammy," replied Johnny, approaching Sean.

"Of course it matters."

Johnny stroked the lapel of Sean's new suit, and when Sean looked down, lifted his finger to strike Sean's nose lightly. Sean laughed.

"Okey-dokey," said Johnny. "I like the boys in my mob to look good."

"Daddy'll like it. Won't he?" asked Sean.

Johnny and Rita exchanged looks. Johnny spoke. "You're going to have a very special first communion," he said.

Paul piped up, "One thing, Sean – you mustn't touch the holy communion."

"Not even if it sticks to the roof of your mouth," added Albert.

"And it will," said Paul. "It always does."

"The best thing is to get a good gob of spit ready. Like this," said Johnny.

He showed, noisily, just how to do it. Paul and Albert joined in, to Sean's delight.

"Sacred Heart," said Rita. "Will you bloody well stop that?"

It was the rule that when Siobhan went into the bedroom during the day, the other children stayed out. There was a tiny table in the corner which served her as a dressing table and on which she would array the few pretty things she had collected. These things she kept in a wooden box, to which Johnny had fixed a lid on twine hinges. Siobhan kept it locked with a tiny padlock which Johnny had acquired from one of his mysterious sources. He had contributed it to Siobhan's box because he already had one which he used to keep his precious things away from prying eyes and hands.

She opened the box and arranged her treasures on the table. An old perfume bottle which Rita had given her, the scent of the long-gone perfume still clinging faintly to the contours and the neck. A small hand mirror with just the tiniest crack in the corner that you'd hardly notice. A matchbox full of cotton wool. A powder puff that, unfortunately, had not been in contact with powder for ages.

Out of a crumpled tissue-paper wrapping she took her favourite possession: a small handkerchief with real lace around the edges. She had found it on a number 14 bus and had washed it and ironed it with great care when she got home. She never used it of course, she just waved it around close to her face and imagined a ballgown to match. She did so now and thought of Scarlett O'Hara, that resourceful women who loved Ashley so much that she would even sacrifice Clark Gable for him. Scarlett had done everything: survived a war, saved the family home and helped her rival give birth to the baby of the man she loved hopelessly and forever. Was there ever such a woman before?

She gazed out into the trees and thought of the sacrifices she would make for the man she loved. And the man she loved would certainly never come from Blackhorse Lane, that was for sure. *He* would live in a big house like the major's, but there would always be sun shining on *his* house. He would ride a pony and trap like the major, but *his* pony would be golden in colour with a white mane. If someone like, well, like Angela fell for *him* Siobhan would make sure that she hadn't a chance – the cheek of her to even dream of it! And to be deserving of *his* love, she would fight to save her family's home. She looked around the bedroom and sighed, waving her handkerchief around close to her face.

Johnny took Sean to the church for his first confession. The walk there took longer than usual. Sean, never a fast walker, dragged behind, his small hand slipping every so often out of Johnny's.

"C'mon. Hurry up. The priest is waiting to hear what evil deeds were done by Sean the Terrible. Villages razed, cattle and horses driven off, churches desecrated."

Unusually, there was no response from Sean.

At the church, the last of the first-confession children were leaving. Johnny led Sean to the pew nearest the box in which Father Mulligan heard confessions. A small girl left the box and headed towards the altar, hands clasped directly in front of her nose, serious with the responsibility of her penance. Johnny nudged Sean, who reluctantly rose and walked to the box. At the door, he turned and looked pitifully at Johnny, for all the world as if he was going to some awful punishment.

Inside the confessional, the top of Sean's head was level with the grille window. The panel slid open and Sean's heart started pounding.

"Bless you, my child."

"Bless me, Father…"

"Well?"

A loud wail echoed through the church.

"Quiet now, my child. What's the matter?"

"I've no sins to give you," sobbed Sean.

On a bright, forgiving Sunday morning, the grounds of the church were astir with children nervous about the impending sacrament and parents anxious not to do much shouting. The young girls were all in white and the boys, in various hairy suits with short trousers, clutched their small missals tightly and fingered the huge rosettes pinned to their lapels. The children tried to muster their limbs into some semblance of order, while the parents tried to instil compliance through whispering, a lost cause to those who were used to imposing it through screaming.

There were two intrusions into Sean's first communion. One was the approach of Skin the Goat to Rita as she entered the church grounds. The Moore children edged away as he spoke.

"Where's Tom Moore?"

"In England."

"When will he be back?"

"I don't know."

"Get a message to him. Remind him of Skin the Goat's deal."

"Who was that?" asked Johnny, when Skin the Goat had moved off.

"Not a nice man. Come on, we'll be late." She hurried them into the church.

The second intrusion, into the service itself, was occasioned by Johnny, who had crept up to the organ loft and was pounding the keys and pushing the pedals of the organ. Since the airflow was not in operation, his antics were silent. However, the regular organist came in quietly and threw a switch as Johnny was attempting an enormous chord. The resultant clamour upset Father Mulligan, who at that moment was trying to insert the round communion wafer into Sean's horribly dribbling mouth. He jumped and the host dropped onto the floor.

Johnny was reproached by many people during the week: the priest, who hinted that he had committed sacrilege; the headmaster, who knew that it was in the blood; Gallagher, who advised keeping his head down; and his mother, who claimed it would be the death of her. His brothers and sisters thought it funny. Sean thought it was dinging.

17

In the space of a single day, the very fabric of the Moore household was torn asunder. It was nothing unusual in Dublin at that time. It was the sort of day that reminded those who lived in Blackhorse Lane and other such noxious nooks and cruel crannies of what was described in many a song as 'The Fair City' that life was *not* fair, that the millstones of poverty and deprivation ground exceedingly small, and that individual dreams or efforts counted for little.

With Siobhan's help, Rita was doling out small portions of stew to the children. Albert looked at his plate and started to protest. A swift kick on the ankle and a ferocious glare from Johnny silenced him. Rita emptied the pot, handed it to Siobhan and took her usual seat. She picked up a mug of tea and sipped it.

"Where's yours, Mammy?" asked Siobhan.

"I had mine earlier. Eat up before it gets cold. Down the little red lane, Sean."

Siobhan and Johnny exchanged glances. Rita took another sip and replaced her mug carefully.

"I was over at Major Brennan's today," she said slowly, not looking at anybody. Johnny froze.

"He's… looking for someone to work in the house."

All the children except Sean looked at Siobhan, who burst into tears and left the room. Rita took another sip of tea.

Johnny was climbing through the high branches of the laurel bushes on the major's estate. Angela was seated on a low branch, swinging her legs.

"We used to make little houses in these bushes and hide there. Papa would pretend he couldn't find us."

"You and…?"

"My brother Darcy."

"What did he die of?"

"I'm not sure, but it was awful. He couldn't breathe."

"You're still sad."

"Yes. I always will be."

Johnny climbed some more and reached the bird's nest he was seeking. He took one of the two eggs out and started to climb down.

"I hope there are no eggs in that nest," Angela called out. "I used to get very angry with Darcy when he took eggs."

Johnny paused. "No. None. I'm just looking."

"I like to think of the little baby birds inside, wanting desperately to fly."

He had started to replace the egg when he saw Rita and Siobhan approaching the major's front door. His foot slipped and the egg was crushed in his hand.

"If that bird is dead, it'll have company when I get down," he muttered.

When he reached the ground, having wiped his hand on a glossy laurel leaf, he stood next to Angela as they watched Rita and Siobhan crunch their way up the drive. They both waved, but mother and daughter were too engrossed in their mission to notice.

"I was doing well at school," Siobhan was saying. "Better than Johnny."

"I wish this family would realise how hard I find all this."

"I do, Mammy. But it's still not fair."

"Nothing's fair, Siobhan. Believe me."

Farrington opened the door for them and silently ushered them into the lounge where the major was having tea.

"Mrs Moore. How are you, Siobhan?" asked the major.

"I'm well, thanks, Major."

"You look well. You should be happy here. The work's not hard."

"She's not afraid of hard work, Major."

"I'm sure she's not."

Angela came in, very dishevelled. The Major looked at her disapprovingly.

"Angela, why don't you show Siobhan the rest of the house while Mrs Moore and I sort out some details?"

Angela led Siobhan out of the lounge and towards the back of the house.

"Johnny and I have just been climbing in the bushes."

"Lucky for some," muttered Siobhan.

"He says he's going to be rich some day. I believe him. Do you think he will?"

"It's not for me to say," replied Siobhan shortly.

"Oh, Siobhan, please don't be angry with me. I know you have to leave school and that must be terrible. But we can have fun together in this big place. Come and meet the cook, who insists that Papa eats only healthy food. He's always complaining. Farrington, the butler and driver, is a grim old stick..."

Chattering carelessly, she led the way. Siobhan followed, excited in spite of her resentment. It would be nice to be surrounded by nice things all day, even if she had to go home to share a bed with Attracta at night. Angela was all right, not so stuck-up she couldn't get along with her. She was dying to see Angela's bedroom; she bet it would have real perfume and lots of lacy things. She might even let Siobhan have a few cast-offs, things she could show off at... oh, she forgot. There'd be no more school. She wasn't going back to school, ever.

The realisation suddenly lay like a lace curtain between her and what she was seeing in the house: the landings as big as the bedrooms at home; Angela's bed that had – yes – a lacy eiderdown and lacy pillows. She would never have such things. She was stuck – a maid for the rest of her life, unless she got married, and the man for her didn't exist in Blackhorse Lane.

The kitchen was clean and bright and smelled of food and not damp. Feeling not a bit like Scarlett O'Hara, she said hello to the cook and was told of her duties. They seemed so light that she almost laughed and wondered how she would fill her day here. Angela was not much help in this, and Siobhan understood immediately that she had never played any part in running the house and had left such matters to others, secure in the knowledge that somebody would take care of her every need. Siobhan was on the verge of dismissing her as a spoiled, unthinking rich girl when she was brought up short.

"Leaving school must be horrible," Angela said as they were sipping some lemonade the cook had prepared for them.

"Yes. I mean, my father is away in England and never sends any money, so we all have to help. Mammy takes in washing but it doesn't pay enough and I have to help out. But you don't go to school, do you?"

"I'm on a long holiday until I go to a finishing school in Devon next month."

"What's a finishing school?"

"I'm not sure but I think it's going to be fun. Papa took me to see it before we came home. They teach social graces and deportment."

"What are they?"

"I'm not sure. Languages, I suppose. But I know a fair bit of French. And music. And dancing. And painting or drawing. And… oh, I've forgotten what."

"And maths?"

"Oh, I don't think there'll be so much of that. A young lady is not supposed to know much maths."

"What's deportment?"

"How to walk, talk properly. Maybe talk to the King if you're lucky enough to meet him. How to behave at social functions."

"Didn't your mammy teach you that? Oh, Angela, I'm sorry. I forgot."

"It's all right. My mama died when Darcy and I were born, so I never knew her."

"Where's Devon?"

"It's in England, and it's so warm all the year round. I met some of the girls. They're from all over – France, Switzerland, Germany – and some are princesses and duchesses. I don't know what they will be like. I hope they're nice."

"Princesses?"

"Yes. I'm sure they'll look down their noses at me from Dublin."

Siobhan was stunned at the idea of people looking down on this rich young girl. No matter how rich you were, was there always someone richer to look down on you?

"Johnny tells me you are very poor."

"Yes. We are."

"It's so unfair."

"It's the way it is all along the lane. As soon as you can leave school you get a job."

"Will Johnny have to?"

"Yes."

The word hung there as they sipped the lemonade. They both knew what it meant for a boy they both admired. They both knew it would clip the wings of an adventurous and intelligent boy, and they both felt pain at the thought. Siobhan knew with utter certainty that that was the way it had to be, and Angela knew just as certainly that that was the way it was.

Johnny was at the mirror hanging on the bedroom wall, talking to his reflection. A yellow ribbon was stuck to the edge of the mirror. He snarled and jabbed a finger at his reflection.

"You're next, kiddo. Somebody's got to bring home the bacon."

His face creased and he looked desolate. Sean came in, clutching a tin can. Johnny switched into his James Cagney act.

"Whaddya want, you dirty rat?"

Sean proffered the tin.

"I'll never be able to spend all my communion money. Keep it, in case you can't get jam jars."

"What do you think I am, taking nickels from kids? I run this neighbourhood, understand? If there are any jam jars around here, they're mine. You got that? Now scram before I squash a grapefruit in your ugly mug."

"What's a grapefruit, Johnny?"

"It's something you stick in a broad's face."

"What's a broad, Johnny?"

"Something you don't want to mess with."

"Is there real people like those in the pictures?"

"Yeah. Plenty."

"Where?"

"In a place called Hollywood. And I'm going to go there and make pictures."

"Will you take me, Johnny, please?"

"They don't take punks."

"But I could be a punk in one of your pictures."

"I suppose you could."

"Will you be able to earn lots of money there, Johnny?"

"Zip the lip! Before I fill you full of lead."

Johnny dived on a squealing Sean.

The blinds were drawn in the shop and in the dim light, Mullarky was filing the bottom off a weight for the scales. There was a soft knock at the door and he put away the weight and the file, took out the book and went to open the door. Rita slipped in.

"Would you like a sherry?" he asked.

"No. What do you want that you couldn't tell me in the day?"

Mullarky waved the book in the air. "We agreed, didn't we, Rita, that the book shouldn't ever get out of control?"

"Yes."

"There's more to your account than I ever give to anyone."

"It's just that Tom hasn't—"

"Indeed, and I know."

"There must be something wrong."

"There's something wrong, right enough. With the book."

"I'm taking in more washing now and Siobhan has a job. I'll soon be able to pay it off. How much is it?"

"It's too much."

"What are you going to do?"

"Well, that depends, doesn't it?" Mullarky's breath became slightly thicker.

"How much is it?"

"Thirty pounds, nearly."

"Sacred Heart…"

18

The Moore children were seated on the mound of rubble in the lane, listening to Johnny.

"Miles and miles, he had to walk before he saw some of the roads he knew. He was destroyed. Lifting one leg after the other. His feet were in flitters. Every step hurt. Would he *ever* reach home? The boy and the mot are waiting. Looking out the window, their eyes glued to the road. Sighing."

All eyes swivelled to the entrance to the lane.

"Where was he at all? Then they saw him at the bend in the road. They look at each other. They can't believe it. It's really him."

Sean's eyes welled up.

"He starts to run. They start to run. She's bawling. He's crying. Lassie is whimpering. 'Lassie,' she says. 'Lassie's come home.' Then they're all hugging and kissing like mad. The end."

It was too much for Sean. He ran, sobbing, into the house. They looked after him.

"He's missing his daddy," said Attracta.

"Lassie. It's a her," complained Paul. "You kept calling her 'him'. Lassie's a girl's name."

"That was no girl dog," said Johnny.

"How do you know?" asked Attracta.

"Well… a girl dog couldn't do all the things Lassie did."

Attracta was indignant. "I bet you she could."

"What sort of a dog is Lassie?" Albert was concerned with more substantial issues.

"A collie," said Paul. "I'll bet it's a collie. Johnny, isn't it a collie? They're trained to chase sheep. They're the cleverest dogs of the lot."

"Go 'way ou'a that. Alsatians are the cleverest," said Albert.

They started to fight over it, barking as they struggled.

"The thing is, there's never any good parts for girls in pictures," said Johnny.

"What about the girl Lassie comes home to?" asked Attracta.

"Ah, she's only there to… to come home to," Johnny said with finality.

Just then Siobhan came into the lane, looking very tired. She didn't greet the others, who watched her silently as she went into the house.

It was cold in the kitchen and Rita was ironing linen. Johnny came in and handed her a packet.

"Mullarky gives me the creeps. Why do you make me go there?"

"Because I bloody well have to! Sean's burning up and the chemist won't let me have any more medicines."

"I hate going to him."

"So do I. But he gives us credit and we need it. Maybe you should start thinking about a job."

"Mammy! When I finish school, I'll earn decent money. But I have to finish."

He stormed out towards the bedrooms. Rita looked at the Sacred Heart.

"He better be right."

Sean was tossing and turning on his pillow when Johnny came in. He raised his head.

"Why don't you tell us stories any more?"

"Ah, sure, nobody wants to hear them."

"I do."

His head fell back on the pillow. Johnny made the effort.

"OK. Trigger and me will head them off at the pass. Then we'll come back and save that purty girl from those durn outlaws. But first, folks, a little song. *West of the Pecos, I gotta go...*"

Sean wasn't really listening.

"Sometimes when we're in bed and it's getting dark," he said weakly, "I close my eyes and count to... to five, and I say that when I open my eyes Daddy will be at the door. Over there. Sometimes I count to six but it still doesn't work."

"Well, pardner, that's what's wrong. You're not counting long enough. You gotta count to eighteen before daddies come."

"I don't know how to count to eighteen."

"Count to six three times, like you were counting heads of cattle as they ride through the range. *West of the Pecos, I gotta go...*"

Sean closed his eyes. "One, two, four – no, three..."

"*West of the Pecos, that's home sweet home...*"

Johnny was looking through the IRA memorabilia. He had just flicked through some blank IRA letterheads when Siobhan came in.

"Why aren't you studying? If it's not the pictures, it's dusty ould rubbish. Will you ever get your head out of the clouds, Johnny Moore?"

"What's eating you?"

"Plenty of things. And they should be eating you too."

"What things?"

"Things like food. Do you ever stop to think about where it comes from? How it's paid for?"

"Mammy does washing," said Johnny uneasily, "and you've been bringing money home. And one day, I'll be—"

"Oh, Johnny Moore, you eejit. Will you ever stop your stories? They mean nothing. The things you tell about only happen in the pictures and I don't care any more. You pay for them with jam jars that you scrounge around for! You don't even know what money is, how it's got to be earned: by doing things you don't want to do but you have to. You're just like your daddy. He sings and you tell stories. And you don't care about the rest of us, just as long as you have your books and your jam jars and your stories."

"He's your daddy too."

"No, he's not. Daddies are supposed to take care of you. Your daddy is over in England somewhere, singing and telling lies – just like you."

Her tears were too much for her and she left the kitchen.

Johnny looked at the items in the case and tried to conjure a story out of them, but he wasn't in the mood. Was he getting too old for all that? *The empty cartridge case, now – where did the bullet from that end up? Come on. Think. In somebody's breast? Through a black-and-tan head? In the wall of a police barracks during a daring night raid?* Nothing. No sign of that lift of the spirit when a good story started to shape up.

What was happening in his life? Why were so many changes taking place? Where was his father? Why didn't he come home and sort things out? Some awful thoughts started to loom in Johnny's head, and he was frightened by the way anger suddenly surged through his being. Families shouldn't break up. It was a father's job to make sure that everybody stuck together until they were adults and starting families of their own. Now Siobhan had left school, he'd be next. He'd end up like Flaherty if he wasn't careful.

He stared at the cartridge.

19

Rita was sorting the linen when Johnny came in carrying Sean on his back. He placed him down by the small fire and started to put on Sean's shoes, which had been warming on the hearth.

"Mammy, Sean's strap is gone again. His shoe won't stay on."

Rita came over and looked at the thin, down-at-heel sandal. The strap was broken beyond repair. She tugged at it gently.

"It's gone beyond fixing. Your feet must be freezing in them anyway."

"Yeah. They are."

Johnny went to a cupboard and produced a piece of chicken wire. He slipped into a John Wayne walk and drawl.

"Guess you oughta be glad there's a handyman around this here house. We'll have that shoe fixed in a jiffy and you can run in the Kentucky Derby after all and bring in that thousand-dollar prize."

He wound some wire around the shoe.

"There, Mammy," said Sean.

Rita took a deep breath, grabbed her coat and left the cottage. Outside the lane she moved hurriedly towards Mullarky's shop, unaware that Johnny had followed her. He peered around the corner to watch as Rita knocked. The door opened and she went in. Johnny settled down to wait for her.

Rita was standing behind the counter, the upper part of her body sprawled across it. Behind her, Mullarky was having his way with her. Her arm rested on a shoebox beside her. She was staring stonily into the middle distance. In her head, she could hear Johnny telling one of his stories.

Stella Dallas stands in the dark outside the window. Inside, her daughter is glowing in the bright lights of her new home. It's easy to see she's happy and loved by all around her. Stella Dallas wipes away a tear and walks away into the darkness her lovely daughter will never know.

Mullarky, panting as he was, was still able to articulate in short bursts of words. "You'll have to confess, won't you? You'll have to go down on your knees and tell the priest that you did this. That you enjoyed doing this. That you wanted to do this. You wicked woman. Oooooooh! Ooooooh! Wicked! Wicked!"

A tear ran down Rita's face as Mullarky finished and tidied himself. She straightened, picked up the shoebox and moved slowly towards the door. Mullarky took the book from under the counter. She turned and saw it.

"You're not…?"

"I'm giving them to you at factory price."

"But I thought…"

"You thought what? Mrs Moore – Rita – I've given you more credit than anyone else in this neighbourhood. And I haven't pressed you."

"Haven't you?"

"Well… not really. I mean, I'm letting you run up as much as you need."

"What could you do if I didn't pay you back?" She flared. "Throw me in jail?"

"Throw you out on the street!"

"You couldn't."

"Oh, couldn't I? Listen, I bought them cottages last year. They're falling down but they're on a grand bit of land. I could throw you out, all of you, but I don't. Out of the goodness of my heart. Ah, Rita. Let's not fight over this. Let's keep on with our... arrangement. I'd never really throw you out. You know that."

Rita looked long and hard at him. Then she took a deep breath. "Get your book ready."

She moved to the shoeboxes and started selecting. Mullarky stuttered in alarm.

"Black brogues. Three pairs. One size four and two size three. Write this down. Factory prices, mind."

In torment, Mullarky wrote in his book.

"And these lovely fur-lined boots. Size five. Now let's have a look at some nice food. Are you getting all this? Am I going too fast for you?"

When she had addressed all her family's immediate needs, Rita left the shop, laden with boxes, and Johnny started after her. Father Mulligan appeared around a corner across the street from Rita. She dropped her head and hurried away. The priest started to greet her, but stopped and looked after her in puzzlement before turning away. Johnny ran after his mother.

Later that day, in the kitchen, the kids were modelling their shoes in great delight. Johnny was putting Sean's new shoes on for him.

"Will you look at this toff?" he said, to Sean's delight.

"Mammy," said Siobhan, "these boots are lovely."

"Now look at this, all of you," Rita called out.

She produced a rich fruit cake and a small bottle of sherry. There was momentary bedlam as they got a plate and a knife. Rita sat to one side and watched them. Siobhan cut the cake and they all got a piece. Johnny prepared a place at the head of the table.

"Would Madame care to take the best seat in our restaurant?"

"Thank you, my good man."

She was escorted to her place. Johnny looked hard at her as she took her seat. She caught his look and blushed.

"The best seat for the best mammy," he said, and Rita smiled at him with a tear glistening on her eyelashes. It was Johnny's turn to blush, but he hid his confusion and poured a drop of sherry into a cup with a flourish. She tasted and nodded. He poured some more. Then he snapped his fingers.

"The orchestra, please, while Madame dines."

The children consulted briefly before Johnny mustered them into a line. Rita glanced at the Sacred Heart and turned her back hurriedly. Siobhan saw the movement and sidled over to her.

"Is everything all right, Mammy?"

"Everything's going to be fine," said Rita as she sipped the sherry and the kids consulted seriously.

"Where did the money come from?"

"Sometimes when it seems so… money just… sort of…"

"Thank Heaven, then."

"No. No, don't thank Heaven. Don't mention Heaven!" Rita said angrily, and took a hard swallow of the sherry as Siobhan looked at her anxiously.

Johnny started to conduct the children and they burst into song:

"*Mairsy doats and dosy doats…*"

Johnny rolled his eyes.

"*And liddle lamsy divy*
A kiddley divy too, wouldn't you…?"

Father Mulligan had had a good crop of confessions this morning. Some were interesting and, more importantly, he felt that he had actually made contact with some of his flock and helped them cope with varying degrees of stress. When that happened, he always felt more satisfied. There was Mrs Fagin, for

115

example; he was pleased with the way he'd handled that. Sixteen pregnancies in fourteen years, several miscarriages and a crop of snotty-nosed but healthy children to feed. Fagin himself was an annual confessor, usually smelling of porter, no matter how early in the day it was. The priest had tried to slip in a word about the size of his family, but it was a can of worms, difficult and dangerous to open.

"Bless me, Father," said Mrs Fagin when she came in. "It's two weeks since my last confession, or is it three? I'm sorry, I can't remember."

"It doesn't matter, my child."

"No, it must be three because Joey and Vinnie and Tommo had the whooping cough, so I couldn't get away. Yes, it was three."

"All right, three."

"I stole some money."

"You stole?"

"Yes, it was about one and sixpence."

"One and sixpence?"

"Yes. They gave me too much change at Guiney's and I... I kept it. But I don't like the lino."

"What lino?

"The lino I bought that they gave me too much change for. It looks terrible, too. Serves me right, doesn't it?"

"Maybe that's your penance, having to live with the lino."

"But it's in the boys' room. They have to live with it. That's not fair."

"Do the boys think the lino is terrible?"

"Ah, sure, they never even noticed it, the lambs."

"There you are then. It's your penance, so."

"So I don't have to give the one and sixpence back?"

"Have you got one and sixpence?"

"No. My husband hasn't worked this month."

"Well, I tell you what. We'll consider it quits. Guiney's have to fiddle the books and you have to live with the lino. Say a Hail Mary anyway."

"Oh, I will."

"I'm sure you will. Now go in peace."

"That's not all. I… I committed the sin of lust."

"Lust?"

"The same day, as I was leaving Guiney's, I saw this dress in the window. Red taffeta, off the shoulder, with a big green frill around the hem. And a lovely little hat with a veil and a feather."

"And you lusted after this dress?"

"Well, my mouth went dry and my hands went wet. I nearly stopped breathing, my heart was pounding and there was a roaring in my ears. Isn't that lust?"

"It sounds very like it."

"I nearly ran back in and put the one and sixpence on it as a down payment."

"Ah, you see where one temptation feeds on another. The little bit of harm you did with the one and sixpence could have turned into a great deal of harm with the red dress. How long would your husband have to work to earn the price of that dress?"

"At the rate he earns, God love him, the rest of his life."

"Anyway, woman, where would you wear such a thing?"

"God alone knows, Father. It's just that… I'd like to see myself in a dress like that just once."

"You could have gone in and tried it on."

"And me looking the way I do? Sure, I'd have to buy a new dress before I could go in to try that one on."

"Say an act of contrition now, my child, and stop worrying."

She did so and he gave her absolution with a will, having built up a good appetite for dinner. He heard somebody enter the box and kneel down heavily. He slid the panel back and recognised Siobhan Moore.

"Bless you, my child."

117

There was a long pause and a soft sob.

"Bless me, Father, for I have sinned. I went with men."

All thoughts of dinner fled, and his good mood and feeling of self-satisfaction evaporated.

"What? What men?"

"Men. I don't know. They gave me money."

"And what did you do with the money?"

"I bought things."

"What things?"

"Food. And cake. And shoes."

Father Mulligan thought long and hard and finally said, "My child, I want you to go home and think about what you've told me. Then come and see me next Saturday and we'll go through it again. But think hard about what you told me."

"Won't you give me absolution?"

"We'll see about that next Saturday, if you have thought about it and if you come. Now go into the church and say a prayer for me."

"For you?"

"Yes. For me. Say a prayer for me and for all the people who don't know what to do to put things right."

She left and Father Mulligan put his head in his hands.

"Dear God. Help me in this," he said to the empty confessional box.

20

Paul and Albert were hanging about in the lane when Johnny came along, carrying three library books and reading one of them. It made his walking quite erratic.

"Tell him."

"There's nothing he can do."

"What happened?" asked Johnny, looking from one to the other.

"He got caned," said Paul. "By Wilson."

"That's nothing."

"One on each hand," said Albert. "And another four because of you."

"Me?"

"He said I was after letting you be a bad influence on me."

"The cave. Now," said Johnny, his blood boiling.

The cave was a rough shelter made of sheets of corrugated iron and hardboard which Johnny had taken from various yards and building sites around the neighbourhood. The sheets, each of a different size, were held together by wire he had taken from several fences. It was carpeted – a fact that Johnny was very proud of – with a scrap of carpeting he had pulled off a slow-moving cart which had passed the back lane some months previously. On the 'door' was a roughly-painted skull and crossbones, in pink, unfortunately, but paint was hard to come by. The cave was tucked in against the wall of the major's orchard and was separated from a service lane by a thin screen of bushes. Access from the lane to the shed through these bushes would have been easy but Johnny forbade this and decreed that the only entrance was to be through a rough tunnel under the branches, up against the orchard wall. This tunnel was some twenty yards long, which Johnny saw as an advantage because the entrance to the tunnel was far enough away from the cave to make its existence a secret.

Inside the cave, Johnny, Albert and Paul were crouched over a small fire. They had strange markings on their faces. Johnny had a firm grip of Paul's hand and was holding a needle in the flames.

"We must seal our fates with our own rich blood and swear to keep the secrets of the brotherhood," he chanted.

He suddenly stabbed Paul's finger with the needle, and then his own.

"Let that blood drip into the flames until we are all blooded. Albert?"

They turned around to see Albert stretched out on the ground.

"Jay. I've never seen anyone unconscious before," said a deeply impressed Paul.

Johnny seized the moment and pricked Albert's finger. He came round and they all mingled their blood, rather messily.

"Now we swear an oath of secrecy on our mother's grave…" said Johnny, and glared at them because they were slow to respond.

"On our mother's grave," they intoned.

"And on the graves of our family for nine generations," Johnny carried on, and Paul and Albert repeated every phrase after him.

"And if I break this oath, I instruct my blood brothers to cut my heart out while I'm still alive and burn it in front of my eyes. So help me, Beelzebub."

"Who's Beelzebub?" asked Paul.

"The Devil," said Johnny.

"Jay, Johnny," said Albert, after a pause. "That's a bleeding great oath."

Johnny produced a map.

"Now. The quest," he said. "We seek the Golden Staff of Knowledge."

During a break the next day, Johnny went striding towards the teachers' room, carrying a piece of paper. Albert placed himself next to a cupboard in the corridor and fiddled with his shoelaces. Paul lurked at the end of the corridor, pretending to read a schoolbook. Johnny scurried into the room, grabbed the cane and scurried out.

Back in the corridor, he walked past the cupboard and slipped the cane behind it. He gave a secret sign to Albert and walked on. Albert counted to five, then grabbed the cane, hurried down the corridor, shoved the cane under a rug and ran on. As he passed Paul, he gave him the secret sign. Paul counted to five, grabbed the cane and ducked around the corner to where Johnny was waiting at an open window. Johnny grabbed the cane and leaned out. Outside, Albert was standing with his back to the window. Johnny stuck the cane down inside Albert's shirt and pushed it down until the handle was at the neck. The tip of the cane poked out below Albert's short trousers. He walked stiffly towards the hedge at the side of the yard and stood with his back to it.

Meanwhile, the headmaster was poring over some sheets of paper in his room, with Gallagher in attendance.

"Moore's marks are a disgrace," the headmaster was complaining. "He's bottom of the class in maths."

Gallagher looked away and moved towards the window, and the headmaster followed him with the incriminating book. As Gallagher looked out he saw a hand – Paul's – come out of the hedge and, with difficulty, extract the cane from Albert's shirt. The headmaster moved over to Gallagher with the book. Gallagher stepped between him and the window, taking the book from his hand and trying to distract him.

"Not all his marks are so low. Some are actually quite good. It's just that he's not interested in some subjects. Certainly not maths."

"Not interested?! What's that got to do with it? This…" The headmaster looked out the window to see Johnny running along outside the hedge. He watched in disbelief as Johnny took the cane from Paul and ran away.

"The little…" spluttered the headmaster.

Two hours later, Rita was standing at the door with Mr Wilson. He raised his hat and departed. She moved into the kitchen, where her children were waiting.

"He says they'll probably expel you."

"Can they do that?" asked Johnny.

"I don't know."

"For a silly little stick?" said Attracta.

"For the Golden Staff of Knowledge!" said Paul.

"I have to go and see the committee."

"They can't expel me. Mammy, I have to finish school."

"Johnny Moore, you'll be the death of me."

21

The headmaster was very dignified, Wilson was grim and Gallagher was amused.

"We don't want such children in this school," said the headmaster.

"I agree," said Wilson. "The Moores are always in trouble."

"Always?" asked Gallagher.

"Well, always at the bottom of the class."

"Johnny Moore has made a mockery of discipline in this school," continued the headmaster. "If we let him get away with this, it will set a bad – a *very* bad – example to the rest of the school. I propose we expel him."

"I agree," said Wilson, grimmer than ever.

"Mr Gallagher? He's in your class." The headmaster was scrupulous.

"If you expel Johnny Moore," said Gallagher, "you will probably be getting rid of the brightest boy in this school."

"The brightest? Look at his marks!" exclaimed the headmaster.

"His bad marks are not necessarily his fault. I have spent forty years trying to instil a rudiment of knowledge and awareness into thousands of children, most of whom are too dim or too undernourished to take much of it in. Every so often I come across a child who's different. Who isn't afraid to speak his mind or to let his imagination run loose, or to rise above the whole snotty-nosed, lousy herd and be conspicuous for something other than bullying. It's my fault if I can't inspire him to do better and get more of the marks that we grudgingly dole out."

The headmaster shook his head. "That's not the point. The point is, we must punish him."

"Yes, I suppose we must. Give him six of the best on each hand – with the cane he stole. He'll enjoy the irony in that."

"Him? Understand irony?" Wilson was scathing.

"If we merely flog him," said the headmaster, "we will do it in front of the entire school. To humiliate him."

"If you must," said Gallagher. "I doubt he'll be humiliated, though."

There was a knock on the door and the secretary peered in. "Mrs Moore's here."

"Send her in," said the headmaster. "At least we'll humiliate *her*. I intend to demonstrate the deficiencies in her child's upbringing."

The door opened and Rita came in carrying the cane.

"Mrs Moore. Please sit down," said the headmaster graciously.

Gallagher rose to take the cane and to move her chair forward.

"Mrs Moore," continued the headmaster, "I hope you realise the seriousness of the situation? We have—"

"Indeed, and I do," replied Rita heatedly. "None of my children have ever stolen anything in their lives. I promise you that Johnny will never, ever do anything like it again."

"Er… quite. We have—"

Rita interrupted him. "Believe me, you could never make him as sorry for doing it as I can. No matter what you do."

"Yes. Well, I'm not so sure about that, Mrs Moore. We can expel him."

Rita was on her feet. "If you expel my Johnny he will never get into another school. That would be all out of…"

"Proportion," volunteered Gallagher.

"Thank you. Johnny, for all his mischief, is a good child. He brings fun and happiness into a house that has not much else to get through a day. He makes people laugh – even me – and that's a rare gift. With an education, he has a fair chance of doing something with that gift. Without one, he will be lost and I will have failed. I'm not having that. Expel my Johnny and you will have me to deal with, and half the mothers in the lane who all like him. And Father Mulligan, who keeps a special eye out for him. And Major Brennan is very fond of him too, I can tell you."

"As… as it happens," said the headmaster, "we had decided merely to flog him for his misdemeanour. In front of the entire school."

"Do that, Headmaster," Rita said. "He'll take it like the man he is. Now, if you'll excuse me, I'll let you be about your flogging."

In spite of themselves, they all rose as she swept out.

Wilson reached for the cane, but Gallagher was too quick for him. He picked it up and swished it.

"Oh, she was humiliated all right. He's my pupil. I'll do the flogging," he said as he followed Rita.

Johnny came out of the school into the yard, flanked by his brothers. He was hugging his hands under his arms. There was a moment's silence; then the boys and girls surrounded him, cheering.

"Dinging, Johnny."

"You should have burned the bleeding thing."

"Hey, Johnny," a girl called out, "will you steal something for me?"

"Johnny," called another, "can I rub your hand for you?"

Johnny and his friends and brothers moved away from the crowd and out of the school grounds. Suddenly Flaherty and his cronies were there and there was a momentary stand-off.

"Hey, Moore, c'mere," said Flaherty in an unusually friendly tone.

He beckoned for Johnny to move around behind a hedge. Johnny stilled his brothers' protests and followed. Flaherty snapped his fingers and a crony handed him a cigarette. Flaherty stuck it in Johnny's mouth and gestured. A crony lit the cigarette.

"You need any help in your next job, Flaherty's your man."

Johnny sucked on the cigarette and tried to ignore the dizziness. He put on a Humphrey Bogart lisp.

"Say, Flaherty, the jam-jar run down to the Manor is getting a little rough. We need some muscle to get the Cabra punks off the beat. Are you with me? I can always rustle up a jam jar or two to make it worth your while."

"Jaysus, Moore – Johnny – just say the word."

Johnny blew a smoke ring, to everybody's amazement, including his own. He stifled a cough and sauntered away from the admiring group.

The headmaster was seated behind his desk when Gallagher walked in with the cane.

"Sometimes I wonder why I'm in this profession. He deserves better from his so-called teachers," he said.

"He stole government property!"

Gallagher looked at the cane with distaste. "He called it the Golden Staff of Knowledge. Wouldn't it be fine if such a thing existed? However, it *is* government property and God knows what evil rituals he committed with it. Better break the spell."

He snapped the cane over his knee, threw the pieces onto the desk and walked out.

"We'll see about you, Gallagher," fumed the headmaster.

22

Johnny was pacing nervously up and down the pavement at the top of the road that led to the Manor Cinema.

"I can't believe I did it," he said to himself. "It'll never happen. Made a complete fool of myself. Rocks in the head, that's what I got."

Flaherty approached, running at great speed. He handed Johnny some money.

"There's your money for the jam jars. Hurry up. We'll be late."

"You go on. I'm waiting for someone."

"Who? Oh."

Johnny didn't answer. His eyes lit up and he ran across the road to meet Angela, who was walking hurriedly towards him. Flaherty's jaw dropped and he turned and ran back towards the Manor. When Johnny arrived at the end of the queue with Angela, Flaherty and his cronies stepped out and ushered them to the front. Any complaints from the other children were dealt with summarily by Flaherty, and even the commissionaire was deferential. Blushing, Johnny directed Angela's attention to the poster advertising the Fred Astaire/Ginger Rogers movie *Shall We Dance*.

Three hours later, in a house under construction, Johnny and Angela were seriously trying to tap-dance on a sheet of plywood. They weren't doing it very well.

"*You say tomato...*" sang Angela.

"*And I say tomato...*" sang Johnny, using the same pronunciation of 'tomato' as her.

"Johnny!" she snapped at him.

She sang the next line, but Johnny kept using the wrong pronunciation.

"*You say potato...*"

"*And I say potato...*"

"*Let's call the whole thing off!*" Johnny finished. "Silly song."

"But the dancing!" said Angela dreamily.

"Yeah," said Johnny as he danced through the shell of the house. "I think this is a great place. I first came here when there was just trenches in the ground. We used to chase each other around them. Then they started to build the walls with concrete blocks and it was great to see the rooms and the doorways, and a machine they had for making the blocks. They'd throw cement into it and slam down the lid, and when they pulled a lever, up would come a block. We used to make blocks with only sand and stack them with the real blocks. But I suppose they could tell them apart because none of the walls ever fell down."

"Did you not get into trouble with the builders?"

"Oh, sometimes they would chase us but we were too fast. The thing is, I could imagine each house being built for me. Come on.

"And this is the parlour," he said, and gestured towards an alcove in the wall. "That painting? Oh, that's my wife. Thank you, yes, she is a fine lady." He gestured up the stairs. "And up there, you'll find four bedrooms. My parents' room is on the right. My father's... away. He travels a lot. I'm expecting him... shortly."

The beauty of the building site for Johnny was that each house that emerged slowly, modest though they all were, served as a canvas onto which he could project in his mind's eye, the ideal home for a family with six children. He could create the perfect layout for each bedroom and would often come when the builders had finished for the day and pace out the rooms in those houses that had stairs and floors installed and imagine the beds in their allotted places: a double bed for his parents, with a dressing table and a wardrobe; a separate bedroom for the girls, with extra space set aside for Siobhan's dressing table and small chest of drawers. The boys would share two bedrooms. He and Sean would have the room at the top of the stairs, in case he had to slip out during the night to patrol the city. He would have his own bed, of course, and his own wardrobe and writing table. Sean would have to do with less space until he grew up. He had tried to work out the colours for each room and the type of furniture, but it was hard and once he got one room planned out properly, another thought would come in. For example, the front room just had to have a gold sofa, even though keeping it clean would be a problem. So, in this benign home-building mood, he would spend many hours roaming and planning.

Suddenly, as he was describing the layout of the finished front room and Angela was agreeing with him in everything, he stopped in shock. Skin the Goat was looking at them through a doorway.

"You're Johnny Moore. Tell your oul' fella Skin the Goat wants his money."

He turned and walked away, leaving both of them frightened.

Johnny was examining the Bolex intently through the glass. It now had pride of place at the front, next to some film cans. Mr Bourke was glaring at him from the back of the window, a cloth clutched in his hand. Suddenly Johnny imagined the Bolex whirring and moving pictures being projected onto the glass. Crouching, he turned around and held an imaginary Bolex to his face. He used his curled-up fingers as a viewfinder. Into the frame came Mr and Mrs Murphy. Ignoring the traffic, he moved towards them, 'filming' away. They looked at him, aghast; a small boy, strangely familiar, narrowly missing death from a passing cyclist, with his hands up around his face. They scurried away and Johnny straightened up, a blissful look on his face.

"Why the feck not?" he said.

That night, Johnny sat himself down at the kitchen table and opened the IRA suitcase. In it was small notebook held closed by an elastic band. A few pages, he knew, were devoted to dates, places and times for meetings, exercises and lectures. The entries were in a very rudimentary code which he had worked out very quickly, but because they concerned events long past, they didn't interest him. Nor could he extract any semblance of a story from them. The people concerned were indicated only by initials and the venues relied on a contemporary knowledge of who lived where and what places were being referred to. But the bulk of the pages were empty and offered up fields of space for him to fill as he wished.

He had decided to keep a diary of his endeavours to become a film-maker and make it so interesting and full of knowledge that it would one day be in the library for the guidance of people like himself who were looking for something useful and interesting to do. The book Gallagher had taken out on the cinema was good but full of very hard stuff to understand, and each piece of information that Johnny got out of it required more information to make it make sense. The best part was what was called a 'glossary', which gave him all the terms and equipment and what they meant. He had already copied many of them into the notebook for future reference. His book would be much more useful to anybody who wanted to make pictures.

The first page was easy:

HOW I MADE MY FIRST PICTURE
BY JOHN MOORE, DIRECTOR

It would be a war picture, with enemy forces invading a land ruled by a lovely princess...

Near the field, Johnny was crouched down in a bush next to the road, holding his homemade camera to his face. In the background, Angela was seated on an improvised throne. She wore a makeshift silver crown and held an improvised sword.

"Ooowa! Ooowa! All the gang." This came from Paul, who was stationed further down the road.

Johnny started to move his hand as if he were winding a movie camera. He pointed the gas mask at the centre of the road.

"*Action!*" he shouted.

An obviously reluctant Albert walked to the centre of the road and stopped, staring into the distance. Johnny swung the camera to point down the road. Around the bend came four of the Cabra boys. They saw Albert and broke into a run towards him, yelling triumphantly. They came to a halt a short distance from Albert as Johnny emerged, still 'filming' away.

"What's that eejit doing?"

"Doesn't matter. Let's beat the shite out of both of them."

They moved forwards. Johnny moved across the road to cover the scene.

"Stop!" cried Angela. "I, Princess Mathilda, forbid you to enter my realm."

Laughing, the Cabra boys moved forwards.

"Bring on the princess' guard. Action!" shouted Johnny.

Out from the bushes came Flaherty and his cronies, with Michael and Thomas, all a bit embarrassed but game.

"You have heard the princess' command," said Flaherty. "Now piss off, the lot of you."

"No," shouted Johnny. "Avaunt or prepare to meet thy doom."

"Av... avaunt or prepare to meet your doom," said Flaherty.

Johnny moved in to get a close-up.

"They're all a bunch of eejits," said one of the Cabra boys. "Get them."

"Wait!" commanded Johnny.

They all paused and looked at him, even the boys from Cabra. In the field, unseen by the boys, the major appeared on his pony. He looked at the scene in amazement.

"I want to hear some insults and boasting from all of you. Action!" said Johnny.

"Forward, men," said Angela. "For the honour of your princess."

"Lily-livered varlets, I will—" Albert started.

"Shall," corrected Johnny.

"Shall leave your bones for ravens to eat."

"Ye hoor's melt," said one of the Cabra boys as he looked at Johnny for approval. Johnny rolled his eyes.

"Worthless dog," bellowed Flaherty. "You will die in our deepest dungeon."

"Ye pack of arse-licking gobshites," replied one of the Cabra boys.

"Better," said Johnny.

"You shall rue the day your mother bore you," said Michael.

"You lousy snot-gobblers," said the first Cabra boy. "You turds. You bastards. You piss-drinkers. You sheep-shaggers. You cat's scutter. You wormy, rotten, stinky, snivelling, humpty-backed sons of bitches. I hope you all have a good dose of diarrhoea and fall back into it."

The proceedings came to a halt. Johnny was the first to recover.

"He has smirched the honour of the princess. Action!"

They clashed joyously, each stopping the punch-up when Johnny directed them to. Angela waded in, plying her sword, albeit rather delicately. Through it all, Johnny was yelling "cut" and "action" to his heart's content.

The major was in shock.

23

The major was standing in front of the fire with his hands clasped behind his back. Angela was standing in front of him, the silver crown in her hand.

"It is not what I am bringing you up to do, playing in the lane. With those…"

"With Johnny! Who is funny and clever."

"Maybe! But there are just too many differences, Angela, between you and him."

"There shouldn't be, Papa."

"Perhaps not. But there are. He comes from a very poor family, and…"

"Yes. And it's not fair."

"Perhaps not. But that's how things are in Ireland. There are a few of us living in comfort and many, many more living in what I can only call squalor. They are Catholic and we are Protestants – another reason why we can live peacefully with them, but there can be no socialising."

"But Papa, you let him into the house and his sister works here."

"Yes, I do and she does, but only within strict and clearly understood limits. It is a Catholic country now and we must keep ourselves to ourselves and not cause any offence. We are lucky that the Irish are not very vindictive and they have forgiven us for the harm we did to them over many years, but we are here under toleration, not full acceptance."

"Johnny and Siobhan accept us."

"Yes, they do, providing we keep our place and they keep theirs."

"We have so much, Papa, and they have so little."

"That's why they welcome any employment we can offer. Siobhan, I'm sure, is very glad of the wages she gets."

The steam, such as it was, went out of this gentle confrontation as she reached out and took his hand. He stroked her hair and sighed.

"What were you doing out there, with a crown, no less?"

"Johnny was pretending to make a picture and I was the princess who ruled the country. Then some Cabra boys came along and I got frightened because they usually cause such trouble, but Johnny told them they were the enemy invading my country and they joined in and did everything he told them to do. It was so funny."

She laughed so merrily at the memory that the major was touched and troubled by her loneliness and hunger for children her own age. Well, she would soon be among her own kind and age and would forget this uncouth rabble.

"So funny," she said again, this time in such a forlorn tone of voice that he bent down and kissed her hair.

"Anyway, my dear, you must not be so free with Johnny Moore from now on. Is that clear?"

"Yes, Papa."

"Now get ready for dinner."

"Yes, Papa," she said again, and with a slight curtsey, she left the room in silence.

The major turned and looked up at the portrait of Darcy, hanging in an alcove that matched the one in which Angela's portrait hung. He looked at it for a long time, sighed and walked to the liquor cabinet.

Outside the lounge Angela caught up with Siobhan, who was moving away from the lounge door. It was obvious that she had heard. They both walked into the kitchen and Siobhan crossed to the table where she had been polishing the silver. Angela threw the silver crown onto the table.

"Maybe your father's right about you and Johnny," said Siobhan.

"Do *you* think I shouldn't see him any more?"

"It doesn't matter what I think," replied Siobhan, looking at the crown and attacking a piece of silver. "Johnny usually gets what he wants, anyway," she continued, and then, under her breath, "even the fecking fairy princess."

To work off his confusion, the major went to spend some time with his pony, which he called Copenhagen in a wry tribute to Arthur Wellesley, the first Duke of Wellington, who rode a thoroughbred/Arabian horse of the same name at the battle of Waterloo.

Wellington was one of the major's heroes, even though he had grave misgivings about Wellington's reluctance to acknowledge his Irish birth and his antipathy to Ireland, which he described as a nation of scoundrels. Although he saw the Irish males as essentially 'cannon fodder' he was remarkably solicitous of their welfare when they served under him. He also championed Irish emancipation but was loath to share seating in the House of Commons with the resultant Irish politicians. A man of great contradictions, and probably deserving of the enormous, brutal and intrusive monument erected in his honour in the Phoenix Park.

Copenhagen always calmed the major down; he was so trusting and affectionate and he had bought him for Darcy, who did not have time to learn how to ride him properly. Angela rode him on the few occasions when she was home from school but there was no real bond between the girl and the pony.

He was walking Copenhagen around the grassy paddock behind the house when a man approached the paddock fence. The major stopped and waited for the man to address him.

"Morning, Major. The name's Gallagher."

"Yes?"

"Have you a few minutes to spare, I wonder? I'm a teacher at the school."

The major nodded and turned towards the house, Gallagher following.

"Your manservant said I would find you here. I hope you'll forgive the intrusion. I came to talk about one of my pupils, Johnny Moore."

"I know him," said the major shortly.

"Then you'll also know he's a lad of great spirit and potential. If a little unruly.

"Unruly, certainly."

They entered the house and moved into the lounge. The major walked to the liquor cabinet and reached for the bottles. He looked hard at Gallagher. It was obvious he was trying to place him.

Gallagher coughed. "I was up before you once."

"So you were. So you were. Drink?"

Gallagher wiped his mouth and shook his head. "On a drunk-and-disorderly charge."

The major walked towards him, without a drink. "Ah. I remember now."

"You were decent to me. Suspended sentence."

"I remember you had had some altercation with that fellow who runs the shop in the lane."

"Mullarky. Yes. But I've come about Johnny... the problem is that his grades and the focuses of his attention are very uneven, which doesn't make him the ideal pupil for a national school."

"I should imagine not."

"The national school system is not designed for such as he. However, he would flourish in your upliftment programme."

"But he's a Catholic."

"There is that slight administrative detail."

"Detail? You do know that the programme is under the aegis of the Anglican church, which, last time I attended a service, was of the Protestant persuasion?"

"Does that disqualify Johnny?"

"Not inevitably, but probably. Besides, there would be resistance from the Catholic church. Our scheme is designed for the upliftment of exceptional and studious children with enrolment at Trinity College in view, and Catholics cannot attend Trinity without official dispensation. How does young Moore, or rather his mother, feel about that?"

"Oh, they don't know about your scheme."

"So they don't know that you're… asking on his behalf?"

"No. I'm sure if we all thought it advisable, dispensation could be obtained."

"*If* we all thought it advisable, and if the child came with a… an appropriate recommendation. However, I don't think that Johnny Moore—"

"Your programme is exactly what he needs. God, it's everything I thought teaching should be. But Johnny's a dreamer and—"

"I'm sorry. I can't see myself recommending a dreamer, and an unruly one at that."

"Why not? Have you forgotten what dreams are?" Gallagher paused. "Sorry to have wasted your time. No. I'll see myself out."

The major bowed slightly as Gallagher left the room. He looked again at Darcy's portrait.

"*I* forget what dreams are? Ha!" he said to himself.

Outside the lounge door Gallagher almost bumped into Angela, who had been listening. He nodded as he passed. She took a deep breath and strode into the lounge.

Johnny and Angela were standing at the gate, he outside, she inside.

"Not talk to me? Ever? He can't do that," said Johnny.

"He's my father."

"It's not fair."

"No, it's not." Sadly, Angela turned and walked back towards the house.

Johnny was silent for a moment, then he called out, "I'll show him. I'll show them all. I'll learn how to make real pictures and then I'll come back and show you."

She broke into a run. Johnny spoke softly to himself.

"Every time you turn around, expect to see me, because one time you'll turn around and I'll be there."

24

It was night. Johnny was running faster than he'd ever run before. Down the lane into the avenue. Down among the more substantial houses. The darkness, the quietness and the stillness did not, as they usually would, excite Johnny's imagination, nor evoke vivid images. He reached the house in question, leaped over the low gate and ran up to the door. He pounded the knocker, sending echoes into the night. He stepped back and looked up at the second-storey window, ran to the door again and knocked some more.

A shaft of light fell on the path behind him and he moved into it. The window opened and Dr Jones called out, "Who's that?"

"Johnny Moore. Sean's worse."

"I'm coming."

Only then did Johnny feel the heaving of his lungs, the rasping of his throat.

Sean was delirious, tossing and turning on the pillow. Rita was sitting on the bed next to him, mopping his forehead with a damp cloth. The other children were cowering against the wall, awed by the seriousness of the moment. Johnny burst in and ran to Sean.

"Didn't I tell you I'd be back in the blink of an eye?" he said into Sean's ear. "The doctor is on his way. He'll be here before you can say 'Johnny Weissmuller.'"

Sean's eyes flickered and he murmured something. Johnny leaned forward to hear.

"No, Sean. Weissmuller."

Dr Jones came hurrying in and crossed to feel Sean's head. "Oh dear, I was hoping…" he said.

Nobody moved or spoke as he took Sean's temperature.

"Way too high. He'll have to go to Clonskeagh. Now. In my car."

He and Rita wrapped Sean in a blanket.

"Where are you taking him?" asked Attracta.

"To the fever hospital, where he'll be well cared for."

He lifted Sean gently and moved towards the door. Rita followed.

"Siobhan," she said, "look after the rest. I'll be back as soon as I can. Children, do what your sister tells you."

Siobhan was washing clothes when Johnny came into the kitchen.

"Shouldn't you be at the major's?" he asked.

"He said I could take time off while Sean's sick."

"You should only be able to get fevers in the jungle."

"Tom Connolly died of a fever two years ago," said Siobhan. "He was Sean's age."

"Why can't we go and see him?"

"It's terrible far. And the visiting hours are late at night, and anyway, they don't like young children in there."

"But Mammy says there's hundreds of children sick in there. They need other children to help them get well again."

"Try telling the ould doctors that. You better give me that shirt, it's manky with the dirt."

"What?! My musketeers doublet, stained with the blood of the cardinal's guards! Sacré bleu! What would the King say?"

Siobhan started to take his shirt off. She was very close to tears.

"Didn't kings have the healing touch in the olden days?" she asked.

"You speak truly. 'Tis said in ancient manuscripts that—"

"I wish we had a king in Ireland right now. You take it off. I can't see the buttons. There's something in my eye."

The double-decker bus had passed two stops before the conductor approached Johnny, who was sitting in the front seat upstairs.

"Fares, please."

"Certainly," said Johnny, and reached into his jacket pocket. A look of dismay came over his face and he searched the other pockets.

"Where can it be? Mother gave me half a crown for the journey."

The singularly unimpressed conductor jerked his thumb.

This little ruse worked on three other conductors until Johnny reached the suburb of Clonskeagh. He always considered the buses to be public property and therefore available to anyone who couldn't afford the fare. As he got off the last bus, Johnny seemingly found a coin in his pocket and gestured with it to the conductor on the departing bus. He even made a half-hearted attempt to run after the bus. Judging by the conductor's face, if Johnny *had* caught the bus, he would have been brained.

He asked directions to the hospital of one of those aged men who seem to be part of the Dublin landscape, untidy, but with a semblance of dignity or at least a calm acceptance of the inevitability of old age.

"Why? Are ye not feeling well?"

Johnny wasn't in the mood for joking. "No. My brother is in there and I've come to see him."

"From where?"

"Blackhorse Lane. Up past the Phoenix Park."

"That's a powerful long way. Come on, I'll show you the way. The bus fare must have been killing."

"I didn't pay."

"And why should you? The buses are there for all of us. Why should the likes of us, the poor people of Ireland, pay the same as the rich people for a public service? Can you answer me that? No! You can't! This country has failed the heroes who died for it. People like Connolly. Sitting down, he was, when the bastards shot him. He died for a socialist state. A state where you and me, son, could use state facilities for free. All! They all died in vain because you, as small as anything that ever fell out of my nose, are expected to pay for public – public! – transport. Is he bad?"

"Who?" asked Johnny, who was still grappling with the image of a seated hero.

"The brother."

"The doctor says he is."

"Ah, sure, what do the doctors know?"

"Dr Jones has always been looking after us."

The old man sighed. "Then you must see your brother. Listen, there's an ould bollix at the door, a bloated plutocrat who thinks he's St. Peter guarding the Golden Gates. Don't you mind him. Tell him Dr Jones told you to come. They're all afraid of the doctors in there. They think the sun shines out of their arses. Tell him your da is in Kilmainham for murder and that your ma has a beat outside the barracks in Arbour Hill."

"What's that?"

"Never you mind. You're too young. He'll know, though."

They reached the massive iron gates guarding the red-brick building and paused.

"There you are. At least the fever hospitals are free. But a hospital shouldn't look like that. It should look like a… I don't know, a hotel, a place you want to enter, but Christ almighty, more people went in there than ever came out. Lookit! The

Gates o' Hell! I tell you, it's not where I'd want to die. Not that your brother will die there, son, I'm sure he'll die – when he does die – in his own bed, surrounded by a loving family. Go on now. Never mind the ould bollix."

He patted Johnny roughly on the back, pushing him towards the gate.

The old man was right: the porter had legs as splayed as the street junctions at O'Connell Bridge. He was also very fat and his enormous stomach seemed to sway in the light breeze as he surveyed the outside world, which, in spite of his most strenuous efforts, would seek to intrude into the inside world of which he was in complete ignorance, never having been further into the hallowed spaces than the manager's office which adjoined the main entrance hall. As he approached this august personage, Johnny kept a wary eye on the stomach which sought to dominate the rather flat suburb of Clonskeagh just as the hilly site of the ancient city of Tara dominated the plains of Meath. This called for guile, of which Johnny had a deeply rooted fund.

"Excuse me, Officer," he said, and paused.

The porter quailed for a moment, torn between being addressed as such by a ragged urchin and gratified by being given such an impressive title. He drew his stomach as far inward as he dared with his contrary bowels and their tendency to respond to such rude constrictions – especially after lunch – with explosive discharges of the gases created by a copious intake of highly combustible fodder. He squared his epaulette-decorated shoulders and stood as upright as he dared.

To Johnny, the upheaval of the man's belly was fascinating as the flabby flesh, which was at his eye level, contracted and endeavoured to crawl up and back over the scarred leather belt that circumscribed the massive girth. It almost made it.

"What do you want?"

"That gentleman at the gate said you were a bollix."

A bollix? I'll bollix him!" The belly lurched towards the gate, closely followed by the porter. The old gentleman in question was nodding and grinning. He suddenly turned and wagged his arse at the fast-approaching porter before moving away.

Johnny ducked through the door and stood looking around. A young man in a white coat with a stethoscope dangling from his neck paused and surveyed him.

"Are you looking for somebody?" he asked.

"Yeah. My brother, Sean Moore. Dr Jones said I could visit him."

"Ah, yes. I'm treating him."

"Is he OK?"

"Well… yes. The fever has abated – gone."

"Thank you. I know what 'abated' means."

"Good. I'm glad you do. Well, I'm gratified to inform you—"

"To tell me."

"Yes. To tell you that he can go home tomorrow."

"He's better, then. That's great."

"Yes… erm… yes, it is."

"I don't know how we can get him home, though. It's awful far."

"Don't worry. Dr Jones says he'll take him. I must say, he thinks very highly of the Moore family."

"Does he?"

"Yes, he does." The young doctor suddenly became very confidential. "You know, he's the sort of doctor I want to be. Works all the hours God sends, never gets paid. Never complains. Will do anything for his patients. He was offered a very senior job here, but he said that he's needed out there."

"Can I see my brother?"

"Yes. He's still in an isolation ward, but you can see him through the glass. I'll show you. Come."

Sean was vaguely aware of his surroundings. Out of the corner of his eye, he caught sight of waving arms. It was Johnny on the far side of a double window that looked out onto the corridor. Sean smiled weakly as Johnny pulled a horrible face and wiggled his thumbs in his ears. Standing at the side of the window, he reached into view with his arm and tapped himself on the shoulder. When he turned to look at the hand, it punched him on the nose and sent him hurtling backwards and out of sight on the far side. Unfortunately, when he reappeared, staggering, a hospital orderly was standing in view. He reached for Johnny, who waved at Sean and skedaddled.

Sean looked at the ceiling and smiled.

At the side of the bed a white cloth had been placed over a wooden crate standing on its end. Laid out on the cloth was a small silver crucifix, two lighted candles, a saucer half full of holy water, a small piece of palm and a folded napkin. There was also a glass vial filled with oil, and next to it lay a ball of cotton wool and a slice of bread. Rita was on her knees next to the bed. Johnny was leaning on the far side of the bed, his head close to Sean, who was lying very still. The other children were on their knees against the wall, in varying states of terror.

Dr Jones stepped back from the bed and said quietly, "The fever's gone, but his poor heart…"

Father Mulligan moved to Sean, murmuring the prayers for extreme unction. He poured some oil from the vial onto the cotton wool and applied it to Sean's eyes, his ears, his nose and his mouth. Pouring some more oil onto the wool, he applied it to Sean's hands, which were folded outside the sheet. Tugging the sheet free at the bottom of the bed, he anointed Sean's feet.

"Ah, Sean, treasure, don't go," said Rita.

Suddenly Johnny leaned over Sean's face. His cry, when it came, was multi-syllabic and as full of pain as a satiated tick is full of blood. It redounded with an unutterable rage; at loss, at deprivation, at deadened ambitions, at dark horizons and darker lives, at unhoped-for dreams and unlooked-for death.

"*Maaaaammmmmmyyyyyyy!*"

It echoed off the wall that bounded the back lane as Tom came hurrying towards the cottage. He stopped, crossed himself and ran into the cottage as all his remaining children started their inarticulate keening.

25

There was a single wreath and a row of jam jars next to the grave. Each jar had a sprig of flowers or greenery in it. Flaherty was conspicuous among the children from the school who stood behind the Moore family. He was looking around the cemetery curiously, never having been inside one before. Some other children came through the gate at a trot and to Johnny's surprise, he recognised the Cabra boys and nodded briefly at them as they slowed down and took their place self-consciously next to the schoolchildren.

The small coffin lay across two planks which straddled the grave, and two cloth bands were threaded through the handles and underneath. Rita could not take her eyes off it. She couldn't believe that her Sean was in there and not at home. She ignored the arm Tom had placed around her shoulders and with which he pressed her every now and then. Johnny stood next to Tom, looking everywhere except at the coffin. In spite of himself, he counted the jam jars, converting them into visits to the Manor. As Father Mulligan started to read the funeral service, he looked at him with relief, glad to hear the comforting Latin mumble.

Father Mulligan closed his prayer book and looked around at the crowd, which waited in respectful silence.

"The history of Ireland can be traced through the eulogies delivered at the graves of her heroes. At school, we learn the words spoken around those graves by their comrades and they become part and parcel of who we are as Irish men, women and children. We respect those dead heroes because they embody the values of a free and proud nation. But what of the unsung? Those millions of ordinary citizens and those who are taken from us even before they realise that they are citizens? Even before they have a grasp of Irish history and how they are part of it? We are about to consign to the bosom of Ireland a young child whose entire world consisted of his parents, his brothers and sisters and the occasional person who took the trouble to find out who Sean Moore was. Well, Sean Moore was a child of us all. A child of God who spent far too few years in this imperfect world. Who wept at his first confession because he had no sins to confess, yet who went to his grave as unblemished as an angel and as a child who was as close to the original state of grace as Adam and Eve. A child who will reap the just rewards of a pure life forever, while we who consign him to the earth labour on in our quest to be as he was. Let us pray that we reach the close of life as pure as he."

As he led the crowd in an act of contrition, Tom, Jacko and two other men stepped forward and grasped the ends of the bands and, with very little effort, raised their burden so that one of the gravediggers could pull the two planks away. The men lowered the coffin very slowly and Johnny started to hum the death march as Sean's remains disappeared into the black clay. The coffin settled, the bands pulled out, the men stepped away. Father Mulligan took hold of the spade that was stuck into the loose mound of earth. He scooped a small amount and tossed it onto the coffin. Rita's shoulders started to shake at the sound.

Tom put his arm around Johnny and leaned down when he heard the humming.

"Easy now, Johnny," he whispered.

"Where were you?"

"What could I do?"

"You could have been here."

Tom eased Johnny towards the grave. He took the spade, tossed some earth in and proffered the spade to Johnny. Johnny stood with his head down.

"Johnny. You're the man of the house now."

"I'm only twelve and a half!"

Tom tried to thrust the spade into his hand but Johnny turned and ran. He ran through the lank grass of the cemetery, along the gravel path towards the trees that stood close together near the church. He wanted to run out of Dublin, out of Ireland. He wanted to run on the prairie, over the foothills of the Pecos, along the banks of the Rio Grande. He wanted to run where nobody had ever run before. Mostly he wanted to run back in time, to when they were a family, to when his daddy sang after supper and Sean listened, enthralled, and begged for another song before he had to go to bed.

He only got as far as the trees where, among them, out of sight of the mourners, he threw himself against one and wrapped his arms around it.

"I better grow up now, Sean," he said. "Because you can't."

Tom was angrily on the defensive. He was seated on the edge of the bed, glaring out into the lane. Rita was in a fury, trying to keep her voice low.

"Hard? Hard?! Life is hard in England? You *worked* in England. You earned money. You fed yourself and you drank in the pubs. And all that time your children were hungry. Going round in rags. Getting sick every minute. Dying!"

In the bedroom next door, her voice was all too audible. Johnny stuck his fingers in his ears and tried to drown out the argument.

"Fix me up, Doc," he said in his Jimmy Stewart voice. "I've got to get back to a pretty young girl in a small town in the Midwest. She's been waiting for me since this war began."

"I've got a steady job now," said Tom. "Not good, but steady. There'll be regular payments. Here." He produced a wad of notes and threw it on the bed. "There's seventy pounds there. That'll keep you going."

"That'll pay my debts."

"You owe seventy pounds?!"

Johnny continued talking softly to himself. "She doesn't know whether I'm alive or dead. But I know just what she'll say when I step off that train."

"How do you think I kept this family going while you were away?" said Rita. "Tell me that!"

"Give me a slug of that whiskey, Doc," said Johnny frantically. "And do what you have to do, so I can go home to my girl."

"But the interest them gougers charge!" exclaimed Tom. "You'll never see the end of it."

"The interest?" said Rita. "No. I'll never see the end of that."

Johnny, quite desperate, threw the blankets over his head.

Early the next morning, before the other children awoke, Johnny was reading at the table. Tom came in and poured himself a glass of water.

"You're up early," said Tom while he drank. "Well, I'm off again."

"So soon?"

"There's nothing here for me."

"There's us."

"You know what I mean. Any word on a job yet?"

There was a silence, and Tom hadn't the courage to break it. Finally, Johnny spoke.

"How long will you be gone?"

"Don't know, son. Say goodbye to the others for me."

He tried to sing.

"And so I go to fight the savage foe
Although I know I'll be sometimes missed
By the girls I've kissed..."

The song died on his lips.

"Yeah," said Johnny.

"Yeah. Goodbye, so." Tom nodded and left.

"Goodbye, Daddy," said Johnny. Then he sang, softly:

"Goodbye, goodbye
I wish you all a last goodbye..."

Johnny and Flaherty were walking towards Mullarky's shop.

"This is dangerous, Flaherty. We'll probably get into trouble for this."

"Great."

"That's why I don't want my young brothers involved."

"Anything to get back at Mullarky. He has them all in his book, I'm telling you. I know my ma only gets credit because she... you know."

"What?"

"I don't know." Flaherty flared up. "How would I know?!"

They walked on, both of them angry and confused. They reached the shop and Johnny took a deep breath.

"I'm going to buy something. You keep your eyes open while I get his attention. I want to know exactly where he keeps that book."

Flaherty's eyes lit up. "Jaysus! You don't mean...?"

"Anybody messes with Johnny Moore's family, messes with Johnny Moore. You got that?"

"Yeah, Johnny."

They entered the shop. Mullarky was stacking shoeboxes onto a shelf from a pile on the floor. Johnny crossed over to him.

"Here, Mr Mullarky," he said. "Let us give you a hand."

He started handing the shoeboxes to Mullarky.

"Oh, thanks. I'm getting a bit stiff."

Flaherty joined in. He was tall enough to place the boxes on the shelf.

"Mammy wants two eggs," said Johnny. "She said you could... erm..."

"What? Oh, OK. The eggs is over there. Help yourself. Two, you said?"

Johnny went to the eggs, turned his back and made a great fuss of examining them. Mullarky looked anxiously at Flaherty, who was diligently putting the boxes in position, his back to the room. Reassured, Mullarky crossed to the counter, looking suspiciously at Johnny all the time.

"The brown ones is nice," he said. "They have a great big yellow yolk."

"Brown ones?" said Johnny, his eyes firmly on the eggs. "Oh, yeah. There's some here all right."

Flaherty's eye was on Mullarky as he took the book out.

"Two eggs. You'll want to wrap them," Mullarky said as he made an entry.

Johnny came over with the eggs and placed them on the torn newspaper that Mullarky had spread out on the counter.

"Thanks, Mr Mullarky. We'll be off, so."

Flaherty muttered a goodbye and followed Johnny into the street.

"He keeps it on a little ledge, right up under the till. Johnny, when are you going to...?"

"I don't know. Soon. Not a word to anyone, OK? I have to work out a plan."

"Me lips is zipped. See you Saturday. Don't be late."

He ran off, laughing. Johnny took an egg out of the paper and crushed it in his fist.

"*This* dead bird is going to have company."

He ran back to the shop, threw the other egg at the window

and ran away. Through the window a puzzled Mullarky watched the egg slide down the glass.

It was late afternoon on Saturday when an angry Johnny came home. He lurched past Paul and Albert, who were sprawled on the mattress, their resentment hanging in the air. Rita was washing as usual when he came into the kitchen. He slumped down on a chair and looked at her sullenly. She let some minutes pass before she spoke.

"Where were you, Johnny? The others have been waiting all day."

"I was working at the abattoir with Flaherty. He's got a full-time job there and he got me Saturday work."

Shocked, she came and sat across from him.

"There was no need for that."

"Oh no? Well, there's a need for this, isn't there?"

He took out some coins and threw them on the table.

"You're working all Saturday? So no more movies?

"*No!*" he shouted, amazed that he could shout at his mother.

She looked as if she had been slapped. Her open, vulnerable expression angered Johnny even more. He wanted this to stop, but he couldn't stop it. He was angry with her, with Mullarky, with Flaherty for what he had said, or rather what he had not said. He was angry with himself for being angry with the one person, he suddenly realised, whom he loved more than any other person in the whole world. He was angry with the anger, and the frustration of that made him even angrier.

"There!" he said, pushing the money towards her.

She grabbed his hand and he tried to pull it away. She turned it over to reveal burst blisters on the palms.

"That's terrible work," she whispered.

"It's not as terrible as what you're doing!"

Her eyes filled. He started to tremble.

"*Where's my fecking daddy?*" he shouted.

Johnny was lying in bed staring at the ceiling, the yellow ribbon clutched in his hand. Albert whispered across the sleeping Paul.

"What's it like at the abattoir, Johnny?"

"Go asleep."

26

Father Mulligan was sitting in his confessional at the appointed hour and for once there was no line of sinners waiting. It gave him time for reflection on his flock and his care of them. Funny people, they were, and when you got a brief look into their souls as they bared them and grovelled in guilt it wasn't a pretty sight. And listening to their descriptions of short moments of shabby pleasure or vindictive jealousy was singularly unedifying. Unlike Copernicus, most of them thought they and their sins were the centre of the universe. *The smug way they behave*, he thought, *you'd never think they were hurtling through space at over half a million miles a minute. Maybe that's what has them confused.*

The opening of the door and the shuffling and scuffling as the next sinner took up position alerted him to take up the weekly burden and the perpetual responsibility. As he slid the grille open he hoped it wouldn't be too onerous.

To his relief it was Whacker Farrington, the unruly Lothario of the lane, always ready to swap a few spits and drop his hand with the local girls – Lord alone knows what gave him such ready access to their bodies. Whacker started his well-aired jargon and routine.

"Bless me, Father, for I have sinned. It's four weeks since my last confession."

"Yes, my son?"

"I committed immodest actions."

"How many times?"

"Three times."

"On your own or with someone else?"

"With someone else."

"This is a very serious sin, my son."

"I know, Father."

"Not only for you, but for the girl. It was a girl?"

"Wha…?"

"Of course, of course. And you led her astray. You must remember, my son, that we are all temples for the Holy Spirit, especially the soft, pure body of that girl."

He realised too late that he should not have mentioned the girl's body.

"You've done this before, haven't you?"

There was a long pause, and he knew he had left a gap for the sweet memory of the sin to come before the mandatory repentance. *You'd think after all these years, I'd know better*, he thought. *Better whip him into line.*

"Yes, Father."

"And you have every intention of doing it again, haven't you?"

"Ah, no, Father."

"You wouldn't lie to me, son, would you?"

"Me, Father?"

"You, Father! You know, don't you, that I can only absolve you from this terrible sin if you have a firm desire for amendment?"

"Yes, Father."

"And that if you have deceit in your heart when you say an act of contrition, it's a worse sin than the one you have confessed to?"

"Yes, Father."

"So you won't do it again?"

"No, Father."

Maybe he believes it now, but when the next battle between the church's strictures and the deep shade in the Phoenix Park is played out the flesh will win hands down. Oops, an unfortunate thought.

"For your penance, I want you to say three – *three* – Nicaean Creeds."

"Wha…?"

"Say the 'I believe in God…' three times."

"I believe in God the Father almighty—"

"Not now! Do you want us to be here all weekend? Say an act of contrition. *Ego te absolvo…*"

Later that morning, Rita entered the confessional and let the darkness embrace her as she knelt down. This, she felt, was the one place where she could let all her fears out and lift the lid on all that troubled her. She could hear the soft murmur of another woman's voice through the gloom and the deep tones of Father Mulligan interjecting every so often. This was the priest who had heard her first confession, and the first confessions of all her children. Not that she would be telling *him* what she wanted to tell. She would be telling God – Father Mulligan was merely the channel for God's grace. That thought made it easier to dwell on what she had to tell God. She bowed her head and inhaled the smells – the dust, the wood, the incense, the smell of burning wax candles and polish. The smells she had grown up with. Here, maybe, she could find the answers to the questions that burned her. Here, perhaps she could throw off the burden of her sins, which, deep down, she knew were not really sins but actions forced upon her…

She suddenly thought that this was a sacrilegious thought and started an act of contrition, but the screen was pulled back and she caught a glimpse of Father Mulligan's careworn face.

"Yes, my child?"

It was too much. She broke into uncontrollable sobs.

"It can't be as bad as all that, my child."

"Ah, it is." There was a pause as long as eternity. "I committed adultery."

A sigh filled the confessional. "A decent woman like you?"

"You know who I am, then?"

"Who heard your first confession?"

"You did, Father."

"Why, in the name of God?

"I had to. I owed… too much money at the shop. There was no food in the house. No suit for Sean. No money from Tom."

"Why didn't you go to the church?"

"I did. They gave me food tickets! For *his* shop! And they made me… feel like a beggar."

"There's no shame in begging."

"Isn't there? You… you won't tell anybody about this, will you, Father?"

"I can't! I can't!" said the distraught priest.

It was a long while before they could proceed.

The bishop and the priest were in the sacristy. On the way through the darkened church, he had genuflected before the altar. His knees had crackled so much that Father Mulligan feared he might never rise to his feet again, but the resolve of this particular spiritual superintendent of the Holy Roman and Catholic church was stronger than his cartilage. He straightened slowly and proceeded towards the light that spilled out through the open sacristy door and brushed the well-polished altar rails.

Inside the sacristy, the dim light from the window was barely sufficient to illuminate their movements. The bishop moved towards the table that occupied the centre of the room. Father Mulligan crossed to a cupboard, from which he took a white cloth and a pair of candles in silver candlesticks. He carried them to the table and the bishop helped him position them carefully on the cloth.

"Draw the curtains fully, Father Mulligan," said the bishop. "We want no eyes prying into tonight's ecclesiastical affairs."

Father Mulligan pulled the curtains closed as the bishop struck a match and lit the candles.

"May the Lord give strength to our hands this night," intoned the bishop.

"Amen, Bishop," replied Father Mulligan.

He crossed back to the cupboard, took out a flat, cloth-wrapped package and placed it on the table. This was followed by two chalices and a bottle of wine. He poured some wine into each of the chalices. They both sat and sipped solemnly.

"Maynooth, 1936," said the bishop. "A rare vintage."

He opened the package to reveal a pack of cards. They each emptied a box of matches onto the table.

"I bought this box today in that shop in the lane," said the bishop. "There's so few matches in it, it's robbery, God forgive them."

The bishop cut and Father Mulligan dealt.

"Any IRA men down your way?" asked the bishop as he gathered up his cards. "Give me three. They've been very active lately."

He tossed two matches onto the table.

"No, thank goodness. Three for the dealer," replied Father Mulligan, tossing in three more matches. "I don't relish the idea of refusing any of them absolution."

"That's the ruling from Drumcondra. Not sure I agree, but there you are."

He threw in his hand. Father Mulligan gathered the matches and the cards, which he passed to the bishop, who dealt and said, "We had an application to have a marriage dissolved last week. A smart, South Dublin surgeon."

"I can open. Give me three."

He threw in two more matches.

"His wife can't have a baby, he tells us," continued the bishop as he equalled the stake. "I'm taking two. When I tell him that's no reason for a dissolution he says, 'I'm leaving her because she's unbearable.'"

"I bet four," said Father Mulligan.

"See you and raise you four," said the bishop. "Because she's impregnable."

"Three tens."

"Three jacks. Because she's inconceivable. Funny way about them down there."

The bishop gathered in the matches as Father Mulligan dealt.

"How's the food-ticket scheme going?" asked the bishop. "I can open. None for me." He tossed in six matches. "I see this fellow Mullarky has put in a bid for supplying the whole parish. What do you think?"

"I'll see him in Hell first!"

The bishop looked at Father Mulligan in surprise.

"Sorry, Jack," said Father Mulligan as he threw in six matches. "I'll see you. I'm recommending that he be removed from the scheme altogether."

"Well, it's your call, Desmond," said the bishop with a roguish grin. "Mine's a straight flush."

He left the matches on the table and they both leaned back in their chairs and surveyed each other as they sipped their wine. They had both been through the seminary at the same time and had remained in touch throughout their respective careers, and their mutual respect and friendship was deep. The bishop spoke first.

"What's troubling you? Do you want to confess?"

"No thanks. Some advice wouldn't be amiss, though."

"I'll do what I can, but you were always the wiser of the two of us."

"And look where it got me."

"Now, Desmond. Don't confuse the kowtowing of the middle classes with respect, or don't think that the acknowledgement of the bishopric has any real meaning. The church in Ireland has always been a sort of bolthole for the well-off when they begin to feel a twitch or two about their excesses. That's the world I move in and I must admit I like it."

He sipped his wine and, to Father Mulligan, he suddenly looked very old. The bishop sighed and continued.

"But you, on the other hand, deal with the deep-rooted needs of this country. You have plentiful opportunities to guide ordinary people on the bottom edge of society and help them cope with problems which seem to them to be beyond their power to solve. That's where the real mission of Christ belongs, not with my snotty-nosed casual Catholics. You don't need to tell me what you heard in confession. I know that's what's troubling you – it was from some poor parishioner driven to do something which he or she knows is wrong but can't see any alternative. Amn't I right?"

Father Mulligan looked at the bishop for a long time before he responded.

"You know, you're lost in the bishopric. You should be out here with me in the..." he looked at the glass of wine "... in the vineyards. Trying to ignore the plump grapes at the bottom of the bunch, bursting with flavour, and probing for the shrivelled grapes that nobody wants to pluck and so must wither and die."

"They're all God's children," said the bishop in a very humble tone.

"Yes, they are. But many of them suck the hind tit, as my grandfather used to say, and they're the ones most in need of succouring. Sorry, Jack, I—"

"Don't apologise! Don't ever apologise to me, Desmond Mulligan. You were always the better priest. Now let us both pray for a righteous solution to the problem you are facing, and for strength to you to help them find it."

They both clasped their hands and bowed their heads over them.

27

In the kitchen Rita was ironing on one end of the table while Johnny was busy on the other. He had commandeered all the shoeboxes from Rita's major shopping expedition and had transformed one of them into a miniature cinema. Inside a hole he had cut in one end, he had stuck a piece of glass. Through slits in the sides of the other end he had threaded a strip of paper. On the paper he had stuck frames out of *Mandrake the Magician*, cut from several copies of the *Evening Mail*. He had taken frames almost at random and written his own script for the images. The paper strip was wound around two thread bobbins attached to the outsides with some wire. A careful winding of one and unwinding of the other bobbin advanced the drawings as Johnny whispered the story to the tin soldier that stood inside the cinema in splendid isolation. A large hole in the lid, covered with tissue paper, supplied the interior illumination until Johnny could work out how to do it with a candle inside. The jerkiness of the paper's advancement annoyed him but he did not yet know how to make single advances in a smooth manner. However, the soldier seemed totally absorbed as Mandrake gestured hypnotically and the leopard-skin-clad Lothar did his bidding.

The door suddenly opened and a shadow fell across the floor. They turned in surprise to see, silhouetted in the hard light, the bulky figure of Skin the Goat. He fingered the faded wreath that hung on the door for a moment and then stepped into the kitchen. He seemed to fill the room.

"Where's that bastard Tom Moore?"

"Still in England," Rita whispered.

Skin the Goat walked towards her. Johnny swallowed and walked between him and Rita. Skin the Goat looked down at him stonily.

"I heard he was back here."

"Only for a while. He's gone again," said Johnny through a constricted throat.

"What's the dead flowers for?"

"My youngest son. He... he died."

"I am owed twenty pounds now, counting all the interest. I've waited nearly a year. I'll come for it tomorrow, same time. Twenty pounds – or there'll be another one of them things on the door.

"You hurt anyone in this family," said Johnny, "and you'll be sorry."

Skin the Goat ignored him and walked out. "Tomorrow," he called over his shoulder.

"Not tomorrow," said Johnny, "but one day, and for the rest of your life."

Johnny had been busy, at school and in the neighbourhood. His stature since the cane incident, the 'film shoot' and Sean's funeral was such that he had become an icon of resistance to all the children who thought they weren't being given a fair deal for whatever reason. They had recognised in him a drive that offered them all some hope of reaching some (mostly unformulated) goal. This was ironic because Johnny saw his dreams drifting further and further away as doors seemed to be closing in his face. However, when he sent out the call to a further adventure, the children responded in sufficient numbers for Johnny to feel reasonably confident of pulling his stunt off without having his head knocked off. Part of him was excited about the plan, in a detached way. The rest of him was in a blue funk.

But the next day, when Skin the Goat turned into the back lane and made for the Moore cottage, Johnny was standing in the gateway with his hands on his hips, one foot forward, the way John Wayne stood when he was about to give some baddie a mouthful of scorn.

"Oh, it's Little Big Mouth," said Skin the Goat.

"Oowa! Oowa! All the gang," called Johnny, a bit upset when his voice crackled in the middle of the call. However, it had the desired effect. Suddenly there were kids everywhere, the Cabra kids to the fore. Each had an improvised weapon: hurleys, iron bars, a bicycle chain, a yard brush and even a bread knife.

"Ye little bleeders," said Skin the Goat, nonplussed for once. "You, Moore – where's my money?"

"Mr Mullarky has it."

"Him with the shop? Why?"

"My da sent money but Mr Mullarky said we had to pay him first. He took it all. There was nothing Mammy could do."

"How much money was sent?"

"A hundred pounds."

"Jesus," said Skin the Goat. "I'll kill him."

He turned away, relieved at not having to work out how to handle twenty-odd kids with weapons. Suddenly Johnny vomited. The boys gathered round in sympathy.

"That's a deadly colour," said one of the Cabra boys as a thin stream of bile dangled from Johnny's mouth.

"Yeah," said Flaherty knowingly. "When me da gets sick for the third time, it's just like that."

Johnny recovered and wiped his mouth, glad that the pounding of his heart had stopped.

"Right," he said confidently, "I'll be needing some of you tonight when it gets dark. Right now, I need Flaherty to do something for me."

The boys took off and Johnny beckoned Flaherty into the cottage. Flaherty sat at the table as he was bid while Johnny ran to the bedroom. He returned with the case of IRA memorabilia and placed it on the table.

"You can write like an adult," he said.

"Yeah. Can't spell but I can write just like a grown-up," said Flaherty proudly.

This was a fact. Flaherty had been called upon by many a mitching or lazy schoolboy to write a note from their supposed parent, excusing their lack of attendance or homework. The handwriting he was supposed to use was a mystery to Johnny. He had started off at school with capital letters, and when the class had more or less got the hang of those, the smaller letters, which, in some cases, bore little resemblance to the capitals, but learn them he did. Then in a later class, he was given a copybook with lines ruled in two colours, and between them he was taught to write in what they called copperplate. This was a spidery form of writing with huge curves in the capital letters and a boring up-and-down shape for the smaller letters.

He battled with these two forms of writing but was totally thrown by the writing classes in Irish. This was a round type of writing with no big letters as such, but round letters that were written a bit bigger. This, he was told, was Gaelic writing and it was part of the proud history of Ireland. The thing was, none of the writing he was taught was anything like the writing he saw in books and newspapers and he wished that the school would make up its mind because he was always getting slapped for writing badly. So he had written a note in the notebook in the big and small writing he was taught most of the time, and this he showed to Flaherty along with a sheet of IRA notepaper, and handed him a pencil.

"Never mind the spelling. Just copy that."

That was a message which started:

Mr Mullarky,
It has come to the notice of the Irish Republican Army...

In the lane that night, close to Mullarky's shop, Johnny, dressed in a trench coat and beret, was being helped by two of the Cabra boys to mount Flaherty's shoulders. Flaherty was wearing outsized boots he'd borrowed from his father, who was lying in a drunken stupor at home. One of the Cabra boys, who had been watching the shop, came up to them.

"He's in there all right. On his own. He's just drawn the curtains," he reported.

Johnny's balance was precarious. One of the boys handed him an envelope.

"OK. Off you go now," said Johnny. "Wait for us in the alley."

The boys ran away and the tall figure moved unsteadily towards the shop. It paused at the window, the shadow falling across the drawn curtains. Johnny banged on the glass and half-pulled, half-nudged Flaherty to the door. He dropped the envelope on the doorstep, banged on the door and kicked Flaherty, who moved away quickly. After a few tense moments, the door of the shop opened and Mullarky looked out, just in time to see the figure disappear into the gloom.

"Who the hell was that?" he muttered.

His gaze fell on the envelope and he picked it up and walked back into the shop. He closed the door and opened the envelope as he returned to the counter. The blood left his face as he read:

...that you are oppressing the descendants of some of the
patriots who paid the supreme sacrifice for our beloved
Ireland. This must stop forthwith. To avoid retaliation we

strongly advise that you destroy your filthy credit book and prove that destruction to our commandant's satisfaction.

Signed, O'Donovan Rossa the Third
Execution detail
Irish Republican Army

"Merciful Christ!" he said as he wiped his face, which was dripping, and ran to bolt the door and turn out the light. He paced up and down the shop in torment, pushing the curtain aside every so often and peering out.

Johnny and Flaherty reached the alley near the shop and scurried up it. Johnny gathered up the skirts of the trench coat and jumped down. They both crouched down next to the Cabra boys in the darkness and watched the shop. They hadn't long to wait.

Skin the Goat appeared out of the darkness and strode up to the shop. He pounded on the door. The curtain was drawn aside slightly and then dropped back in place. Skin the Goat pounded again.

Inside, Mullarky was panting in terror. "Jesus preserve me," he whispered. "Skin the Goat! An IRA commandant!"

He grabbed his book, ran to the door and pushed it out through the letterbox. Skin the Goat leaned down and picked up the book, just as Mullarky found his voice and screamed.

"Honest to God! I didn't know it was IRA business."

At the mention of the IRA, Skin the Goat drew him up sharply.

"IRA?" he muttered. "Fuck that! I don't need them in my life."

He moved away rapidly. As he passed the alley he threw the book into it. Johnny grabbed it.

"Flaherty," he said, "I need one of your matches."

The boys watched the book burn slowly and took turns to

blow on it to keep the flame alive as it ate its way through the pages. Flaherty took a bent cigarette butt from his pocket and lit it off the flames. He settled back and looked at Johnny.

"You know wha'?"

"What?"

"You're like one of them fellas in the pictures."

Johnny's heart swelled, but he kept his face expressionless and his eyes on the burning book.

"Alan Ladd," said Flaherty finally. "And do you know why?"

Johnny could barely answer. The number of times he had played at being Alan Ladd! And here was Flaherty looking into his soul.

"Alan Ladd always knows what to do," continued Flaherty. "With the crook, with the mot, with everybody. The minute he walks in, they all look scared, 'cause they know somebody is going to get the shite beaten out of him."

Johnny screwed his eyes up and looked at his partner through the smoke of the campfire. Flaherty was thick but loyal and had helped him through some tough assignments all right, and could handle a gun and a broad and could always be relied on to cover his back when all hell broke loose.

"And he never smiles," mused Flaherty. "He's not sad. He's just…"

Just tired. Tired of hunting the crooks, dodging the cops, rescuing the girl. But there was always another scrape to get out of, another crime to avenge, another girl to take care of…

"There's women in the lane who'll be glad that's gone," said Flaherty, grinding the ashes of the book to powder.

And they must never know. They must never guess that the quiet man that breezed into town had saved them all from shame and poverty. Never. Johnny stood and hitched his trousers.

"Let's get out of here."

They walked off down the mean street in a bunch.

28

Through the open windows the children could be heard calling out the multiplication table. Gallagher came into the empty playground and moved behind a building at the rear. He looked around to see if anybody was there, produced a baby Powers and emptied it in one slug. As he lowered the bottle and wiped his mouth, he saw the headmaster watching him from a window. The headmaster looked rather pleased as he beckoned Gallagher inside. In his office, he and Wilson confronted Gallagher. The headmaster immediately went in for the kill.

"Since your reputation preceded you, I knew it wouldn't be long before you made a show of yourself. First of all by your drinking, and then by encouraging that young thug Moore in his mischief."

"The drinking is, I agree, a fatal weakness of mine, caused by a pain I wouldn't wish even on you." Gallagher had decided to go out with valedictory glory. "But encouragement is my strong suit. It is the secret ingredient that makes teaching so rewarding. It can sometimes be misplaced but it is never wasted."

"Well, it was certainly wasted on Moore." Wilson couldn't resist chipping in. "He's a disgrace. But we'll soon be rid of him, I'm glad to say."

"If I said that we, the three of us, are the disgrace in this matter, you wouldn't know what I was talking about, would you?"

"I certainly wouldn't. I tried with him. Lord knows I tried." Wilson was the soul of martyrdom. "Headmaster, you know I tried!"

The headmaster felt they were drifting off the point, which was to send Gallagher off with a very large flea in his ear.

"That's beside the point. The point is that you have dragged the reputation of this school down in the community and in the department." He decided that a touch of martyrdom on his part wouldn't go amiss. "A fine reward I have reaped for giving you this chance to redeem yourself."

Gallagher was too astute to let him get away with this. "You had nothing to do with the placement. Stevenson appointed me."

The headmaster sat a little straighter at the mention of the very influential department head. "*Mr* Stevenson will no doubt be very disappointed."

"He will, and for that I am truly sorry. He is a good and sincere friend."

The headmaster felt the high ground slipping away from underneath him. "I will emphasise that I will have only the good of the school in mind when I write my report." A worrisome thought suddenly struck him. "I... I'm sure he will agree with me. After all—"

"Oh, don't worry. He'll agree. He and I knew that this was a last gesture of goodwill on his part. For his sake, I won't cause any further trouble for the department. I resign forthwith."

The headmaster and Mr Wilson were highly indignant that the high ground was now occupied by this abject failure of a teacher.

"Headmaster!" Wilson bleated, and stopped, not knowing exactly what to say.

The headmaster felt cheated, but he knew the workings of the department better than Wilson. He mustered what dignity he could and nodded in what he believed was a gracious manner.

"That would be best for all concerned," he said, hoping the interview would close on that magnanimous note, but Gallagher wasn't prepared to let that happen.

"The truth is," he said, "the profession has failed me and I have failed the profession."

"The profession failed you?! This noble profession has no place in it for the likes of you, as your descent from the inner-city schools demonstrates so well."

"It *was* a noble profession once. And in some schools, it still is."

"And none of those schools, including this one, wants the likes of you teaching the precious pupils entrusted to us."

"Precious?! Yes, they are precious. Especially in a poor community like this, where the school affords the only possible escape from grinding poverty and ignorance. But you, sir, have failed probably the most precious pupil this school has ever had in its trust. Good day to you both."

He walked out on two frustrated teachers.

A test paper lay face down before each child. Wilson was striding amongst the desks, poking the plumper boys.

"While Mr Gallagher is... indisposed," he hissed with satisfaction, "the headmaster thought it a good idea to hold tests on several subjects to see if any learning has been accomplished in this class this year."

He stopped beside Johnny and glared at him, or rather, at his thin, vulnerable neck.

"These tests will determine which of you are better off earning a living and not wasting both your time and ours. Turn over the papers."

It was a maths paper. Johnny looked at it in horror. The figures squirmed before his eyes.

Johnny had met Gallagher outside the school, he thought by accident, and they were walking through the park. Johnny had been prattling on about his maths paper and was rather surprised that Gallagher had not responded.

"Johnny, I'm leaving the school," Gallagher announced abruptly.

Johnny stopped, shocked. "You can't!"

He started to hurry away and Gallagher moved after him, puffing and pushing his bicycle.

"Please slow down. I've been… well… 'sacked' is a reasonably accurate description of what has happened to me. The headmaster discovered my predilection for… both kinds of ardent spirits."

Johnny stopped in his tracks and watched as Gallagher sat down on the stump of a newly felled tree.

"What are you going to do?"

"I am now unemployable. It was my last chance with the department. Fortunately, or otherwise, I have an older sister who owns a boarding house in Morecambe – an indentation in the English coast which is, in all seriousness, called a resort. I'm moving there."

Johnny was suddenly angry. "How am I going to learn how to make pictures? You told me to study!"

"And you must."

"How? What?"

Gallagher stood up and started walking. He spoke softly, as if Johnny were keeping pace. Which he was. "I had a son, just like you. Don't ask me about his mother. She was… well, she was not around. My son was bright, just like you. He was full of curiosity, too, just like you. Always in trouble but always able to talk his way out of it.

"Then I took him on a cruise down the canal, even though

it wasn't school holidays. There was me and a companion, a botanist, and my son. We were going through the Bog of Allen on this converted barge I had borrowed and which my son soon learned how to steer. The canal there was straight for several miles. My son was at the tiller. All he had to do was keep it in the middle. I had taught him the steering, how to read a chart – everything he needed to get us through the Bog of Allen. The botanist and I were at the front, enjoying the incredible peace and quiet and the amazing amount of flowering plants. With the talking and a faint wind blowing, we couldn't hear the engine… and we couldn't hear what must have been my son calling for help.

"It wasn't until the barge bumped into the bank that I thought of looking back. The canal is paved all the way but in the bog, the weeds along each bank are thick and it's hard to stand. Especially when you're a small boy."

He stopped walking and talking and his face closed up, as if shutting off a sight and a memory. Johnny spoke first.

"Canals don't go anywhere, do they? Not like rivers."

"You're right, Johnny." Gallagher pulled himself together and walked on. "Canals just slosh around from lock to lock. I suppose all the water does eventually reach the sea but it's an inadvertent journey at best. Rather like my life since… since the Bog of Allen."

He sighed very deeply. "How are you going to learn how to make pictures? I don't know, Johnny. I wish I did. But you'll never make it if you don't get an education – a good one, which you will not get at that school."

"Why is that? We're supposed to learn things at school. It's not fair."

"No, it's not."

They had reached a major street. Gallagher lined up his bicycle.

"Well, I must be off. I'll say goodbye now, Johnny, and I'm sorry I can't be here for you any more."

He threw his leg over the bicycle. Johnny looked at him

seriously as if weighing something up in his mind. Then he held out his hand.

"Goodbye, Mr Gallagher. And thanks."

Gallagher shook his hand and then pushed himself forward.

"Goodbye, Johnny. And keep your head down or they'll chop it off."

Gallagher rode away, feeling that he was deserting another boy who had called to him for help.

In the Moore kitchen, Albert, Paul and Attracta were busy with pencils and round, paper milk-bottle tops. Johnny was drawing on a large piece of cardboard.

"Johnny, how many of these feckin' things do we have to make?" asked Paul.

"Don't say 'feck' in this house," they all intoned.

"My hands are falling off," said Albert.

"Quit complaining and get on with it."

The next morning the headmaster walked towards the school gate, puzzled. The children were coming in, each with a bottle top pinned to their chests with the letter *G* inscribed on it. The headmaster went out and across to the plantation. Behind it, he found Johnny handing out the badges. Hanging from the hedge was a movie-style poster which read: *THE GREAT GALLAGHER: the best teacher in Ireland*, accompanied by the slogan: *A giant brought down by pygmies*.

"Moore. My office. Now."

Within a few minutes Johnny was standing on one side of the desk, the headmaster was seated on the other and an indignant Wilson was lurking. The headmaster looked at the pile of badges and the crumpled-up poster.

"Your abysmal marks alone would have been bad enough. Twenty out of a hundred! But this is the final straw. And I can't say I'm sorry..."

In the foreground, under the branches of the trees, Johnny turned to take a last look at the school. In the background, in sunlight, the schoolchildren were playing in the yard. In his ears rang the voice of the headmaster:

You are past the compulsory schoolgoing age, Moore. You can either take the route usually taken by such as you and leave, or I shall expel you. Either way, I don't want you in my school.

He turned and started the long, long journey home.

Father Mulligan was going home too and, although it was a moment's walk from the church hall to his house, it felt like a long and an arduous journey. It had been a draining evening. Some time ago he had given permission for a haphazard gathering of elderly men to meet once a month to discuss the issues of the day in the light of the church's teachings. Most times he left the group alone to ponder what was happening and what they should think about it all. Their level of assessment and interrogation were abysmally low since very few of them were even literate, but it was his job to keep an eye on what they perceived as their Catholic duty. The path to error in such matters was slippery and the men required guidance but, Lord, it was tiresome and took more energy than he could spare at the close of a long day.

Suddenly, Mullarky appeared in his path, looking very agitated.

"Father, Father. I need protection. I need help from the church."

"Oh? Why?"

"It's Skin the Goat. He's after me."

"Skin the Goat only goes after those who owe him money and the church doesn't concern itself with gambling debts. Although it might have something to say about gambling."

"I don't gamble. Gambling debts? Who said anything about gambling debts?"

"Then if he's after you, you should go to the police. They'll help you. Now, goodnight, I have to—"

"I need the church's protection, Father. I always look after the church's interest, so I do."

Father Mulligan thought it was time to do a little needling.

"Do you now? Oh, the bishop is a customer of yours, isn't he?"

"Oh yes. A grand man. A saint. I've had the pleasure of serving him now and then, and all the clergy around here. And the parishioners. It's important that everybody knows that. I was only saying—"

"The bishop said a funny thing to me last night. He said that there were so few matches in a box nowadays."

"Did he now? I'll talk to the suppliers about that. But Father, I need to do more work for the church. Get more involved. The food tickets, now. Have you any word on this year's contract? I've opened up new lines of credit with every wholesaler in town. I've placed orders too – and paid up front. And the church takes care of its people. Everybody knows that. Amn't I right?"

Father Mulligan felt his mood lightening. "Oh, haven't you got my letter yet?"

"What letter?"

"The bishop has decided – no, I'll be straight with you: *I* have decided – to award the entire contract to O'Gorman."

"Why? Merciful Heavens, why?"

Father Mulligan burst out laughing. "I can't tell you. Ha! I can't tell you."

He moved onto his front path, leaving a distraught Mullarky gasping for air. Still laughing, he crossed himself and said in a giggly undertone, "Sorry, Lord, for enjoying that so much."

He had a little trouble getting his key into the front-door lock.

29

Rita and Johnny, both dejected, were in the kitchen.

"What would the Lone Ranger do?" said Rita, trying to coax a smile from Johnny.

"Right now, he'd be feeling very lonely," he said.

"I did what I could last time. I can't do it again. I'm too…"

"I know. I'll look for a full-time job."

"Where are you going to start looking?"

"I don't know."

He really didn't know. The abattoir beckoned, but the thought of a full week's work in that environment of death appalled him. He was far too young for anything other than a casual job, without benefit of any form of social registration. Such formalities only kicked into effect at the age of sixteen.

Regarding his dream of being involved in pictures in some way, he saw the cinemas as the sole manifestation of the movie industry in the city. Perhaps a casual job could be got in one of them, and from there he could investigate the job opportunities somewhere else. He had read enough to have some idea of the process of making pictures and getting them seen by audiences, but he knew that this knowledge, patchy as it was, was no qualification for a casual job. In fact Flaherty had shown by his physical strength and unquestioning obedience that he was more employable than Johnny was. And without an education…? His heart sank when he thought of it, but he stopped the thought and concentrated on the search for job opportunities in descending order of desirability.

The starting point was logical. The Manor felt strange on a weekday afternoon. There was no noise, no teeming children, no bustle nor excitement. One or two adults passed in and out of the cinema in a desultory fashion, not at all like the children did.

The commissionaire was leaning on the side railings smoking and looking very bored, as if he missed the children. In fact he watched Johnny approach in disapproval. Children were Saturday fodder. Children didn't belong in the Manor on a weekday afternoon. Children were noisy and ruined the picture for adults. Children were disgusting, no end of trouble and diseased. In the weekday quiet, the commissionaire seemed very small to Johnny, not at all the frightening guardian of the revered cinema. He hadn't really looked at him in isolation for many years, not since his first visit to the Manor, when he had appeared gigantic and much to be envied. He had always been part and parcel of the Saturday tumult and not a distinct human entity. Today the dandruff on the back of his collar was particularly abundant, the tobacco ash on the front was rampant and the grease stains on his blue coat multitudinous. His yellow fingernails, scrawny wrists and bony shoulders made him seem very vulnerable and Johnny suddenly wondered how he could muster such mastery over a horde of children every week, many of whom, Flaherty especially, could have knocked him down with ease. However, he was part of the Manor machine and Johnny addressed him with respect.

"I want to work in pictures."

"Would you ever feck off?" was the immediate and final

answer. The commissionaire threw his cigarette butt away and slouched towards the nearby shop.

Johnny ran up the steps to the ticket office. This was a dull wooden structure inside the doors and to one side. In it resided the cashier, a blowsy woman who chain-smoked, making the glass-fronted cubicle so full of smoke that she drifted in and out of vision like a fish in a cloudy fishbowl. Johnny peered through the rounded hole in the glass and perceived that she was reading *Radio Fun*, a comic that he used to like. It featured the current performers on BBC Radio: Arthur Askey (Big-Hearted Arthur), Tommy Trinder ("You lucky people") and Petula Clark (Radio's Merry Mimic). He used to follow their adventures regularly before he switched his allegiance to movie stars.

He tapped on the glass and was rewarded by a glimpse of her face and a billow of smoke through the window, which made him cough. Her dim eyes swam behind her tortoiseshell-framed lenses until they found him. Since he didn't proffer money, her conditioned response didn't kick in. She looked flummoxed.

"Wha'?"

"I don't suppose you know where you get the pictures?"

"What pictures?"

There was definitely no answer to that. So that she wouldn't think he was trying to get in without paying, he gestured at the door to the manager's office, which had a useful sign reading *Manager* above it. She nodded and he knocked, not in any expectation of an answer since, in all the years he had been coming to the Manor, he had never seen the manager. However, a thin voice responded.

"C-c-c-come in," it said.

Johnny opened the door and entered to be rewarded with a smile on a very wrinkled face above a bow tie. The smile faded as it perceived Johnny, but the wrinkles took several seconds to relapse into what seemed to be a habitual configuration.

"We don't g-g-give m-m-m-money back," said the more concerned wrinkles around the mouth.

"I don't want money back. I want to know where you get your pictures."

"You b-b-better ask the pro-pro-pro—"

"Projectionist?" offered Johnny.

Some of the wrinkles were grateful, some were offended.

"Yes. The p-p-pictures are his c-c-concern."

The wrinkles turned away, as did Johnny.

At the top of the metal staircase at the side of the building, Johnny banged on the metal door so hard that it opened slightly. He pushed the door back and entered to see a wizened little man struggling with an enormous reel of film. It was full almost to overflowing and the man was hugging the reel to his chest with one arm, while he tried to stop the wayward loops of film from cascading onto the floor. Johnny was so mesmerised by the glistening loops with their captive images that he stood very still.

"Catch the fecker!" cried the projectionist. "I've gotta thread it in *now*."

Johnny made a grab for the film and immediately cut his finger on the edge. He wrestled with the almost-live ribbon and managed to still its wild squirming.

"Give me the end," the projectionist bawled, and Johnny did so with alacrity. The projectionist slipped the reel onto its rest, threaded the front end of the new reel into the whirring machine and relaxed as it engaged seconds after the last image on the tail end of the old reel materialised on the screen. There was a moment of palpable camaraderie as the projectionist checked the focus and Johnny sucked his finger. While Johnny basked in the success of the struggle, the projectionist took the old reel off the projector and slipped it onto a rewind spindle.

"Love stories!" the projectionist said with scorn. "Miss one single frame and the old bats with the perms are incon-fecking-solable. Who are you?"

"Where do these pictures come from?"

The projectionist pointed at some cartons. "Them boxes," he stated as he rewound the film.

The Royal Cinema, on the Liffey's south bank, was something else. A gorgeously dressed commissionaire, without a single trace of dry scalp or slovenly braid on his person, was striding across the top step, eyes peeled for any who might lower the tone of an establishment which offered dancing girls, a live concert and a feature film, all in one show. Johnny was suitably diffident as he approached.

"Mister, do you know anything about the pictures you show here?"

"Only that you can't afford to see them," came the condescending reply.

As Johnny was trying to frame his next question, a dapper man in a dark suit passed. He paused as he witnessed the stand-off between his large commissionaire and the small boy.

"What is it, son?" he asked.

"I'm looking for a job. In pictures."

"In pictures? What do you mean?"

"I'm not sure. I've just left school and I don't want to work in the abattoir."

"And you think pictures might be a better alternative?" asked the man with a smile.

"It's just that… I like pictures and I want to work in them."

"Let's see now. We just show the pictures. We don't even choose which ones, and we have all the staff we need. Our distributors, the people who supply us with the pictures, are in Middle Abbey Street. You could try them. They might have something."

"Where do *they* get the pictures?"

"Most of the ones we show come from America. Some from England."

"Are there any made in Ireland?"

"Not that I know of. I've never seen any."

"OK. Thanks."

The man wrote the name of the distributor and the full address on a slip of paper and Johnny took it and headed towards Middle Abbey Street.

On the third floor of a gloomy building he pushed open the distributor's door and went in. A young blonde woman was sitting behind a desk, filing her nails. There was nothing in the room to indicate the nature of the business carried out there.

"Yeah?" the woman asked.

"I don't suppose there's a job for me here?"

"Yeah. You can file me nails for me."

For the first time ever, Johnny entered Bourke's photographic shop. Mr Bourke was mounting a large portrait of a bride.

"Ah, it's the boy who keeps dirtying my window. What do you want?"

"I need a job. Have you one?"

"There isn't enough round here to keep *me* busy."

Johnny turned away, disconsolate.

30

The abattoir was a creepy place, sidled up to the avenue, the dark secrets of its death-dealing hidden behind a stalwart door and small, barred windows high in the dressed stone wall. It was across the road from the cattle market, but none of the children in the neighbourhood ever saw cattle being herded in. It was as if some weird osmosis transported the beasts from the cattle pens to death row on a level of experience beyond human perception. On Saturdays, Johnny's duties had been restricted to shovelling offal into chutes and channels on the outside of the main buildings, an unpleasant task in itself, but removed from the real, fatal activities within. Two days in the atmosphere of sweaty, brawny men wielding long poleaxes, of bellowing cows and grunting sheep, of razor-sharp cleavers and knives and of slippery, bloody floors and tiles traumatised him beyond measure.

At close of business on the second day, Johnny came out of the building and leaned against the wall. He was very pale and the perspiration was dripping off his face. He was breathing deeply, on the verge of throwing up.

"Hold on there. Wait for me."

Flaherty emerged, carrying two bulging, wobbling, bloodstained paper packages. He caught up with Johnny and they walked out onto the road.

"It's great to see them bullocks drop dead on the floor. Like a snot," said Flaherty. "Here. Take this home to your mother. Great tripe, this. Great eating on it."

Johnny nearly vomited.

"You all right?"

"I'll get used to it. Come on. Let's get out of here."

He took one of the packages and they headed home. Flaherty stuck a cigarette in his mouth and lit it. On an impulse, Johnny took the cigarette and pulled on it. As he did, he saw Angela being driven past in the major's car. They looked at each other, she in shock; he in shame.

"Hey. Isn't that—"

"Yes," said Johnny, cutting him short. "Let's go."

He took another drag on the cigarette and walked swiftly ahead. He felt he was walking away from a whole way of life, into a dismal space that smelled of failure, effort and grinding, unutterable boredom.

Angela was the most dutiful of daughters. Since the death of her brother Darcy, she had felt a great responsibility towards her reserved father although she had not had much opportunity to demonstrate it to him. After a period of mourning deemed adequate, she had been packed off to the same boarding school in England which her mother had attended. There she had come in for a fair amount of teasing about her Irishness. Not enough to make her bitter, nor yet not enough to engender any clear feelings of Irish nationalism. Her father, she knew, considered himself Irish although he had gone to school and university in England, and certainly subscribed to the tenets of upper-class English society. He was more aware of the King's birthday, when it came round, than any major Irish anniversary, and he took the *London Times*, late though it was in delivery.

This slight ambiguity rubbed off on Angela and she thought that, when she was in Dublin, she was residing in some distant English suburb. She had been comfortable with the girls in her school, two of whom came from Scotland and had very much the same perspective on their homes as she did. It wasn't until she came home for a long stay that she realised how Irish her thought patterns were. She had related immediately to Johnny and enjoyed his typically Irish mixture of fecklessness and seriousness. The fact that the major was invariably genial, even gracious to the Dublin folk among whom he moved, meant that she was not at all snobby and saw nothing untoward in being friendly with Johnny. When he had indicated the social barriers that lay, as he perceived, between Johnny and her, it had come as a shock. And when he had ordered her not to see Johnny again, she had decided to let time go by, believing she could gently persuade her father to be gradually more accepting of Johnny, so that she could reinstate the relationship without upsetting him.

However, when she saw Johnny walking away from the abattoir, smoking, she knew instinctively that he had left school and taken a job. She had understood the dreaming side of him and was aware that, without an education, he had no hope of ever achieving his dreams.

Her father had often spoken about the upliftment programme and was very proud of it. Angela knew that Johnny would thrive in it and set about doing all she could to have him accepted. She copied out some of the programme details at her father's desk and decided that she would approach Johnny and work out a plan. Her faith in his cleverness was such that she knew he would find a way to impress the selectors, especially her father. The major had already said no once but she could rely on his sense of fairness, and she was sure she could change his mind for him. Difficult it would be, but not impossible.

So it was that Angela was sitting at the kitchen table across from Johnny, who was very quiet, and Rita, who was reading Angela's notes.

"Sacred Heart, Johnny! This programme sounds wonderful," Rita exclaimed. Then she turned to Angela. "But your father said no."

"And we must think of a way to make him say yes. You'll get the best education in Dublin."

"Miss Brennan, Johnny's a Catholic. The programme is only for Protestant children."

"Not only. Usually. I've read all the rules and Papa once told me about a young Catholic boy he's very proud of. He has gone on to great things in medicine."

"He'll be mixing with Protestant children," Rita said musingly.

"I'm a Protestant."

"Ah, love, I don't mind that. But the church would, I'm afraid. However, don't you worry about that. Getting him accepted is the thing. Eh, Johnny?"

Angela caught Johnny's eye and smiled encouragingly. "Johnny," she said, "what would Gary Cooper do?"

Johnny was silent.

"We need your help in this, Johnny," said Rita. "Cat got your tongue?"

"Mammy, I'm working now."

"Do you want to spend the rest of your life killing cattle?" Rita snapped.

He looked at her forlornly.

"Don't give up now," she said. "This is your last chance. We have to have Father Mulligan's permission. I'll go and see him."

There was a long pause, and Rita and Angela let it last. They could almost see the struggle taking place in Johnny's mind: the dulling of his imaginative side by the brutality of the abattoir and all that it stood for, versus the faint, distant glimmer of hope raised by Angela's proposition. All of the dreary reality of Dublin, accepted as normal by such as Flaherty, pulled him down while the thought of a really good education strove to raise his spirits upwards.

"No. I'll go," he finally said.

Rita smiled with relief.

"And then I'll have to see about the major," he continued, and Angela smiled with relief.

"Yes," said Rita.

"You will," said Angela.

They both felt it was going to be all right.

31

To say Johnny was nervous about facing Father Mulligan was an understatement. The priest represented all that was unchallengeable in his world. A strict religion, an even stricter God and the awesome power of the sacraments served to render the priest highly formidable and to be approached with a great deal of respect. Father Mulligan had always treated Johnny with genial casualness but the power was there, the unspoken contract and the understanding that that the priest could bind and loose with impunity.

Now Johnny was going to ask him to alter a major rule, or practice. The thought made him slightly light-headed. Why was life so complicated? Why was doing what you knew was right so difficult? Why was there always either a person or a custom standing in the way of getting what you wanted? Did it mean that what he wanted was bad? Was he being sinful in wanting an exciting and challenging life? Was he meant to stay in his place like Flaherty, content with the prospect of a job, any job, a few bob in your pocket and a few cigarettes every day? Was his life going to be as disappointing as his father's, whom he now admitted had run away from his responsibilities and left them all in the lurch? Would he have to do that: slip off some early

189

morning and leave them all behind? He knew he couldn't. No matter how little he was earning now and for the foreseeable future, he was needed at home. Why was it all so complicated? He realised he was going round in circles. *Whoa! Stop. One thing at a time. Get Father Mulligan out of the way somehow.* That's what he had to do right now. The rest would have to wait.

He was at the church, and he passed the statue of Christ dead in His Mother's arms. He looked at His sorrowing face, debating whether or not to pray for some guidance. But He seemed to have so much on his mind already, slumped as he was, dead as a doornail on His Ma's lap. Johnny sighed and headed for the side door of the church.

Father Mulligan loved his holy vestments. The smooth feel of the silk and satin, the rough texture of the gold braid; the delicate needlework carried out by loving hands in some convent – a labour of love if ever there was one. He was packing them away in the deep, dark cupboard which smelled of lavender and herbs put there against the moths. No nose-wrinkling smell of moth balls for these vestments. He folded each one carefully and laid it in its appointed place, as several priests had before him and, please God, as plenty more would after him.

The door creaked slightly and he turned to see who was opening it. Johnny stood there looking unusually subdued.

"Johnny. What brings you to the tradesman's entrance?"

"I need to talk, Father."

"Is it confession you want?"

"No."

There was a long pause as Johnny tried to get his thoughts in order. Father Mulligan gave him time, finishing the packing away.

"Father, I'm working now."

"So I heard."

"I was sort of expelled out of school."

"I heard that too. A shame."

"Yeah, it is. The thing is..." Suddenly it all came out in a rush. "There's this scheme run by Major Brennan – well, he's involved in it. It lets young boys go to school, a special school where they can learn all the things they want to learn and they get to go to university and all. And I want to be on that scheme 'cause I'm not going to work in the abattoir all my life."

"I've heard of that scheme, and a very good scheme it is. But it's run by the Anglican church and it's not for Catholic boys."

"But it is – I mean, Catholics *can* go on it. There've been many."

"The Catholic church is very reluctant to let its children come under the influence of other religions."

"Ah, you wouldn't want to worry about that, Father – sure, nothing'd change the way I feel about... God and the Catholic church and... and all."

"The thing is, Johnny, you're very impressionable at your age. I can't let you place your immortal soul in jeopardy."

"I just want a decent life."

"My child, your life may be your concern, but your soul is ours."

"I didn't mean to—"

"And if you go on this programme without a dispensation from the church, you will be committing a sin. A serious one."

"There are worse sins."

"Don't you go telling me about sins," snapped the priest.

"But you can let me go. I mean, going without your permission would be a sin but you can get me a... dispensation, can't you? Then it wouldn't be a sin."

Father Mulligan sighed. "I also know the detrimental effect endless poverty has on the faith of the people around here," he said at last. "And I don't want you ending up on the building sites of England, where your faith will have to be very strong to survive."

"So you'll get me a dispensation?"

"Well, it's not up to me entirely. I'd have to go to the bishop to get his permission, and after it all, if you *do* prove good enough for Trinity, the archbishop himself will have to make the final decision. So you see, it's a very serious matter, young man."

Father Mulligan stood up and strode around the sacristy. He was angry: with Johnny for putting him in a spot he never thought he would ever be in, and with himself for being angry with Johnny. No matter how a priest tried to avoid the great, the serious, the essential conundrums of faith, they rose up without warning and demanded to be dealt with. He stopped and looked at this scrawny supplicant and was not surprised to meet a steady, enquiring gaze.

"But you'll try?"

"I suppose I must," Father Mulligan finally said.

Later that morning, as the period of confessions was coming to an end and Father Mulligan was looking forward to a light lunch and a bottle of stout, the door opened and a wave of cheap perfume filled the confessional. He sighed and slid the panel open.

"Yes, my child?

There was a long pause before the response came.

"I'm a prostitute, Father. I've come for confession."

There was a longer pause before Father Mulligan replied.

"I see."

"Do you? Well, it's a year since my last confession and I've… done it… a fair few times since then. Do you want to know how many times?

"No, no, no. I… I gather you do… it… regularly?"

"Of course. Otherwise, why do it at all?"

"Quite. And do you repent of it?"

"Of course I bloody repent. It's a hard way to live."

"Then you must turn your back on your way of life."

192

"And if I did that, how would I live, with no man to look after me and a child up for adoption in a convent in Cork?"

"Then you're turning your back on Christ and his forgiveness."

"Maybe he turned his back on me." This time the pause was much longer. She continued, "Does that mean you won't hear my confession?"

"I'll hear it. In fact, I *am* hearing it. But I can't give you absolution if you continue to live the way you do."

"There's this one fella – he doesn't live a million miles away from here – he comes to see me every Friday night and I know he goes to confession, probably here, every Saturday and communion every Sunday. He tells me he'll never give me up. I wonder what he tells the priest?"

"In his heart, he himself knows that he is not making a good confession."

"That's all right, so."

"What's all right?"

"In *my* heart, I know that I make the best confession I can. Every year, in a different church."

"You're putting your immortal soul in jeopardy."

"So is everybody I know, Father. Anyway, I put my soul in jeopardy the first time I ever went into an air-raid shelter with a fellow. Can I say an act of contrition now? It'll make me feel better."

"You can."

He listened as she ran quickly through the prayer, speedily and accurately. Strange how they never forgot. He murmured absolution and was struck by how he ran through those words.

"Go in peace, my child."

"I'll try, Father."

She left Father Mulligan alone with his troubled thoughts. *And tomorrow morning, when – if – she comes to me for communion, and I put the host on her tongue, what'll I be doing:*

condemning her to Hell in the next life, or helping her survive in this one?

He was about to leave the confessional when the door opened and somebody slipped in. He slid the panel open. It was Siobhan. *Guide me, oh Lord, in this moment*, he thought.

"Bless you, my child."

"I'm back, Father."

"So I see. And have you thought about what I said last week?"

"Yes, Father."

"And…?"

There was a long silence and Father Mulligan let it hang in the gloom.

"I didn't go with men, Father." There was an incipient sob in the words.

"I know you didn't, my child."

"It's just…"

"Take your time."

"What do you do, Father, when you know something is wrong and you don't know how to stop it?"

"I ask myself that question, in this confessional, every Saturday."

"Do you?" How could this priest, who looked after everybody in the lane, not know what to do?

"Yes. I hear the sins of the world and I give absolution and I don't know how to stop the sinning. Some sin from wickedness, some from carelessness, and some sin because they feel they have to, for the sake of others."

"Does that make it right?"

"No, it doesn't. But it does explain why careful, God-fearing people sometimes do what they know is wrong because others are suffering. That is something I understand, and I hope that the absolution I give them will give them the strength to stop sinning, and if in their heart of hearts, they intend to sin no

194

more and trust in God to help them, then that will make it all right. Do you understand?"

"I… I think so. But Father…"

"Yes, my child?"

"I lied to you last week."

"But I'm sure it was in a good cause."

"Oh, it was, Father. But I'm sorry anyway."

"Well, three Hail Marys will make that all right. Now say an act of contrition."

Siobhan said the prayer with such fervour that he felt the tears fill his eyes as he gave her absolution.

32

The bishop's house was a large, ugly red-brick structure in a quiet South Dublin suburb. It had extensive gardens, indifferently kept by a team of three gardeners who kept the grass short, the bushes neat and the occasional flower beds colourful throughout most of the year. There was a house staff of three who kept the bishop, the Most Reverent James Driscoll, DD, in a state of suffocating cosseting. His quarters in the rambling house were spread out over three floors and were used sparingly, and only when some official occasion was created by his priests and attended by clergy or laypersons of note. The rest of the time he spent in his bedroom, his study and a comfortable drawing room next to the back door and overlooking a small, fruitful orchard.

It was here that he and Father Mulligan, both unbuttoned, were ensconced in two armchairs pulled up close to a glowing fire. A small table stood next to each of their chairs, on both of which was a Waterford crystal glass of very acceptable wine. The remains of the simple but wholesome meal had been cleared away and the two men were looking into the embers, one with calm satisfaction, the other in deep contemplation. Father Mulligan broke the silence.

"A little scrap of a thing called Sean Moore died a while back and the family was in bits. He came to his first confession just before he died and he said a thing that made me feel... well... lost for a while. He bawled and said, 'I have no sins to give you.'"

"Desmond, we have all had youngsters upset at their first confession."

"So have I, Jack. But it's what he said: 'I have no sins to give you.' It was as if he perceived it as some sort of tithe, something he owed me, the church, something I needed to do my job." He paused and the bishop observed him closely. "Sin. Do I need sin? Does it keep me in business? Is this whole..." he looked around "...edifice built on sin?"

"You're getting close to heresy, Desmond. And I'm not sure it's right to discuss such matters after a bottle of heavy Burgundy."

Father Mulligan smiled and sipped some more wine. "Perhaps not. But in a way, it ties in with another... conundrum that's bothering me."

"Another sin?"

"Yes. Trinity College."

"That old chestnut again. Tell me about it."

"There's another member of the same family. He's twelve and a bit and—"

"He's a bit young for Trinity. Is he a boy genius?"

"No."

"Good. They're a curse."

"Not a genius, but he's the brightest boy I've seen in the parish. Very popular, very inquisitive and always up to something unusual. I'll tell you now: he goes to the pictures almost every week, uses jam jars to get in and—"

"Jam jars! They used to save and swap them when I was a boy. What's the value of a jam jar now, I wonder?"

"A penny ha'penny. Two will get you into the Manor. Anyway..."

"Sorry, Desmond, I'm interrupting. Carry on."

"The thing is, he tells the story to the family when he gets home, and he'll tell it to his schoolmates for half a sandwich. The whole lane knows about it and admires him for it."

"And he wants to go to Trinity?"

"No. He knows nothing about Trinity. But he does know about an upliftment programme that is designed to prepare young boys for Trinity. I've heard about it. The man behind it in our area is a Major Brennan. I'm told the boy and Brennan's daughter are great friends."

"I've heard about that programme too. Do you think the boy...?"

"Johnny Moore."

"Do you think Johnny is right for the programme?"

"Undoubtedly. But is the programme right for him? That's the question."

They both sipped their wine and looked into the embers for a long moment while the bishop absorbed this.

"And do you, Desmond, think there's no opportunity for Johnny to get a good education in the national school system?"

"I doubt it. He's just been expelled. The only thing our national school system seems to encourage is conformity and obedience."

"Is he a troublemaker?"

"No. Just high-spirited." He looked slyly at the bishop. "As you were at Blackrock."

"But I got my high spirits under control."

"That's because you had good – great – teachers, and the right sort of companions to share your thoughts with. Like old McQuaid."

The bishop laughed. "Ah, Himself. Yes. We were bosom companions for a while, but he galloped ahead." He looked with suspicion at Father Mulligan. "And Trinity is his bête noire, as they say. Hmm. Is that why you brought it up?"

"No. No. No. No."

"You're as manipulative as you ever were."

"Johnny and Trinity need not trouble Himself. Not for a few years at least. What I'm concern about is the programme. I want him on it, and you have the authority to allow that."

"Is it the only way for him to reach his potential?"

"Yes. There's no way he could afford the sort of schooling you had and the programme is fully funded."

"If…" The bishop let the word hang in the air. "If I allowed this, it would be under the same conditions that Himself laid down for Trinity. He'd have to keep up his religious duties, regularly and frequently. He'd have to stay away from any group, or indeed lecture, that promotes any ideas contrary to the Catholic faith, and take advice and guidance from a priest on this. And he must hang about with other Catholics regularly. Do you think this Johnny could manage all that?"

"Yes. He could."

"Well then, see if you can get him on the programme, and I'll sort it out this end. Now, let's finish off this wine and get you home."

Father Mulligan thought briefly about sharing with the bishop the problem that the prostitute had raised in confession but, in the companionable silence, with the soft sigh of collapsing embers, he had time to dwell on sin and its… architectural, that was the word, ramifications. From the 'sin' that Johnny was contemplating and which he had indicated that he would commit even if clerical dispensation were not forthcoming, to the pragmatic fornication that the prostitute had resigned herself to, sin, it seemed to the priest, was like a vast cathedral, like Chartres, which he'd had the privilege of visiting when he emerged from the seminary.

At its heart were the nave, the altar and the choir, all existing under a logic-defying vault held aloft by faith, built by divinely driven masons and attesting to the reality, the affirmation and the praise of the ultimate truth, while around it, in the purple gloom, wove the aisles, the transepts, the ambulatory, the dark places where uncertainty dwelt. And when one had absorbed the underlying tensions of it all, there was the labyrinth in a key, confrontational position, to challenge certainty. There was a single entrance to the south-west that led to an empty space in the centre, neither of which would lead to infinitely anymore than a child's game of hopscotch.

Intimidated by the magnitude of this image and what it represented, and the fumes of the Burgundy, Father Mulligan emptied his glass and started to get to his feet.

Mr Bourke was reading a magazine when Johnny burst in.

"That Bollix in the window."

There was a pause as Bourke looked at him in surprise. "Ah… yes. The Bolex. I've seen you looking at it. What about it?"

"It's 8mmmmmmmm, isn't it?"

"Eight millimetre, yes?"

"Does it work?"

"Oh yes."

"And do you have any film for it?"

"One roll, black and white. Years old but still all right. You seem to know a lot about it."

"A little. Can I borrow it? And the film?"

"Why on earth should I do that? It's for sale."

"Nobody around here would buy it."

That was undeniably true. Bourke was nonplussed for a moment.

"What do you want it for?"

"I want to make a film. A story."

"Do you have a script?"

"Yeah… well, I know what I want to shoot."

"How long will this… story be?"

"How long is the roll of film?"

"It'll give you about eight minutes"

"It'll be an eight-minute story, then."

Bourke stood looking at Johnny, remembering. He finally spoke. "Do you have any idea how a film is made?"

"Yeah. I read a book."

"I must be mad."

"Does that mean you'll lend me the camera?"

"I suppose it does."

Johnny opened the squeaking gate of a two-storey terraced house on the outskirts of Cabra. It was a dispiriting street of corporation houses showing the neglect usual in a street of people who had no distinct interest in their area. There were no tended gardens, even though the soil was rich and ready to respond to any gardening endeavour. It was better, much better than the lane, but it had an unkempt surliness about it helped by the dulled, neglected windows and the sagging and torn net curtains. Bicycles there were aplenty, some whole and functioning leaning against walls, some dismantled and rusting lying on the scrubby grass which poked through the spokes and bars and gaping sockets. As he stood there, the sound of a violin came from a half-open window on the second floor. It was accomplished, if sporadic and repetitive, as if the player wanted to get each phrase perfectly right. He approached the scarred front door and pounded on it, since the knocker had long since fallen off.

After a few minutes, a distorted face appeared in the ribbed and wired glass panel of the door and its eyes wandered over all within its compass before settling on the shape of the figure on the front step. Having regarded this shape and decided that it represented no immediate threat, the face receded and a hand fumbled and fiddled with the lock. The door opened and the face, now recognisably human and belonging to a blowsy middle-aged woman in a dirty housecoat, addressed him.

"Whatcha want?"

"Does Mr Gallagher live here?"

This sparse answer seemed to appease some inner rumination because the woman stepped back and opened the door slightly wider.

"Mr Gallagher!" she bellowed.

A nod of the head granted access and Johnny slipped in and stood by the wall. The violin music stopped at the shout.

"A boy to see you!" screamed the woman, who slammed the door, turned and made her way to the back of the house. A creaking of floorboards and the opening of a door and Gallagher stood at the top of an oilcloth-covered staircase. He was holding a violin in one hand and a bow in the other.

"Moore. Well, I'm blessed. I never thought to see you again. Come up. Come up."

Johnny climbed the stairs and followed Gallagher into a front bedroom. It was crammed and chaotic. A single bed, a chair and table and a doorless wardrobe comprised the furniture. The rest of the room was a precarious shambles. Clothing, boxes, suitcases and assorted items littered the floor so copiously that distinct pathways had been formed from the door to the bed, from there to the table and chair and from there to the wardrobe and window, on the ledge of which stood a spindly rubber plant in a dark brown tub. Gallagher made his way to the chair and sat down. Opposite the chair stood a music stand with a printed score on it. He gestured towards the bed.

"Behold the bed of Odysseus and Penelope. I'm growing the olive tree for the bedpost but it's taking the deuce of a time. Please be seated and tell me how you found my Attica."

"I don't know what you're talking about, Mr Gallagher," said Johnny as he took a seat on the sagging bed.

"I'm sorry, Moore. My extensive general knowledge is all I have left."

Johnny looked around at the squalor and thought that the

men who had the greatest influence on his life had failed in theirs, like his father. Mr Gallagher waiting to go to his sister. Mr Bourke with the holes in his socks. And Father Mulligan a parish priest in a very poor parish, and they said that he had gone to school with the bishop *and* the archbishop! Oh yeah, there was the major too. He did well, but he had lost his only son and bullied his daughter. But Johnny needed them all. Sometimes it was all too much to handle.

Gallagher sat quietly and looked at the various emotions moving across Johnny's face, and suddenly he had the surprising thought that this child could save him. He seemed to represent all the children he had taught and tried to point in the right direction for them. Just after he had said goodbye to the boy, here he was, making demands of him, as every child should do of those who appoint themselves as their teachers. At this moment, what he said to Johnny seemed like some emotional pivot, a moment in time when a whole life, perhaps two, were in the balance. He started carefully.

"How did you find me?"

"There was a file on you in the headmaster's office."

"That's supposed to be confidential. How did you get your hands on it?"

"I didn't. I got Albert to get it and read it."

"The was very… enterprising of you and Albert."

Johnny shrugged, as if raiding a headmaster's office was an everyday occurrence.

"Why did you come?" Gallagher asked.

"I'm going to make a film. Mr Bourke is going to lend me a camera and he's going to teach me how to make an eight-minute film. The thing is, when I do, I need to show it to the major first of all. My marks are no good and they won't get me onto his programme. But a film will. Then I need to show it to Father Mulligan, so he'll feel OK about letting me do the programme. He has to see the bishop about that so I suppose I'll have to show it to him too. And he said the final decision is the archbishop's, so he'll want to see it."

Gallagher looked out the grubby window at the dismal street and then turned and faced Johnny who, in his innocent ignorance, was about to challenge half of Dublin. He had to play a part in this mighty endeavour, no matter how small.

"What do you want me to do?"

"Well, when I finish the film, you can help me get those people to come and see it. I don't know where yet."

"That I can do, although I have crossed swords with the major and I'll have to work on that. And there's an old friend of mine in the Department of Education who has a lot of strings he can pull. I'm sure he would like to see the film, and maybe he could put out any fires in the department that someone might try to light."

"Like the headmaster."

"Like the headmaster. He's a bit like a crab in a bucket."

"How?"

"Well, they say that if there are lots of crabs in a bucket and one tries to climb out, the others will pull him back."

He paused as Johnny digested this.

"Jealous?"

"Exactly. Have you written the story of the film?"

"Not yet, but I know what it's going to be. Remember the figures I drew on my schoolbook?"

"Yes. The prodigal son, as I remember."

"Yeah. I haven't worked it out yet but I know it'll work."

"There's another way I might be able to assist. Have you thought about music in your film?"

"Erm… No."

Gallagher ran his bow over the strings of the violin in a deft arpeggio.

"I used to be a very good violinist and I still keep my hand in, in spite of the old dragon downstairs. I think some dramatic violin music would help your film."

He played a plaintive passage. "For example, when he leaves his father, you'd require some pathos."

He played a riotous few bars. "And when he's living it up, a tarantella."

He played an appropriate piece. "And then when he comes home for forgiveness…" He played a quivering, sad lament.

Johnny looked and listened, mesmerised by the possibilities. "That's great. But the last bit – play it again."

Gallagher obliged.

"Great. But at the very end it would have to be…"

"Triumphant?"

"Yeah. Triumphant."

Gallagher played a rising crescendo and Johnny nodded thoughtfully.

33

Bourke placed the Bolex and its battered carrying case on the counter, and opened the case. There was a well-thumbed instruction book inside, which he took out and flicked through.

"This camera changed the film industry. It's a marvel of simple, direct technology and very sturdy, which is why I am taking the risk of lending it to you."

"Don't worry, Mr Bourke. I have an assistant. He's not very bright but he's strong, and if I put him in charge of the Bollix—"

"Bolex. A long 'O'; *oooooo*."

"Bolex. He'll guard it with his life."

"In that case, I suppose I can lend you a tripod too. And I have a spool of exposed film to practise on – a wedding I covered some years ago but they never came to collect it. Now, have you some time to spare right now?"

"Yeah. Plenty of time."

"Then let me show you how the Bolex works."

There began a trip down memory lane for Bourke, and a trip into the future for Johnny. The morning flew by for both of them. And the next morning and afternoon, as the capability of robust and well-made camera revealed its secrets. Bourke first loaded the roll of exposed film into the camera, slowly and carefully, and demonstrated the foolproof spring-winding mechanism. Johnny repeated each movement several times until he got it right. His ready understanding of the mechanics excited Bourke, who grasped that he had a ready and an intelligent young boy to deal with. He insisted that Johnny follow the instruction book page by page, putting the camera through its paces in logical sequence. He also apportioned pages each afternoon for Johnny to memorise.

Johnny had, until then, never handled any piece of equipment more complicated than a cumbersome old bicycle that his father had acquired some years ago and had ridden until it was stolen outside a public house along the quays. He loved the shiny aluminium body of the Bolex, which was covered in what Bourke said was Moroccan leather, and the chrome-plated metal parts. He marvelled at the manner in which the end of the film was automatically threaded throughout the entire mechanism. The three lenses could be brought into play on a rotating turret and the results could be focused on a magnified ground-glass screen. Like any impressionable boy, he wondered at the various features when first exposed to them and immediately accepted them as a natural part of the new life of possibilities that was unfolding in his hands. Through his enthusiasm and quick absorption, Bourke was reminded of his own initial excitement at discovering the technicalities of film-making.

"I was an apprentice cameraman in England when I was a few years older than you," he announced when they took a break from reassembling the Bolex, which he had ordered Johnny to take to pieces and lay out on a sheet of brown paper affixed to the counter.

Every piece they had separated from the camera was placed on the paper and a frame drawn around it that matched the shape of the piece. He had instructed Johnny to write the name of the part on the paper too, corresponding to the instruction manual. The outer case and the external parts, such as the winding handle, the turret and lenses and the eyepiece, were easy enough to remove, study and understand, but the mechanical innards were a different matter.

"I was taught how to understand every single part of every piece of equipment I was expected to handle. And I handled about six different cameras in my career, all of which I could break up and put together very quickly. Even in the dark. Remember that a film camera has a lot of work to do. It has to pull film through a gate at exactly the right speed and allow light to fall on each frame perfectly. And it has to do this in totally lightproof conditions. So you see how each part was made to a very low tolerance..." He looked at Johnny with raised eyebrows.

"No mistakes at all."

"No mistakes at all." In his mind, Bourke dwelt briefly on the cameraman he was apprenticed to for so many years, whose low tolerance was legendary, even in an industry in which brutal treatment of the apprentices was the rule and definitely not the exception. "These parts," he said, gesturing to the finely-made mechanical parts, "can be changed from Bolex to Bolex without any adjustment being necessary. The gate, the feed mechanism, the clutch and this beauty, the motor, which will be driven by a spring mechanism, are all integral to getting the perfect image onto the film, twenty-four times every second, or even faster if you want to slow the action in projection."

They both looked over the parts, Johnny stroking some of them and weighing others in his hands as he admired the mechanical precision.

"How many Bolexes are there?"

"I don't know. Thousands, hundreds of thousands. This one was made fifteen years ago, according to the plate at the bottom of the casing. And I suppose dozens of people used it, some roughly, some carefully, for all sorts of pictures."

"What sort of pictures did you make?"

"Well, when I was finally out of my apprenticeship – this was in London, mind – I was employed as a grip…" He paused.

Johnny didn't blink. "In charge of all the camera equipment."

"That's right. In the film unit of the Post Office under a great documentary film-maker called John Grierson. After that I was focus puller, and then a gaffer—"

"In charge of lighting."

"On a documentary on the Arran islands by another great called Robert Flaherty."

Bourke reminisced for some time and Johnny, although he was examining each camera part as he readied himself to reassemble it, was hanging on every word. Finally, he put down the part and turned to face Bourke.

"How did you…?" he started to ask.

"End up here?" Bourke got up to make a cup of tea and took his time over it. He enjoyed teaching Johnny. He answered every question Johnny asked and fed him the information he needed to carry out a task, and the boy didn't have to, as Bourke himself had had to, wait for a vicious blow if he made a mistake. He knew that Johnny would want to know how he had gone from a successful and exciting career in British film-making to a photographic shop in a seedy backwater in Dublin and, having got to know Johnny's directness, he knew that this question would be asked. So it wasn't until he had sat down again and sipped his tea that he looked Johnny in the eye.

"Colour," he said.

"Colour?"

"Colour."

"I don't understand."

"Why should you? I'm colour-blind." He sipped his tea and waited while Johnny absorbed the implications of this piece of information. It didn't take long.

"And they started making colour films."

"They started making colour films. All that I knew, and I

knew a lot, became irrelevant, useless. I was like a blind man. I literally didn't understand half of what my fellow technicians were talking about. I knew a lot about light in monochrome; I knew how to light a person's face well because I was a fan of von Sternberg, who made Dietrich look like an angel in black and white. I worked out his lighting technique and used it in my portraits. I could also – and this was very useful – see a scene in black and white the way a black-and-white camera would see it. On set or location, I could see the various shades of grey clearly. Most directors and camera operators have to use a monochrome glass to see that. But I could see it and light for it." He sighed. "Which was all very useful until colour came along." He sipped his tea wearily and looked around at some of the framed wedding pictures and portraits that hung on the wall. "Fortunately, none of my customers want colour. Not yet."

Johnny was devastated at the thought. To have learned so much and to have it all become useless! This was worse than never having learned at all. It seemed that the entire world was stacked against anyone who wanted to know, to learn and to work their way out of being poor. Here was this man who knew so much, and here he was in a shop full of stuff and portraits that nobody wanted. If that was the case, what chance had he, Johnny Moore, of succeeding? Was he wasting his time, learning all this very hard stuff?

He sat so long in silence that Bourke began to worry about him. Would he be discouraged and give up, angry at the unfairness of it all, as he himself had when he was banished to a half-life in a half-lived-in city?

Johnny finally shuddered, shook his head and looked at Bourke again.

"Well," he said, "this film is black and white."

Bourke felt so relieved that this skinny little boy with a fire in the belly that he hadn't seen before was giving him a new purpose in life. He turned away to the crowded shelves and took out a flat cardboard box. In it was a framed board covered in black velvet with several grooves running across it. A smaller box contained many white capital letters, each of a size that fitted snugly into the grooves.

"Your title cards," Bourke said. "I suggest that you shoot them separately here in the shop where you can light them properly. It'll save time on the shoot and you can cut them into the film at the edit."

"I'll do them first."

"Good idea."

Bourke took up the unopened roll of 8mm film and turned it in his hands.

"This is Super 8 film stock. Shooting for Super 8 will give you four minutes of filming. However, if you set the camera correctly, you will get eight minutes of filming. You will run it through the camera until you reach the end and then you will take it out – in complete darkness – in the lightproof bag I will give you, and reverse it in the camera. You will then run it to the end. When we send it off for processing in this envelope, they will split the film down the middle and join the two lengths together. This will deliver eight full minutes. When you have discarded the shots you don't like in the edit, you will end up with a four- to seven-minute film; shorter if you are really critical and ruthless in throwing away the bad stuff. So, an edit forces you to be highly critical of what you shot. It's a wonderful process. You have to switch off the ego, face the fact that some of the things you really liked when you were shooting don't work. The good, really good films are made in the edit. You got that?"

"I got it."

When Bourke felt reasonably confident that he could let Johnny loose with a roll of unexposed film, he started to worry about the story that Johnny wanted to tell, so at the end of one of the sessions he told him to come with a story. He wasn't going to let him shoot at random. The story must be written and if possible each scene should be drawn, no matter how simply.

This gave Johnny a lot to think about and, as he walked home, he thought long and hard. First of all, there would be no sound so the story would have to be told in pictures. He had seen some short silent movies at screenings of religious-themed films during meetings in the tiny hall that abutted the church, and understood the principle of simple actions, a lot of overacting with waving hands and arms, and supporting cards with words that explained what happened in between or what was going to happen, or the words that some of the actors were supposed to speak. But where to start?

34

When Johnny came into the kitchen, Rita was sitting at the table, sipping at a mug of tea. He greeted her and started for the bedroom, but Rita stopped him.

"Johnny, what are you doing with yourself these days? I never see you from one end of the day to the other."

"I've been going to Mr Bourke's every day. He's—"

"Is he offering you a job at all?"

"Ah, no. Sure, there's never a customer."

"Well, what are you doing there?"

"He's teaching me about cameras and… film."

"Film?"

"Yeah. How pictures are made."

"You and your pictures. You should be looking for a job."

"I've tried, Mammy. There's nothing, only the abattoir and I can only handle that—"

"I know. Saturday is enough of that. Maybe you should look at the Tin Box Company. That'd be better."

"Not much. I'm sorry, Mammy. I know we need the money but I have to try something. Something better." He flushed heavily. "Mammy, was it always like this?"

"Yes. It was just as bad when I was your age. I had to leave school like Siobhan and get a job with the Tin Box Company. All the girls in the lane did. They were hiring a lot then. But you're right. It wasn't much better than the abattoir. It was dangerous. The rolls of tin were heavy and only the men were allowed near them, with big thick gloves, but when they rolled out the tin, it was as sharp as anything I had ever seen and the women had only thin gloves when we fed it into the machines. The edges cut our hands something terrible and we were given plasters to put on them. There was big blades – guillotines, they called them – and when they came down, they could cut through sheets of that stuff like anything. Bars came down too, to push our hands out of the way.

"We were all told how to be careful and not wear any loose clothes or long hair hanging out, but Lena O'Driscoll, God love her, had lovely red hair and she kept letting it loose, 'cause she fancied the foreman. And one day she leaned too far over the machine and the guillotine caught her hair and it was gone in a second, and the front of her head too. She was sent home with three months' wages and the foreman never gave a damn. We got a talking-to from the boss. I stayed there until I had Siobhan. Yes. It was always as bad."

"What happened to Lena?"

"Not sure. She lived with her old aunt in an old cottage off the lane. She stayed to herself after that. Don't think I ever saw her again. Lovely red hair, too."

"It's not fair, is it?"

"Fair?!" Rita poured another mugful of thick, stewed tea and ladled in the sugar.

"Did you ever have dreams, Mammy? I mean…"

"I know what you mean. I did. Lots of them. When I first met your daddy."

Johnny scowled.

"Now, don't be hard on him. He left school as soon as he could and went from job to job and never got anywhere. What he really wanted to do was sing. He had a good voice, you know, before he started to smoke, but it needed training and where was he to get the money for that in this place where every Irishman sings his head off? He even joined the choir at the Pro Cathedral, hoping they'd train him, but they just put him among the other men and told him to learn the words and stay in tune."

"He wanted to sing for a living?"

"Yes. We used to talk about it a lot. Him singing in a band, or in the ould concert rooms or even the Theatre Royal. Judy Garland sang there, did you know that?"

"Judy Garland? From *The Wizard of Oz*?"

"Yeah. She sang from the balcony to the crowds who couldn't get into the show. Your daddy dreamed of singing there one day. You're not the only one with dreams. He used to listen to all the music programmes on the radio and bought sheet music for the songs he loved to sing, but he couldn't make head nor tail out of them and his father burned them all when he heard how much he'd spent on them."

Johnny was stunned to hear this. His daddy has always seemed so carefree, even in adversity. His daddy with a dream?

"I never knew. He never told us."

"That was because it had all been knocked out of him before you were born. If you'd seen him before he gave up, always singing along softly with Peter Dawson on the radio – he idolised him – or Richard Tauber. He thought he was the greatest ever. He never liked John McCormack though. He invented his own breathing exercises to make his voice carry but they made him dizzy so he gave them up. That's when he started to smoke."

She was lost in remembrance and her face softened as she spoke. Johnny could hardly breathe.

"When I met him, he still believed that a chance would come. He cycled all over Dublin to choir practice after choir practice but it was always the same: 'Join the men and stay in tune.' Never a chance to get better. He even said that he might as well stand on O'Connell Bridge with a cap at his feet. That's how desperate he was. I don't blame him for running away. All them dreams."

The silence hung between them. Johnny broke it.

"I'm going to make a picture, Mammy. Mr Bourke is lending me a camera and some film."

"What good'll it do you?"

He looked steadfastly at Rita, who was disconcerted at his stare. It was as if he was looking straight through her.

"I don't know," he said finally. All I know is I have to do it."

He walked out of the kitchen. Rita looked after her eldest son and felt very sad. He was by far the brightest in the family, ready to try anything, afraid of nothing and amazingly concentrated when he was doing something that really interested him. And here he was dreaming about making films. Just like his daddy; reaching for the moon. *Please, Sacred Heart, help him. He deserves it.*

That night Johnny couldn't sleep. He took his old schoolbag to the kitchen and out of it took a school jotter, which he wouldn't be using any more, and the textbook in whose margins he had animated the story of the prodigal son so long ago. He also took out the tattered New Testament which he had kept safely all these years.

"Read the parable again," Bourke had said. "Read it carefully and work out how much of it you can fit Into a few minutes."

He read it again and looked at his crudely animated version in the schoolbook. He counted the scenes he knew he had to shoot. There were six: the son getting his share of his father's money and leaving home, the high living that the son went through, the hard times that came, the son eating the pigs' food, the homecoming and the eating of the fatted calf. Then he divided those scenes into the few minutes he had to play with and found that he had about forty whole seconds for each scene.

More than enough. In fact, he could shoot extra scenes of the high living and the celebrations.

He found a strange satisfaction in the way he could pin a story down into such clear steps, and in the jotter, he started to draw the first scene, which was the prodigal son leaving home and saying goodbye to his father and mother. The drawing was crude but clear and it allowed Johnny to plan the movements inside the frame. The scene also called for some props and a title card, which he decided was going to read *THE PRODIGAL SON: A BLACKHORSE LANE PICTURE.* He took up the title-card holder and slotted the white letters in. Then he sat for a long time looking at the card and thinking about what it represented.

He worked almost all through the night and when dawn was breaking he had his story, scene by scene, and the words of the cards he would have to put in and what they would say to keep the story going. He thought of his father's breathing exercises and his frantic search for a place to learn how to sing, and how he had given up and started to smoke; and he swore to himself, John Moore, director, that he would get, somehow or another, the additional information he'd need to learn it all. He had learned an awful lot in the past few days with Bourke. But he had to know it all.

35

"Stop laughing, Flaherty, or I'll brain you."

In truth, Flaherty was managing to keep a remarkably straight face, even though the beard made out of very hairy twine tickled his neck, and even though the blanket, held around his torso by an old bicycle inner tube, kept slipping off.

It was when he had to put his arm around Siobhan that the giggles started. Siobhan, on the other hand, was grandeur itself. Rita had entered into the spirit of the enterprise and made her up to the nines. An old patchwork quilt, artfully tucked in and pinned, made a robe of great dramatic effect. A crown of daisies was perched on her clipped-up hair and several rosary beads took the place of jewellery on her bare arms. Johnny had wanted everybody to go barefoot, but Siobhan wasn't having *that*. She pranced around on a pair of Rita's high heels with the innate skill of every little girl, and was as affected as anything and gracious to one and all. Johnny wore one of Tom's old tweed caps backwards as he peered through the eyepiece of the tripod-mounted Bolex.

"Get into position," he bellowed. "Rolling camera. Action!"

It was no good. As soon as Flaherty's arm descended on Siobhan's shoulder, he started giggling again. Johnny stopped the camera and approached the apologetic Flaherty.

"Right. Try laughing instead. You're a rich man and you've plenty to laugh about."

"OK, Johnny. I'll try that."

"OK. Rehearsal. Action."

Flaherty embraced Siobhan, bellowing with laughter. They were standing in front of the pedestrian park gate, which Johnny had chosen as the portal of Flaherty's home. Down the lane and into the shot came one of the Cabra boys, who had delighted Johnny with his ability to pull expressive faces. He hadn't objected to dressing only in an old sheet, with bare legs and shoulders. He strutted up to Flaherty and held out his hand. Flaherty, ha-ha-ing like mad, took a bulging bag with a dollar sign drawn on it out from under his blanket and handed it to the Cabra boy. The Cabra boy took the bag and kissed it as he turned away down the back lane. Siobhan started sobbing while Flaherty waved gaily after the Cabra boy, laughing uproariously.

Johnny looked long and hard at Flaherty.

"Sorry, Johnny."

"No. It's all right. It was only a rehearsal and we're all new at this. Only, it doesn't seem right for you to be laughing when your son is leaving home."

"Only... me arm around a mot! It feels funny."

"Imagine you had your arm around your oul' fella."

"Him? Sure, he'd kill me if I did."

"Yeah. But you wouldn't be giggling."

"You're right."

"OK," said Johnny. "I'm going to shoot this."

They took up their places again as he wound up the camera.

"Stand by, everybody," cried Johnny. "Rolling camera." He focused on Flaherty and Siobhan, started the camera and yelled, "Action!"

They were all on cue. Siobhan and Flaherty looked suitably gloomy and, as Johnny panned with the Cabra boy down the back lane, the latter waved the bag over his head, gave a cheeky little skip and banged his heels together in mid-air. Johnny stopped the camera and tried not to smile.

"Cut. That's a take. Next scene."

The next scene was in Cummiskey's, thanks to Jacko's influence. He and the barman stood to one side while Johnny rehearsed the Cabra boys around a table in the corner. When Johnny was ready he took up his position behind the camera and nodded at the barman, who took up a tray containing several pints.

"Stand by with the pints. Rolling camera. Action."

The barman, after a nod from Johnny, stepped into the scene and dispensed the pints. The boy playing the prodigal son tossed a handful of milk-bottle tops covered in gold and silver paper onto the tray and the boys lifted the glasses and saluted each other. The prodigal son knocked back a mouthful as Johnny zoomed in on him.

"That's enough," said the barman.

"Ah, leave him be. I'll finish the rest," said a laughing Jacko.

"Wait. Nobody move," said Johnny.

His eye was on the prodigal son, whose face was turning a pale green. He had guessed right. The boy swung away from the table and Johnny zoomed in on the stream of black stout that issued from his mouth.

"That's it. One last heave."

The boy obliged.

"Cut."

The manager of Switzers was intrigued. Johnny had mustered his crew on the pavement outside the department store and he had been directed to the manager's office at the back of the store.

"A picture?"

"Yeah. And there's a shot in it where the main character – the prodigal son – is spending all his money."

"The prodigal son spending his money at Switzers?"

"Yeah. He would if he was born now and not thousands of years ago."

"I suppose he would." The manager examined Johnny's deadly-serious face. "So you want to shoot him walking out of the shop?"

"Yeah. With parcels. Empty boxes or bags, like. Nicely wrapped if they're boxes."

The bemused and amused manager had three large packages made up, gift-wrapped and each with a ribbon tied in a big bow. He and several assistants and customers stood around the doorway as Johnny got the camera into position across the street. Johnny snapped his fingers and Paul rushed up with a megaphone made out of cardboard and gummed tape.

"Stand by," he yelled into it. "Mr Manager, remember to shake his hand and hand him the last parcel. And nobody look at the camera. Action!"

The prodigal son appeared from the shop, staggering with two parcels. The manager followed him, shook his barely-offered hand and placed another parcel on top of the two clutched to the prodigal son's chest. As the laden figure walked away, the manager waved after him with a very sincere smile on his face.

"Cut," yelled Johnny. "Thank you, everybody."

"They don't have to be real Knickerbocker Glories."

The manager of Caffolla's Ice Cream Parlour was indignant.

"Not real?!" he said. "We serve the best Knickerbocker Glories in Ireland. There's no way I could have false ones served in this establishment."

"But I don't have a budget for props."

"Do you have a budget for anything?"

"No."

"I didn't think so. Let's consider three Knickerbocker Glories as Caffolla's contribution to the founding of Ireland's film industry."

So, an awed prodigal son and two of his similarly-dressed Cabra cohorts polished off the gigantic ice cream treats in the window of Caffolla's while Johnny filmed it from the street. Afterwards, in the street itself, Johnny also got a shot of the prodigal son vomiting into the gutter the unfamiliar contents of his stomach.

The carriage ride was more difficult. Johnny approached several of the carriage drivers outside the Phoenix Park racecourse before he found one willing to oblige. The most the driver would wear from Johnny's improvised wardrobe was a sort of poncho made from an old sheet with a hole torn in the middle. He initially refused to wear a turban and grudgingly agreed to drive bare-headed.

"If any of the drivers see me like this, I'll whip the skin off your back," he growled, cracking the whip above Johnny's head.

"They won't. We'll shoot it on a back road," Johnny assured him.

After a few rehearsals, the driver had entered into the spirit of the thing and was anxious to get it right. Johnny placed the camera on the ground, so that the 'crowd' comprising six children in blankets filled the foreground. On cue, the driver, haphazardly turbaned, drove the cab past, his face averted rigidly at a strange angle in his efforts not to look at the camera. The prodigal son and his cohorts leaned out the window and tossed the prop coins at the crowd, shouting and laughing.

The next scene with a major set-up was in the pigsty up the lane, from which emerged a smell that made the uninured blink. The prodigal son entered into this scene with remarkable enthusiasm. All he was required to do was to slyly eat some of the food he was feeding to the pigs by throwing handfuls of it into a trough. But when he had done that, he dropped to his knees next to the pigs, thrust them aside and shoved his head into the mess. Johnny was so surprised he almost missed the shot.

The prodigal's homecoming and his loving welcome by his parents evoked Flaherty's propensity to giggle and Johnny had to get him into a proper laughing mood again.

The fatted calf comprised two of the Cabra boys inside three sacks which Johnny had borrowed from the market gardener. They stank of fertiliser and the two boys could only manage one or two minutes at a time inside them. The calf's face and lethal horns had been made by Johnny out of cardboard and his dwindling stock of gummed tape. Flaherty took to the killing of the fatted calf with all the professionalism of an abattoir employee. He had brought along one of the knives from the abattoir to do the job but Johnny persuaded him that the cardboard one would look better on the camera. Unfortunately, Flaherty stabbed with such ardour that the cardboard knife crumpled in rehearsal and the shot was held up while Johnny took it home to repair it.

All these were captured in sequence on the film, with several black frames between them as Johnny closed the iris at the end of each shot and opened it at the beginning of the next.

36

Gallagher and Bourke walked up the gravel path that led to the single-storey house in which Father Mulligan lived with an elderly housekeeper. It was in a pretty bad state of repair and some of the roof tiles were missing. There was no garden to speak of, merely a few bedraggled bushes and a bird bath with no water in it on a crooked pole next to a net-curtained window. Bourke used the door knocker while Gallagher looked around the premises, unimpressed. The door opened to reveal an old woman in a floral dressing gown and bedroom slippers.

"Father Mulligan is expecting us. Mr Gallagher and Mr Bourke," said Bourke.

The old woman stepped to one side and gestured for them to enter. The hallway was gloomy and the walls needed repainting. She stepped ahead of them and turned into the front room. They followed her into a sparsely-furnished room with sagging wallpaper and a faded and stained black-and-white illustration of St. Anthony being tempted in what was supposed to be a desert. Two highly-polished silver candlesticks with half-used candles festooned with wax drippings stood side by side under it. She indicated a couch and two armchairs covered in cracked leather.

"Take a seat. I'll tell him you're here," she said, and exited.

The two men sat down and regarded each other. Gallagher pulled his coat lapels together against the chill of the room, then stood up and made for the well-stocked bookcase that dominated the room. It held a remarkably wide selection of books: scientific and theological volumes filled the top two shelves and most of them had several scraps of paper as bookmarks protruding; there were several large art books on the lowest and deepest shelves and in between, he quickly scanned through a comprehensive selection of major literary works in fiction and non-fiction. The priest was a remarkably well-read man, it seemed. His eye alighted on a well-bound volume of Rabelais, and he prised it out and flicked through it. It was a 19th-century edition of *The Life of Gargantua and of Pantagruel* illustrated by Gustave Doré, which Gallagher was sure was on the Index of Forbidden Books. He opened it and started to examine the illustrations. Bourke sat looking with interest at the snail tracks on the dingy carpet.

It was less than a minute before the door opened and Father Mulligan came in and shook hands with both of them, pressing Bourke back down into his seat as he sought to rise.

"Gentlemen, welcome. It's not often that the seniors of the parish gather together; one caretaker of the minds, one caretaker of the images and one caretaker of the souls of the people." He crossed to Gallagher, who was reluctantly closing the book. "Ah, you have found my weakness."

"There are worse weaknesses."

"Indeed there are, as I am reminded every Saturday morning in the confessional."

"Surely you don't come across transgressions as… gargantuan as those related in here?"

"If I did, my Saturdays would be much more interesting."

"Maybe we have lost the art of the thundering sin."

"I fear we have, they are mostly of the paltry sort in the lane. Now, what can I do for you?"

Gallagher replaced the book and opened the discussion. "Mr Bourke and I have had a long discussion about one of your younger parishioners."

"Johnny Moore? Don't look so surprised. There isn't another child in the lane that anybody outside their immediate family knows, and I sometimes think even they tend to get them mixed up."

"Yes. Johnny Moore. A boy I came to know just a few weeks ago, but I have become very involved with him."

"Most people do. It's very interesting. Mr Gallagher, you have him under your wing. What's his secret?"

"His curiosity, perhaps."

"I'd agree with that," Bourke chimed in. "I've been teaching him the secrets of cameras and his reach is never greater than his grasp."

"And why are you doing that?"

"He's making a film."

"A film?!"

"Yes. I was as surprised as you are. He'll succeed, too. He has a way of breaking up everything you teach him into bits that he can understand and relate to and then apply them."

"Do you find him the same in a classroom?"

"Yes. He's a highly desirable pupil for a teacher and he believes, and I tend to agree with him," Gallagher said, "that a film will indicate his worth to... certain people."

"Including Major Brennan," said Father Mulligan.

"So you know about Johnny's desire to—"

"To join a programme which is designed primarily for Protestant boys."

"Primarily but not exclusively," Gallagher interjected.

"I am all too aware of that. The Catholic/Protestant divide is Ireland's great dilemma. It's been with us since the Reformation and I fear it will not go away as long as Ireland perceives itself as a Catholic country and as long as the Irish people turn to the Catholic church for spiritual guidance. As a priest, I have to balance the relative value of the mind and the soul of the individual, especially in a young boy. It is an awesome responsibility and it has caused me great unease. It seems as if, for various reasons, the school system has not coped with Johnny. He *is* a square peg in a round hole. The major's programme would, I believe, be able to cope with him and harness his... what did you call it? Curiosity in the pursuit of knowledge, a well-rounded education and fulfilment as useful citizen. But – and I cannot stress this enough – it is my responsibility to ensure that he does not stray from the church or its teachings."

"So what do you think you will do?" asked Gallagher.

"Johnny has already asked me to obtain the bishop's permission for him to participate."

"And will you?"

"I'm seriously considering it."

Gallagher stifled a laugh. "For such a skinny little urchin, he creates serious waves."

"He does," said Bourke. "I wondered why for a while but now I think I understand. He persuaded me to give him a crash course in a very complicated camera, which he has mastered in a matter of days. He reminds me of me when I was still eager to learn."

"And me of when I used to love teaching."

They were all silent for a while before the priest stifled a laugh.

"Well, he has the three of us in thrall to him, exerting ourselves to further his desires. He's either a supreme manipulator or..."

He paused and Gallagher stepped in.

"Or a remarkably clever young boy chafing under the bonds of poverty and determined to break free of them."

"All of us seem to be agreed on that," said Bourke.

"Yes, we are," said the priest. "Consider all we have done for him."

"And all we still have to do," said Bourke.

Father Mulligan looked at him in surprise. "There's more to be done?"

"Yes," said Bourke, rising to his feet. "Making a film is all very well but every film needs an audience."

"Are we expected to raise an audience too?"

"We are," said Bourke. "This film must have an impact on everybody who has a stake in his future."

"If we do raise an audience, will the film be worth it?"

"I honestly think it will. I've seen the rough footage and for the work of a twelve-year-old, it will be remarkable when it is edited."

"And when it has music added," said Gallagher.

"Music? I don't know about music."

"I have agreed to play violin music when it is shown."

Bourke was impressed. "That would make an enormous difference."

Father Mulligan looked at the two enthusiastic, elderly men in surprise. "Will you look at us? We're still under his spell." He thought a bit while the other two waited. "Well, the church hall can be organised."

"I can rig up a projector and a screen."

"And I'll be the orchestra. It'll be such fun."

Fun? thought Father Mulligan. *When did I last see any of that in the lane?*

Then, swept up in the dream list of invitees, Gallagher said, "I have a friend in the Department of Education who I think could be persuaded to attend. And if he came, I think I would ask him to invite the headmaster of the school. That would be one in the eye for him."

"A cousin of mine works as a reporter for the *Evening Mail* and he owes me."

Father Mulligan felt he must recover some of the high ground, so, much to his own surprise, he announced, "I wonder if I could persuade James Driscoll to come?"

"Who's he?" asked Bourke.

"The bishop," said Gallagher in stunned tones.

They all toyed with the incipient excitement of the event until the priest brought them down to earth.

"Then there's the major," he said.

Gallagher was silent, as was Bourke. Gallagher was the first to recover.

"I had a… sort of fall-out with him."

"And he's not enamoured of the Catholic religion, I'm told," said the priest.

"Will you look at us?!" exclaimed Bourke. "The three wise men of the neighbourhood and we're afraid of a superannuated officer of the British Army. He's just another threshold guardian, a gatekeeper to a cave. Like Cerberus who guards the entrance to Hades, like the dragon who guards the golden fleece. They're there to test us, to teach us how to fight or find the skills necessary to move further towards our goal. Like you, Father, with your absolution which you only grant to those who deserve it, who deserve to reach their goal. If Johnny is worthy to be on this programme, he must prove himself to this threshold guardian."

The other two looked at him in amazement.

"Sorry," Bourke said. "It's something I just remembered from my studies on storytelling. I thought it might be useful right now."

"Quite," said Gallagher. The priest said nothing.

"Now that that's settled," said Gallagher, "let us beard this threshold guardian in his cave."

37

"A film?"

"Yes."

"An eight-minute film?"

"Maybe even shorter."

"Because," said Bourke, who had been chosen as the frontman for the Major Brennan confrontation, "because films are so difficult for anyone to make due to the various aspects that demand competence, such as storytelling, photography, directing actors, editing and such. For a twelve-year-old child to make a film, admittedly with some assistance, is phenomenal. I know this because I was in the business for thirty years and I never had the confidence to make one."

"Is it any good?"

"It succeeds in achieving its own goals."

"I'm not sure what that means."

Gallagher took up the cudgels. "It succeeds in what it set out to do: to amuse a varied audience with a simple and effective story told in pictures."

"So it's a comedy."

"Yes," said Bourke. "The most difficult type of film to make."

"And you would like me to come and watch it?"

"Yes."

"Why can't I watch it here?"

Father Mulligan thought it was time to chip in. "Because seeing it in front of an audience will give you a measure of its effectiveness."

"I understand, Father. I also understand that you three worthy people are under the impression that it will persuade me to recommend Johnny Moore to my committee."

"That is its sole purpose."

"Three community leaders promoting the fortunes of a young, slightly unruly boy. It's hard to credit."

Father Mulligan leaned forward earnestly. "It is important to us, to me personally, to help Johnny succeed. It's so seldom that I find any spark of originality, of latent talent and relentless ambition in my parish that when I do come across it, I consider it my duty to promote it as a clear demonstration of the power of diligence and hard work."

"Not to mention the ability to recruit such eminent ambassadors," said the major drily.

"That too," said Gallagher. "It's a necessary ingredient in success."

The major rose and paced around the study, which he had thought would be more appropriate for such a meeting. His eye caught sight of the old rifle which Johnny had admired and handled with such assurance. He stopped his pacing and faced the others.

"Gentlemen, forgive me for being so inhospitable. May I offer you some refreshments? I have so many thoughts buzzing around in my brain that I feel a cup of tea and some reflection would be beneficial in the matter."

He pulled on the bell rope that dangled from the wall next to the mantelpiece and Farrington appeared as if he had been waiting outside.

"Tea for us all, if you wouldn't mind, Farrington, and some currant cake."

Farrington bowed and backed out of the room and the major carried on his pacing. In his heart he knew that Johnny was a boy eminently suited to the programme, but two things concerned him. One was the thought that the Catholic church, so embedded in the Irish psyche, was once again taking advantage of the resources of the Protestant community and its largesse; the other was his latent fear of the obvious attraction that Johnny had for his daughter. He knew it was mutually childlike and innocent but such a relationship was against his better judgement. It came perilously close to the barrier that existed between Catholic and Protestant and, as a member of a precarious minority, it behoved him to keep them apart so that his plans for Angela's rise in society would not be imperilled.

He was no nearer a decision when Farrington ushered in Siobhan, who was carrying a tray of tea things while Farrington had command of the cake. She was better turned-out and better groomed than she had ever been at home and she carried herself with a quiet confidence. She curtsied to the men and Father Mulligan smiled warmly at her.

"Siobhan, how well you're looking. I'm delighted to see you."

"Thank you, Father," Siobhan replied as she blushed and carried on setting out the cups and pouring the tea.

The priest was thinking that a position as a housemaid was as much as most of his female parishioners could ever hope for, and a great sadness descended on him. Was this servant status all that could be hoped for? He stifled his incipient anger and pulled himself together.

"Mr Gallagher, Mr Bourke, this is Siobhan Moore, the sister of our young hero."

The men murmured at her as she passed out the tea, the plates, forks and slices of cake. All eyes were upon her but she bore it with equanimity and smiled at them as she followed Farrington out of the room while they sipped and ate.

"I hope she is satisfactory in her position?" the priest said to the major.

"Very," he replied. "But we're all considering a much higher status in life for her brother, are we not?"

More largesse, graciously handed out, thought the priest while he smiled at the major. *Was it all for this? What have we gained from our independence? More crumbs from the tables of the ascendancy?* Realising that he was on a mission, he finished his tea and placed the cup and saucer carefully on the desk. He smiled benignly at them all, but out of the corner of his eye, he saw that the major was looking closely at him.

"Father…" the major said, and waited until the priest had given him all his attention. "I sense your unease and I respect it. We are both, as it were, on opposite sides of a painful divide. But we are no longer the ascendancy and the Land Acts sorted out the imbalance of land ownership and weighted wealth All we have left are our shabby gentility and a way with horses, so we look after our own as best we can. But…"

The priest made as if to interrupt, but the major continued.

"But we are few and, I admit, so are our problems. While we have the luxury of funding and forwarding the fortunes of our few children, your church and your government have the enormous task of lifting millions out of grinding poverty and into some semblance of a fulfilling life. I am more aware that perhaps you think of your personal nurturing of the denizens of the lane and I am offering my assistance in the advancement of at least one. So the three musketeers have not struggled in vain."

The priest bowed deeply, but said nothing. Gallagher and Bourke exchanged relieved glances and the major turned towards the half-closed door and raised his voice.

"I wonder what my eavesdropping daughter has to say about that?"

The door slammed open and a flustered, red-faced Angela stepped inside, straining to throw herself at her father.

"And what do you think I should do, Angela?"

"See the film, Father. Oh, please do. I know it will be good."

"How do you know that?"

"Because Johnny made it."

"You see, gentlemen: my daughter is a member of the Johnny Moore fan club."

"Will you come to the screening?" asked the priest.

"I suppose I must," said the major.

Angela threw her arms around his waist and he smiled down at her, but the priest caught the sadness in his smile. As well he might, because the major saw another part of his traditional life slipping away.

38

The annex at the back of Bourke's shop contained tottering precipices of shelves on three of the four walls. Comprised as they were of thin planks of grainy and grimy pine, they sagged alarmingly as they spanned the yawning gaps between the uprights, threatening to void their loads onto a floor that bore its own burden of unidentifiable things among boxes of wood, cardboard and occasionally metal. The annex contained a lifetime of once-crucial professional equipment, joyfully acquired and tenderly operated, now wearing a thin shroud of dust that denoted years of disuse and neglect. It was a catacomb of outmoded paraphernalia, souvenirs of long-forgotten technologies, of no value other than sentimental, of no practicality other than cannibalisation of parts. But each item had its allotted space on the shelves and the floor and each had its indelible presence in the memory of Mr Bourke. So, he showed not a moment's hesitation when he entered the annex and reached for one of the faintly-printed cartons.

He placed it on the tiny, cluttered desk in the corner and opened it. Out came a complicated piece of equipment with a small glass screen and a pair of arms in front and to one side of it. Bourke placed it on the desk, clicked the arms into rigid positions and lifted and slapped down two metal plates that lay side by side on the base directly in front of the screen.

"And now, the edit," Bourke said as he plugged the machine into a wall socket.

The screen lit up and the machine's purpose became clear. He tore open a two-coloured envelope and tipped out a grey spool in a white cover. Taking off the top, he extracted a reel of film and began to thread it onto the editor, the full reel on the left arm, the loose end of the reel on the right arm. As he wound the reel across and back with the revolving winders on each arm, against the lit-up screen, the images became visible on the film.

"I have often wished that we had a chance to edit our lives. A way we could replay all the things we did over the years and allow us to take out those deeds that did us no good and probably a lot of harm. There, Johnny Moore, is your film, ready to be moved around, manipulated, placed in a new and different sequence that makes more senses of the actions that took place in front of the camera."

Bourke moved away and Johnny took his seat in front of the editor. Moving the winders backwards and forwards, he very soon got the feel of the editor and the operation. Then he played through the film, right to the end, every scene, every cutaway, everything he had shot, lost in all the exuberance of the wonderful, exhilarating, sheer creative power of film-making. There, flickering before his eyes, were his neighbourhood, the people of Blackhorse Lane, his friends and erstwhile enemies, all cavorting, laughing, enjoying themselves, making fools of themselves, exuding goodwill, full of love of the occasion, of the moment, of the opportunity to show off, to pretend, to act the eejit, to do whatever the hell Johnny Moore asked them to do. Hamming. Hogging the screen. Demanding to be looked at, admired for their bravery, their acting skills, their face-pulling, their sheer, unadulterated temerity to be in a picture.

He finished the run-through and sat for a long while, savouring the moment and the satisfaction of having captured the underlying humanity of Blackhorse Lane and all who lived and suffered and survived in it. He knew with utter certainty that, whatever else he achieved, in the long, dismal journey of their impoverished lives, he had recorded what they would consider and remember as their finest hour.

"OK," said Bourke. "First, the titles. Cut them all out and hang them here, on those nails. You did shoot them in sequence?"

"Of course. And I numbered them. How do I take them out? Oh, I see."

He had identified the little guillotine on the base, so, running to the last title, he placed it on the pins that ran along the side and pressed the blade down firmly. The film cut cleanly and he took the titles off the winder and hung them on one of the nails, where they dangled down to the floor behind the desk and into a large cardboard box on the floor. Under Bourke's instructions, he cut a strip off some exposed film as a leader and attached the first title to it by laying it on the pins, dragging an abrasive strip of metal backwards and forwards across the tip, applying soft cement to the rough edge, placing the end frame of the title on it and slamming down the metal cover on the join.

"There," said Bourke, "your first edit. Now, since you shot everything in sequence, including the cutaways, you can't get confused."

Johnny viewed the first scene and its cutaways several times, working out when to cut and listening to Bourke's sensitive suggestions. There was the key scene with Flaherty and Siobhan looking suitably mournful as the prodigal son came up and held out his hand. At that point Johnny edited in the close-up of Flaherty taking the bag out from under his cloak and handing it over. Then back to the main shot as the son walked away down the lane. The cut didn't work. At all. The taking out of the bag was OK, but the handing of it to the son was the wrong angle and so his walking away jarred worryingly.

Bourke said nothing as Johnny viewed it again and again. He tried cutting back to the main scene later, but that meant the son was too far away. He seemed to have jumped the distance. Bourke went to put on the kettle, leaving Johnny to work it out for himself. It didn't take long before he heard Johnny mutter a stifled curse, and then give a light laugh. When he came back into the annex, Johnny had just finished a revised cut and he sat back and grinned at Bourke.

"You look as if you won the sweepstake," said Bourke.

Johnny's grin grew wider as he rewound the film and gestured towards the screen. Bourke saw immediately that Johnny had understood the mechanics of movement. He had inserted a close-up of Siobhan's sobbing face after the bag handover and when the action returned to the main scene, the distance travelled by the son looked and felt natural. Johnny had stopped the scene as the son banged his heels together.

"You see what you have done? You have used the power of film to make time shorter or longer. The son obviously moved some distance away while his mother was sobbing. That, my boy, is a cut. Now a cup of tea."

While they were drinking the tea, Bourke carried on his tutorial.

"There are many films out there that have been saved by the editor, just as your scene as shot was saved. Don't worry. Everybody makes the same sort of mistake in their first effort. You will never forget what you have just learned. That scene tells its own short story and the audience will believe it, even though it couldn't possibly be true. That gurrier—"

"Flaherty."

"Flaherty is no more a father of that son than I am, and yet the audience will accept that miscasting immediately and become involved in the story you are telling. They will fill in the gaps. They will imagine what the players are saying and they will accept any shortcomings in the film-making process because they know you made it and they know it is your first film. That's how understanding audiences are, and that's why you should never lie to them. They know the story and they just want to see what you do with it, so they are receptive to the emotions you are showing, in spite of the bad acting. They will understand the sorrow of the mother and sympathise with her, and they will understand the freedom the son has been given and will laugh at it. Especially the little jump and heel-tap at the end."

"Yeah. I like that. It's short, though."

"It is a bit, but the audience will get it and smile, or even laugh. If we had a budget, we would have printed that last shot several times so it froze on the screen and then faded to black. But you'll do such things on your next films."

"Will there be other films?"

"Of course."

"How do you know?"

"Because it's your destiny, and because you have been bitten by the film-making bug and you'll never be cured."

And so they went on, constructing every scene with all the care and attention they deserved. Johnny's delight was never-ending. At every stage of the edit he was enthralled at the power of film to tell a story; at the need to make every scene, every shot and every insert or cutaway have a clear-cut job to do. Time and again, he was disappointed at the way the pace of the action fought against the mood of the scene. *If only*, he told himself, *if only I could shoot that scene again*; to make it slower when there were some serious things being done; faster when the actions – such as the feasting and farting about during the riotous living sequence. Then a fast pace would have added to the fun.

He asked Bourke about the speeding-up of action that he had seen in some old silent movies, but Bourke was scathing.

Speeding up was cheating; a cheap way to get a laugh. He described how Chaplin, when he had control over the screenings of his films, refused to play his films at the fast pace that modern twenty-five-frames-per-second projectors demanded and had them screened at the slower pace at which he had shot them. The humour or pathos or sadness were in the original filming and acting and not in a false, imposed freneticism.

To his surprise, when Johnny had watched the final five-plus minutes of the film for the fourth time from start to finish, he found himself moved, even tearful at the story. Bourke, who had joined him in the watching, picked this up.

"It's moving, isn't it?"

"Yes."

"Well, it's a great story that's been told again and again for the past two thousand years. Its power and meaning won't fade away. And you've done a commendable job on it. Congratulations."

"Thanks. It's all thanks to you, but."

"No, it's not. Robert Flaherty had a very interesting philosophy. He said that your mind should be as innocent and sensitive as unexposed film to see what is really going on in front of the lens. I've just found out how true that is. So thank *you*."

39

The church hall had never been so full – or so noisy. It felt as if every child in North Dublin was there. Flaherty was lording over them all, a film star in the making. He had wanted to come in the costume he had worn in the film but had been dissuaded by Johnny. Having established his dominance of the cast of the film, he now strode among the unruly children, trying to muster in them some semblance of order. He was fighting a losing battle when a hush fell over the seething throng. He turned, expecting to see Father Mulligan claiming his authority but instead was confronted by a figure who had terrified him for about half of his not-very-considerable years on earth. It was the Manor Theatre's commissionaire in all his tatty finery, free this time from the dandruff that had embellished his shoulders since time immemorial. Nodding at Flaherty as to an equal, he turned to the other children and with gestures that demanded instant obedience, he directed them into the rows of chairs that filled the back of the hall. They scurried to obey. When Rita and her other children arrived, were ensconced in the front row by Flaherty and the commissionaire.

As all this was happening the triumvirate of Bourke, Gallagher and Father Mulligan entered and moved towards the long wooden pew that had been manhandled from the church for the occasion. It stood four-square at the front, facing the screen that stood against the back wall. Behind the pew was a small table on which stood the projector, towards which Bourke made his way. Below and to one side of the screen were a chair and a music stand, towards which Gallagher made his way, clutching his violin case. Father Mulligan made his way to the pew and fussed with the miscellaneous assortment of cushions that were strewn on it, particularly a small mountain of the better cushions constructed in the centre.

The children watched in hushed attention at the actions of such lords of the neighbourhood, turning their heads to witness the entry of some more lordly ones. Leading the group was the headmaster, with Mr Wilson in attendance. They were accompanied by another man in a business suit, to whom the headmaster was embarrassingly obsequious. Behind them was a thin, bearded man in a strident sports jacket with an impressive array of pencils sticking out of his sagging breast pocket. Gallagher strode forward to meet this group and, nodding casually in the direction of the two teachers, clutched the hand of the man in the business suit.

"John. Thank you for coming."

John shook the offered hand heartily and laughed. "Only Declan Gallagher could get me all the way out here."

"I don't think you will consider the trip wasted."

John turned back towards the two teachers, still clutching Gallagher's hand. "When I heard it concerned an erstwhile pupil at their school, I invited these two along."

The headmaster smiled through gritted teeth and nodded at Gallagher. Mr Wilson was more effusive.

"When Mr Stevenson indicated his interest in attending this… we… I was only too happy to…"

An icy glare from the headmaster silenced him. Father Mulligan descended on them.

"Gentlemen. Thank you for your attendance. Please come this way."

He ushered them to the pew at the front, placing the headmaster to one side of the mountain of cushions in the centre where, he felt sure, he would be most intimidated and uncomfortable. He turned to the other man.

"I'm sorry, we haven't been introduced. I'm Father Mulligan, parish priest."

"And I'm John Stevenson, Department of Education."

They shook hands as Father Mulligan placed Stevenson on the other side of the cushions with a gap between them and him. He had plans for that gap.

"You'll be most comfortable here," he said as John seated himself.

Bourke had commandeered the sports jacket and taken it and the wearer to the projector table, next to which were two chairs.

"What the hell am I doing here, Bourke?"

"You might get a little human story for your paper out of this."

"I get a nosebleed when I'm surrounded by such holiness."

"Then it'll be gushing out of you in a minute when the bishop arrives."

"The bishop! Christ! I'll never live it down."

"Shush, Jack. Here he is now."

Into the hall and Father Mulligan's warm welcome strode the bishop in a plain, dark suit with a clerical collar, a touch of red below it and a miasma of self-importance such as only a highly-placed cleric in his own bailiwick can muster. A dim-looking priest was at his heels. Mulligan ushered the bishop to the mountain of cushions and seated him with all due deference.

"Gentlemen, the bishop," he said. Then, looking up, he saw the major enter with Angela beside him. "Excuse me," he said, and scurried away as the pew-load of people muttered politely at each other. The dim-looking priest moved anxiously over to stand against the wall, where he had an unobstructed view of the bishop.

"Major, thank you for coming. Angela, my dear, you look so nice. Come."

He ushered them to the pew and placed the major and Angela on the other side of the bishop, knowing that they would have *so* much to say to each other. They had, too, and were soon in a deep conversation which seemed mutually fascinating.

Father Mulligan looked around. Gallagher was seated on the chair, tuning his violin softly and excited in spite of himself. He had watched the film several times and devised a suitable accompaniment. Bourke was at the projector and… where was Johnny? He moved over to Bourke and whispered in his ear.

"Find Johnny. He's not here. I'll start the proceedings."

A startled Bourke rose to his feet, looked around and made for the door. Mulligan moved to the front and stood there until the noise abated. The commissionaire strode to the back of the hall, dispensing glares in all directions.

"Good evening, Your Grace, distinguished guests, ladies and gentlemen, boys and girls…"

Outside the hall, Bourke stopped and listened. From amongst the few gravestones that lay alongside the church itself, he heard someone retching. He ran to the spot and found Johnny doubled up and voiding the contents of his stomach onto the lank grass.

"Johnny. Come, lad. Father Mulligan is introducing your film. Everybody is there, including the bishop."

That last bit of information started the retching again, but there was nothing left in Johnny's stomach.

"Play the film. I'll be in later."

"You're coming in now. You have to. I know you're nervous. It's natural."

"It's just a lousy, childish film. They'll just laugh."

"Of course they'll laugh. It's a supposed to be a funny film."

Johnny stared at him. It was time to be tough.

"Why do you think I spent so much time on this, and so much money? Yes, money. You owe me, Johnny Moore. This is the last important thing I'll ever do. Don't spoil it. Get inside. Now."

It worked. Johnny spat, smoothed down his shirt and went towards the church.

Father Mulligan was waffling a bit and looking anxiously towards the door. His relief was palpable when Johnny appeared.

"And here he is. Jonathon Moore, Blackhorse Lane's first and foremost film-maker."

The kids went wild and shouted out encouragements and 'well done's at the top of their voices. Johnny bowed and grinned sheepishly and made for the back of the hall where he positioned himself next to the light switches. Bourke responded to Father Mulligan's beckoning and joined him at the front. He cleared his throat and spoke from a full heart.

"We're going to see something very interesting this evening. The product of a mind so innocent – or rather ignorant – of the complexities of film-making that it has the courage to attempt what a more knowledgeable mind would baulk at. We are going to see the first film made by a boy born to be a film-maker. A born storyteller who has found a new way of telling them. One of the distinguished guests here asked me what this evening is all about." Here he caught the eye of the major. "I think it's all about determination."

Over the applause, he went to the table and switched on the projector, and Johnny switched off the lights. The hall was hushed as the images appeared on the screen. At the first title, the kids erupted and from then until the end of the film, there was bedlam as they were swept up in the story, the imagery and the magnificent cheek of the Blackhorse Lane boy who had dared to make a film. Gallagher excelled himself, inspired by the occasion and the situations that Johnny had created on the screen, which demanded the most imaginative music he had ever played on his violin. He held the long, triumphant coda at the end as long as he dared, but it was drowned out by the cacophony from dozens of throats.

Flaherty stood up at the back. "Show it again!" he bellowed.

"Yeah, again. Show it again. Show it again. Show it again."

It became a chant as the kids took it up and started stamping their feet. Bourke caught Father Mulligan's eye, who Father Mulligan looked at the bishop, who nodded. Father Mulligan nodded at Bourke, who had rewound the film and inserted the beginning into the projector feed. As the film rolled, Johnny switched the lights off again.

The reaction was different this time. The kids didn't laugh so much at the first appearances. They laughed at the actions, especially those of the prodigal son, and screamed as he buried his face in the pigswill. A hero had been made that night. They cheered and clapped when the son was welcomed home, and when Johnny switched the lights back on, a group of boys, led by Flaherty, descended on him and bore him aloft in a triumphant march around the hall. The people on the VIP pew, led by the bishop, rose to their feet and clapped as Johnny was borne past them. Rita and Siobhan stepped out of their places and reached for his hands. He held them tightly, at some danger to his precarious seat, then he hushed the children's exuberance and dropped to the ground.

Approaching the pew, he shook hands with the dignitaries, all of whom – excepting the headmaster and Mr Wilson – doled out some congratulatory comments. The major was last to shake Johnny's hand, and he held on to it while he fixed the boy with a steady gaze.

"Mr Moore, congratulations. I think it's time you and I had a confidential talk. Come to my place tomorrow at 9am." He turned and bowed respectfully to the bishop and strode out.

Angela bestowed a beatific smile on Johnny and followed her father.

The bishop moved to Father Mulligan and murmured in his ear. Father Mulligan looked hard at him and nodded. So are destinies decided by those in positions of power.

40

Later that evening, the three men went back to the priest's house for a glass of some ferocious cooking sherry, over which they tried to describe how they felt about what had happened that night. They had all experienced it – and Johnny – through different prisms. But they all knew, or thought they knew, what the screening had meant in their lives.

Father Mulligan knew he would spend the next few years keeping an eye on Johnny as he passed through the major's programme, enrolled and started at Trinity College and kept up regular if not fervent contact with the various Catholic bodies and societies that existed in the purlieus. He kept the rest of the Moore family in his thoughts and prayers as they passed through the various stations of their lives. As to any further contact between them, he doubted if Johnny Moore, the renowned Paris-based film-maker, would spare a thought for his ecclesiastical roots.

Gallagher, in a spirit of resignation, went to join his sister in a gaunt boarding house in Morecambe and stayed there, strolling along what the locals called 'the sands', playing his violin occasionally, thinking regularly about Johnny and wondering where he was in his career. Some years later his sister died and left the boarding house to him. He moved into a residential home and when he died a few years later, his sole beneficiary was Johnny, who was contemplating the production and direction of his first major film. Gallagher's bequest funded the venture adequately and raised Johnny to a more prestigious level of film-making.

Bourke continued in his shop, barely making a living and more than appreciative of the clippings, sent religiously by Johnny, from the various film magazines and arts pages of popular journals as each of his films was released. Some of the clippings were in French because Johnny had decided to operate from Paris where his sort of modest, art-house productions were appreciated. None of them was ever screened in the Manor.

Angela went to finishing school as planned, but she kept up a deepening relationship with her father by post and on her occasional visits home. The major became proud of Johnny's advancement and looked forward to having the two youngsters in his home and driving them about in the trap, now pulled by a younger pony. He was disappointed in that.

As to Johnny, he made short-term and long-term friends and acquired the knowledge which opened up all the possibilities he required. Professional, proficient teaching developed his innate abilities into clearly defined skills. Apart from the academic studies, at which he began to excel, he did woodwork, drawing and sculpting. There was a demanding and innovative photographic course which taxed him to the limit and he loved every minute of it. But he could have been on the moon as far as the average Dubliner was concerned.

Each time he revisited Blackhorse Lane he was greeted by his friends as if he had been in prison and had missed the most important events of the day. Flaherty, whom he saw less and less frequently on his visits, was especially interested in the unfolding fate of the denizens of his own world. He assumed that Johnny would be fascinated by what had happened to the heroes and villains of their childhood. He wasn't, and he cared about none of them except his mother and siblings, all of whom drifted along in their familiar ruts, free, at least, from penury when Gallagher's bequest came through.

He never went to the Manor again.

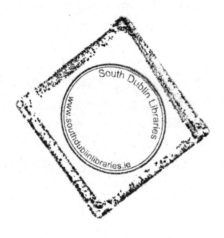